BLINDED BY THE SIGHT

BLINDED BY THE SIGHT

S. L. SMITH

For Julie –

Best wishes,

S. L. Smith

NORTH STAR PRESS OF ST. CLOUD, INC.
Saint Cloud, Minnesota

First Edition, September 2011

Printed in the United States of America

Published by
North Star Press of St. Cloud, Inc.
P.O. Box 451
St. Cloud, Minnesota 56302

www.northstarpress.com

For my parents, John and Jacquelyn Smith,
my inspiration and loyal supporters

ONE

WHAT'S THE STORY?" Pete Culnane asked as he approached the crime scene.

"There's a lot of buzz about the victim, Lieutenant," said Tony Barnett, an eager one-year veteran of the St. Paul P.D.

"Oh, a celebrity? Professional athlete? Politician? Someone on the ten-most-wanted list?"

"No, but the face is familiar, and we've been trying to figure out why. The consensus is he was homeless. Some of us are sure we've seen him hanging around Reaching Out, the soup kitchen on West Seventh."

"And?" Pete asked.

"And he's wearing a diamond ring to die for. Sorry, poor choice of words. I mean, it doesn't make sense to be homeless and have a ring like that."

Pete looked at the crumpled body lying face down in the dirt and construction debris at the Upper Landing.

This once-pristine spot along the Mississippi River, on the southern edge of downtown St. Paul, was littered with remnants of the most recent reclamation of the waterfront by developers. Further desecrating the natural beauty was the throng of St. Paul police, including members of the Homicide Unit and the Crime Lab.

If memory served him well, this was the first time in Pete's years with the St. Paul P.D. that the Upper Landing was the scene of a murder investigation. He wondered if, with all this construction, it might be a harbinger of things to come.

For the past few years, the Upper Landing beckoned developers with the promise of obscene returns on investments for those with stashes of cash or the connections to tap into the well-healed, or those creative or dishonest enough to make something out of nothing. However, that was only the first step. Developers also had to be willing and able to withstand the political haggling and the interminable delays. This process would test the patience of a saint, and most developers had more than death and a few miracles separating them from beatification.

With the burst of the real estate bubble, this project wouldn't meet original profit expectations. It was anyone's guess whether it would make or lose money. Pete wondered if there were enough baby boomers willing and able to pay the exorbitant prices these units would no doubt command. He understood that real estate was a matter of *location, location, location*, but he had a hard time grasping a half-million or more for a glorified apartment with an association fee that rivaled his mortgage payments. He didn't identify with those who had that kind of money. He wasn't sure he even wanted to join their exclusive club. So far, Pete had been successful in maintaining a simple lifestyle despite a series of promotions. He was a saver, not a spender.

This August afternoon, the smell of money wasn't what drew the police and onlookers to the shadow of the High Bridge. The smell was anything but sweet, unless a buzzard was conducting the assessment.

"Warm enough for you, Lieutenant?" Tony quipped.

"And then some, Tony." Pete knew the names of all but a handful of the most recently hired men and women working for the department, right down to the dispatchers. He was respected by all but a few of them.

After taking a minute to inquire about Tony's wife and children, Pete asked, "Any details other than what the kids reported?"

"Carney and Houston haven't been here very long." With a flip of his chin, Tony indicated the two gloved men from the St. Paul Homicide Unit near the body. Carney was scouring the area adjacent to the body for trace evidence, while Houston flashed pictures. "I bet they'd sacrifice a day of vacation to be in an air-conditioned office right now, and it's supposed to get even hotter."

Tony continued, "The Homicide Unit and the Crime Lab are already well represented. Carney said the victim should have showered before his last dance. I realize it's a survival tactic—this can be a tough business—but don't you think they get a little carried away with the gallows humor?"

"Try their jobs on for a couple of years and get back to me on that," Pete replied.

"Yeah, I guess you're right. Anyway, did you notice the furring strips and cans over there?" Tony pointed towards the river. "Everyone seems to think they were used for target practice and they had to have been set up recently. Otherwise they'd have been cleared away before now. Seems like a crazy location to be taking target practice, don't you think?"

Pete looked in the designated direction. After surveying the surrounding area for other garbage, he said, "I agree, Tony. The proximity to the body seems more than coincidental. If the victim came across someone, or several someones, taking target practice, was that enough of a reason to kill him? It seems a bit extreme, even knowing it's illegal to shoot a firearm down here."

"Yeah, it doesn't seem like enough of a motive for offing someone."

"But Tony, let's look at it from the reverse position. What if someone saw the victim down here shooting a gun? Might that person think it was a matter of kill or be killed?"

"Are you suggesting this was self-defense?"

"I'm not suggesting anything, yet. I'm just trying to look at all the possibilities. It's usually the angle you fail to consider that comes back to bite you."

Tony broke into a knowing grin. "Amen, Lieutenant, amen. That being the case, how about the bodies of those four homeless men they found in Minneapolis this summer? Last I knew, three of them died of so-called natural causes, and the fourth was beaten to death. Maybe those natural causes had a little help. Do you think there might be a link to this guy's death, what with them all being homeless?"

"Good question. You working on a promotion?"

"Who isn't?" Tony smiled. "Please keep me in mind, if you have a chance to make a plug. Anyway, other than what I've already told you, about all we've accomplished is to have the paramedics verify that the guy's past tense. We barricaded the area, and Carney and Houston are scouring the vicinity for evidence. I haven't heard anything of interest yet, other than the target practice setup. I've been keeping an eye on the area and haven't noticed any clustering behavior. That's always a sure sign somebody found something."

"How about the medical examiner, or one of his investigators?" Pete asked. "Any word on when one of them will arrive?"

"Yeah, any minute now." Tony fanned the air in front of his face. "Andrew Walker's on his way."

Noting Pete's arrival, Carney and Houston halted their efforts and approached him and Tony. Thanks to a heat index of 104 degrees, their shirts clung like suction cups to their middle-aged chests and abs. The Twin Cities was in the throes of a scorching heat wave.

"Any conclusions yet?" Pete asked.

"In addition to the fact that the guy's dead?" Carney asked as he worked at loosening the grip his shirt had on his torso.

"We don't even have a good start yet," admitted Houston. "We have a couple of folks looking for shell casings and trace evidence. We're waiting for someone from the ME's office before we touch the body. In the meantime, although the bullet wound in his back looks like the point of entry, we won't know for sure until we turn him over. But then I'm preaching to the choir, aren't I?" He grinned.

As Pete assessed the body, he unconsciously stroked his upper lip. His cheeks puffed and he blew out a long sigh.

Judging from the face-down position of the body, it looked like the man died instantly, crumpling like a rag doll and falling forward. His arms were at his sides, so it seemed he made no attempt to break his fall. However, Pete considered, the body may have been moved, even dragged here and posed that way or unintentionally left in that position. The surrounding surfaces lent no immediate clue along those lines, but they might know more once the ME and Homicide Unit finished their work.

Relying on a limited view of the victim's face, Pete guessed the man to be in his mid-to-late twenties. He wore two short-sleeved T-shirts. The outer one bore nearly imperceptible signs that the original color was teal. The collar was stretched to twice its intended size, raising the question of whether someone grabbed it to stop the victim and/or wrestle him to the ground. The collar of the inner, once-white shirt more closely approximated its original shape. The man's jeans were filthy and torn. He wore scruffy New Balance shoes, but no socks.

His hair looked dishwater blond, but by all appearances no part of him had experienced the cleansing effects of water in days. And here he was, lying face down in the soon-to-be front yard of someone with far greater means.

"Do you mind?" Pete asked Carney and Houston, nodding towards the body.

"Wouldn't matter if we did," acknowledged Houston. "This is your baby."

"Don't want to interrupt if you're in the middle of something." Pete shrugged. He could afford to be amicable, and he knew it. This group had an enviable track record because they worked so well as a team and with the ME's office.

"Have at it," Carney said. "We're interested in your read on this, and we've done about all we can until the ME arrives."

"Careful what you wish for," Andrew Walker called out as he approached the group. Wearing scrubs, the investigator from the ME's office was better dressed for the task at hand than the others. He signaled Pete to proceed and asked Carney and Houston about their investigation.

O BSERVING FROM THE SIDELINES, Martin Tierney, Pete's partner, watched Pete remove his stylish aviator sunglasses, crouch down and methodically view the body from every conceivable position—including a few that his own body couldn't easily withstand. Although five years Pete's junior, Martin was often mistaken to be several years older, and that was a kick in the teeth.

For Martin, it was a lucky day anytime he was partnered with Pete. Although Pete intimidated him, Martin learned a lot on those assignments. He wondered how lucky or unlucky Pete felt about those pairings.

Martin appeared to be monitoring the proceedings. Truth be told, he was preserving his knees and staying out of Pete's way.

As he stood there, wiping sweat from his face, fidgeting and wishing Pete would finish up, Martin looked over at the two young boys who had reported the body. They now observed the scene from their perch atop a hill, on the northern edge of the Upper Landing.

Earlier, when he'd verified that they were the ones who called 911, they had added, a little too quickly, that they arrived after the fact and hadn't seen anything. Due to their ages, Martin wouldn't question them until their parents were present. Hence, he settled for their names, addresses, and phone numbers. After wrapping things up here, he and Pete would take them home, speak with their parents and question them.

One of the boys, Bill Brown, looked emaciated enough to be anorexic. The other, Tim Grey, looked like a master of the binge-eating part of bulimia.

It bugged Martin that the string bean had a cell phone. *Does everyone have a cell phone these days? What is this world coming to when preteen kids (at least they appear to be preteens) have their own cell phones?* His wife didn't get one until their son started school and she returned to work.

Martin didn't understand kids these days. Much of the time, that also applied to his son. Hard as he tried, it just wasn't like when he was a kid. Today's kids were exposed to too much, and too many parents were afraid to say "no." That made parenting more difficult. He wouldn't dare share that perspective with Pete, who seemed to be in LaLa Land when it came to kids. But Martin found consolation in the belief that Pete would one day get his comeuppance.

Martin tried and failed to find a dry spot on his hanky. It was crazy to wear a suit in weather like this. He had contemplated coming as he was when he got the call, in khakis and a polo shirt, but changed his mind. He knew Pete would look like he was wearing a designer suit and, well, the wonders of peer pressure. In another fifteen or twenty minutes he'd probably pass out from heat prostration and wind up in the emergency room at Regions Hospital.

After a few hours, Martin's suits always looked like he'd slept in them. That bugged him to no end, because Pete, even in this heat, looked like he'd just stepped off the cover of *Gentlemen's Quarterly*. Martin wondered how he did that. The one time Martin asked, Pete only told him to stop buying his suits at Kmart. *Big help! Kmart doesn't sell suits. Do they?*

STILL SQUATTING NEXT TO THE BODY, Pete swatted a hand past both sides of his face for the umpteenth time, trying futilely to interrupt the banquet he provided for all of the mosquitoes in the upper Midwest. It looked to him, even with the limited information available before they turned over the body, as though the man was found shortly after death, cutting down on the likelihood that he was shot anywhere but here.

The man's appearance stood in stark contrast with the diamond ring he wore. The incongruity puzzled Pete. If the man was masquerading as homeless, he had to know the ring was a dead giveaway. If he *was* homeless, why didn't he use it to better his lot? And wouldn't he worry about being rolled for it? Speaking of which, his ring finger looked chafed and red—like someone tried his or her best to pry that ring off his finger.

Deciding he had as much information as he could get from this vantage point, Pete stood up and stretched his legs, relieving some of the tightness in his knees. For the first time since he arrived, he was aware of something other than the dead body and the surroundings as they related to it. Now he examined the area as a factor in the homicide rather than coincidental to the act. Did the man die because he was in this location, or was he destined to die, making the location secondary? Did it have to be one or the other?

Pete's thoughts kept returning to the man's ring. Learning about that ring, he believed, would be critical to the investigation.

As he strode back to join Martin, Pete noted that the Upper Landing was now a beehive of police and ME activity. This area had been known as Little Italy before a series of floods devastated first the homes and, ultimately, the Italian community once located here.

The intermittent baritone blasts from the tugboats, along with the occasional squawk of an egret, the screeching gulls, and the drone of diesel engines, created a symphony that was punctuated by the whine of a passing speedboat. Pete considered that the creak of the cables linking the barges rounded off the opus nicely.

WHERE MARTIN STOOD, A DOZEN YARDS UPWIND, the smells of death and homelessness were overridden by river smells—especially the diesel fumes and stench of dead fish—and the smells of construction.

Martin believed he and Pete were as different as the two boys standing on the hill. Martin's dark-brown hair was straight as a plumb line and each day he fretted that the part on the right side was widening. Pete's hair was close to the same color, but the similarity ended there. His was a mass of waves so thick that an aspiring wood tick would have his work cut out for him. Martin was extremely sensitive about the thirty extra pounds he carried, primarily above his drooping belt buckle, whereas Pete looked more like a marathon runner.

As much as he liked and admired Pete, Martin was bothered by the way he measured up in comparison. He felt his shortcomings were prime examples of the inequities of life. Whereas he was dealt a pair of deuces, Pete was dealt a full house.

Martin greeted him with, "So, Pete, did you see that ring?"

"Hard to miss. It looks like he or someone else tried to get it off. I wish I knew which. Anyway, the kids who reported the body must've been the first and last to come across him. Otherwise, it's a crapshoot whether it would still be on his finger."

"Or if it was," Martin offered, "whether his finger would be here with the rest of him. How many carats do you think it is? Even from here, it makes my wife's engagement ring look like something out of a box of Cracker Jacks."

"But, Martin, I could swear you told me that's where you got it and that you were sick of popcorn, peanuts, and candy-coated snacks by the time you got the prize you wanted."

Martin let the remark pass. He was accustomed to Pete's good-natured jibes.

"Seriously, Pete, how big do you think that rock is?"

"I have no idea. I've never paid any attention to carats. The only diamond I ever bought was Andrea's engagement ring, and we picked it out by looking at the styles in my price range, not at the carats."

"You may not have looked at carats, but I can guarantee she did. Women pay attention to those things."

"Apparently women aren't the only ones. Maybe this guy's wife bought it for him. Only, he's wearing it on his right hand, and he isn't wearing a wedding ring."

"You don't suppose its cubic zirconium?" Martin asked.

"That seems more probable than wearing a ring like that and living in the streets, but it sure looks real."

"Yeah, but I guess it's almost impossible to tell the difference, unless you are a jeweler or have one of those eyepieces they use. If it's real, he must have a nice, fat bank account."

"Or had one . . . or maybe it was a gift. Anyway, Tony said the consensus is that he was homeless, based on other dealings with him."

"Tony?" Martin asked.

"Yes, he's standing over there." Pete indicated Tony's location. "Haven't you met him?"

"I'm sure I have. I just don't remember his name. Why would anyone live on the street, instead of cashing in on that ring?"

"Hard to say. Sentimental value? Maybe he believed his luck was about to change, and he could tough it out until then. Or maybe he felt that selling it was tantamount to throwing in the towel. Then again, maybe he isn't homeless. However, his clothes exude the sour smell that goes way beyond sweat. There's a raging infection on the first knuckle of the index finger on his left hand. Looks like he wasn't doing anything about it."

Pete asked, "Are those boys on the hill the ones who discovered the body?"

"Yeah. They said they were riding their bikes down here and came across it."

"Those look like mighty expensive bicycles," Pete said.

"They are. The skinny kid bragged that his folks paid more than a grand for his. He said it's a Jeep Rubicon Sport mountain bike. I've never heard of that brand. Have you?"

"No, but I've never been in the market for a thousand-dollar bike. Martin, why would a kid ride such an expensive bike down here? Unless you're looking for an obstacle course, what fun would it be, and why risk damaging it? I wonder if they're lying, if they spotted the body from up there, then came down."

"That's not what they claim."

Pete looked up the hill at the boys who, he noted, seemed oblivious to the proceedings on the Upper Landing. They busily sifted through the sand at their feet, as though in search of something. More accurately, one sifted. The heavier boy's efforts were interrupted by a series of nervous glances, encompassing all of the surrounding area, except the immediate vicinity of the body.

"Why would a homeless person hang around here?" Martin asked. "You have to admit it seems like a peculiar spot. With all this construction, I'd be amazed if this was one of the usual hangouts."

"Why's that? This might be their best opportunity to get a look at the condos. Or maybe he was meeting someone. Tony found evidence that someone was taking target practice. See the remnants over there?" Pete pointed at the clutter of cans.

Just then, Carney signaled them. Pete and Martin walked over to the group gathered around the body. Walker and Houston had the photos they needed. Houston had some video, and Carney had gathered the trace evidence in the vicinity of the body. With the preliminaries completed, all three men conferred with Pete and Martin.

The five men decided it was time to turn over the body, once Houston removed the man's wallet from his back pocket. The picture on the driver's license looked like a younger and somewhat more affluent version of the man lying at their feet. The license identified him as twenty-nine-year-old Bradford Wilson Winthrup, who lived on Lake Shore Drive in Chicago.

"Great. That's convenient," Martin moaned. "Will we be going there?"

"Let's see what develops," Pete offered.

As soon as they repositioned the body, Carney shook his head and muttered, "We were right. Some coward son-of-a-bitch shot him in the back."

It was now apparent that the bullet hole in the man's back was the entrance wound. There was no evidence of injury on the man's front or sides. That meant the bullet was still in the body. Cuts and bruises on the man's forehead and cheeks showed signs of healing, indicating they were acquired a few to several days before death.

Carney, Houston, and Walker continued their examination of the body, clothing, and the space where the body rested.

Having observed Martin's nervous shuffling for the last several minutes, Pete said, "You're looking mighty antsy. What's up?"

"Marty's at second base in about an hour. It's the first time he's starting. I've been working with him on his fielding. He'll be really disappointed if I miss the game. My track record this season is less than stellar."

"There isn't much more we can do here," Pete said. "Carney said he'll accompany Walker when he takes the body to the ME's office and stick around for the examination. They know how to reach us if they need to, so why don't you head out."

"What about the boys who found the body? I said we'd take them home."

"I'll handle it."

"But it won't look good if I disappear," Martin added.

"Don't be so paranoid. How will anyone know where you are? For all anyone knows, you're checking out leads."

Easier said than done, Martin thought. Working in the shadow of a guy like Pete wasn't easy, and leaving now wouldn't improve the situation. But then there was Marty. Since Martin's promotion to investigator, he seemed to be forever putting his son on the shelf, and their relationship was showing the effects. That hurt.

W ALKING MARTIN TO HIS CAR, Pete smiled when he saw that the boys were waiting on the hill for him. *Good.* He was confident they knew more, much more, than they'd said.

Two

PETE PICKED UP THE PACE as the two investigators approached Martin's car, and Martin puffed from the strain of keeping up. That was because Pete's legs were much longer than his, Martin rationalized.

"Slow down, would you?" Martin panted. His fists pumped back and forth at his sides in an effort to hasten his stride. "You're killing me. Why are you in such an all-fired hurry? I'm the one who has to make it to the game."

"I'm anxious to get a few answers. The sooner I start, the sooner I'll finish." And he didn't want the boys running off, before he delivered them to their parents.

Martin got in the car, and Pete told him to enjoy the game. Then, without waiting for a reply, he closed the door and headed for the boys.

When the hill where the boys spent much of the afternoon came back into view, his smile evaporated. Sprinting to the spot, he scanned for any sign of them or their bikes. Once there, he did a slow, methodical 360-degree turn, searching for any sign of them. Finding nothing, he clenched his fist and punched the air fiercely. He was obligated to notify their parents about their discovery. Furthermore, he wanted to be in their faces and question them. The time required to accomplish that had just grown exponentially.

How did they vanish so completely and so quickly? They'd promised Martin they would hang around until someone could accompany them home. What changed that? If they saw the murderer, didn't they realize their lives were in danger? No, that was overly optimistic. They might be in danger even if they didn't see anything. The subject had only to suspect they'd seen something. That was usually enough.

Pete pulled a small spiral notebook from his pocket and dialed the first number Martin got from the boys. He listed it as the cell phone number for the thin kid, Bill Brown.

When the phone rang a third time, he began holding his breath. "Come on, answer the phone, Bill," he whispered.

Bill wasn't listening.

Pete was transferred to voicemail. He hung up without leaving a message.

He dialed Bill's home number. The woman who answered didn't know a Bill Brown. She didn't know any Bill described as between eleven and fourteen, slender, and around five-feet-tall.

Biting his lower lip, he dialed the home of the second boy, Tim Grey. The phone rang, and rang and rang. The longer it rang, the harder Pete's fingers drummed his kneecap. *Come on, come on, answer,* he thought. It didn't happen, and after eighteen rings he gave up. Not even an answering machine. Didn't everyone, at least everyone in the likely age group of the boys' parents, have an answering machine? Right now he'd favor a law, mandating that all parents have one—and checked it for messages.

Much as he hated to, Pete decided to call Martin. He wanted one more piece of information he hoped his partner obtained.

"Yeah?" Martin interrupted the second ring.

"Were the boys' bikes licensed?"

"Why are you worrying about that?"

"They took off, and at least one of the phone numbers they provided is incorrect."

Martin said it had surprised him that a thousand-dollar bike was not licensed, and neither was the other one. They went back and forth several times, with Martin worrying that he better report in.

Pete grew impatient, trying to convince Martin it wasn't necessary—at least not yet. He wanted to hang up and get back to his search for the boys. He had a hunch.

Had Martin been there, he'd have seen the ripple of clenching muscle in Pete's jaw and known it was time to back off. It was an obvious indication that the man's patience was wearing thin. The debate ended when Pete told Martin he'd call if the situation changed.

As Pete ran to his unmarked vehicle, a nondescript white Crown Victoria, he wondered if he was too interested in Martin's relationship with Marty. Pete always assumed he'd have a kid or two. He now worried that it would never happen. He wasn't even dating anyone. He'd heard about a woman's biological clock. Well, his psychological and biological clocks were clanging away.

The latest word out of the scientific community was that autism was more common among children conceived by fathers over forty. What next? Add that to the fact he'd soon have to marry a woman ten years his junior to avoid the health issues attributed to mothers approaching his current age. He couldn't picture himself married to a significantly younger woman.

Almost as important, he couldn't picture himself being sixty when his kids graduated from high school. He wanted to play ball with them and teach them how to ski, the way his wife, Andrea, taught him. He wanted to wrestle with his boys when they reached their growing spurts and wanted to take him on. All boys did that when they were fifteen or so, didn't they?

He remembered the first time he semi-seriously wrestled with his dad, having over-estimated his own strength and his father's decline. He shook his head at the fond memories of the years when he had first tried on adulthood.

Was he overreacting now, because of this not-quite-midlife crisis he was experiencing? No, he decided. Although it was undoubtedly affecting his judgment, Pete was convinced there was a basis for his concern about the boys.

To avoid burning more time, he sped to headquarters. All the way, he thought about the wrong phone numbers, and two boys with colors as their last names. Not good. Not good at all! He was furious with himself for letting them get away. He found some consolation in the fact that the prefixes of the home phone numbers and the addresses they provided were in Mendota Heights. This suggested they lived in, or at least were familiar with the suburb south of St Paul.

After reaching the office, he spoke with dispatch. The cell phone number Martin got from the boys was the phone used to report the body. Using that number, he again tried to connect with the boy whose name was, perhaps, Bill Brown.

Once again he was transferred to voicemail, and once again he hung up without leaving a message. If the boys were, in fact, lying about their other phone numbers and names, would scaring them gain their cooperation or make them less accessible? He had to think about that.

Meanwhile, he enlisted the help of another investigator, Sergeant Penney Zimmerman. She saw him at his desk, frowning and running his fingers through his hair—a sure sign he was flustered. She stepped up to offer a helping hand.

Pete explained his predicament and, while he watched, she checked the Internet for the addresses the boys provided. One was a vacant lot. The other was nonexistent. Numbers didn't go that high on that street. She confirmed that both the real and made-up addresses had to be in Mendota Heights.

He asked her to come up with a list of all Browns, Greys, and Grays, in Mendota Heights, Saint Paul, and surrounding suburbs.

While Zimmerman did that, Pete contacted dispatch and issued a "be on the lookout" (BOLO) for the boys and a silver Jeep Rubicon mountain bike. The BOLO was broadcast immediately to all officers on shift and would be read at each shift's roll call.

At a loss for anything else to do for now to locate the kids, he contacted Minneapolis Homicide to get information on the four homeless deaths on the other side of the river. A cop named Delano put him on hold for several minutes. When he came back, he told Pete that three of the deaths were ruled natural causes. They were still investigating the fourth. Tony was right. The fourth man was beaten to death.

"Do you have personal property sheets for the four of them?" Pete asked. "A homeless man was shot to death over here today. I'm wondering if there might be a link."

"A link?"

"Yes, to your murdered homeless man."

"I can get them, but I think you're spinning your wheels," Delano said.

"Perhaps, but I'd like to know if any of the four had valuable jewelry, or if their families reported missing jewelry."

"You're kidding, right? They were homeless. Valuable jewelry doesn't really fit the profile."

"That's what I thought, until today. Just do me a favor and fax me their sheets."

Pete pressed his luck by asking for the dates and times of death for all four men and when the beaten man died, relative to the other three.

Delano sighed long and loud, but looked it up and told Pete the beaten man died first. Furthermore, two weeks passed between the death of the beaten man and the first death from natural causes. The three who died of natural causes did so in a period of twenty days. The first two died with a day between them, and the third died the day before yesterday. He told Pete, "Things must be even less interesting over there than I've been led to believe. Maybe you should quit that job and come over here, where you won't have to make work."

"Yeah, yeah," Pete muttered as he hung up.

Pete hurriedly removed his suit coat, rolled up his sleeves, loosened his tie and got a less-than-fresh cup of coffee. He used a people finder on the Internet to check for a phone number for the victim. There were times when computers came in handy.

Dialing Winthrup's home number, Pete was treated to a message that the number was no longer in service. He'd anticipated as much, considering that Winthrup was homeless, but Pete hoped for something more than the computerized voice that gave no additional information. So, he went back to the Internet.

This time he looked for a phone number for Shoreline Estates. In addition to Winthrup's street address, his license said, "Shoreline Estates #2402." It had to be an apartment or condominium complex.

Google maps indicated that Lake Shore Drive, the address on Winthrup's license, bordered Lake Michigan. That real estate had to be even pricier than the real estate along the Mississippi, causing Pete to again wonder about Winthrup's current physical state. Thankfully, the Internet also provided a phone number for Shoreline Estates.

A man answered Pete's call, saying, "We're full up. Not expecting any vacancies for at least ninety days."

After identifying himself, Pete explained, "I'm looking for some information about Bradford Winthrup."

"That makes two of us," an irritated voice shot back. "Winthrup disappeared without paying for two months. I started the eviction process, and he vanished. I can't wait to get my hands on him."

"When did you last see him?" Pete asked.

"About three weeks ago."

"Do you have any information on his employer or his work number?"

"Yes, but it won't do you any good. He isn't there anymore. I found that out when I tried to garnish his wages."

Pete explained he still wanted the information, and the man, whose name he learned was Vernon, retrieved it for him.

"According to our records," he said, "Winthrup worked for ACS Marketing."

"Do you know what ACS stands for?"

"It doesn't say. It may not stand for anything other than ACS."

Pete asked about an emergency contact and learned that Winthrup updated it a couple of weeks before he disappeared. When Vernon had called the contact number, he was connected to the Minnesota Governor's Office. The address turned out to be the Minnesota State Capitol building.

"On an off chance," Vernon said, "I asked for Lori Winthrup, the name of his emergency contact. The governor's receptionist didn't know anyone by that name."

"Is there any way for you to retrieve the old information?" Pete asked.

"None. Believe me, I tried. We pride ourselves in running a near paperless office. By the time I knew there was a problem, the backup, too, was updated."

"How well did you know Winthrup?" Pete asked.

"Not very. He was friendly enough when he came to the office, but we never got beyond small talk about the weather and the Cubs, those sorts of things."

Through a series of questions, Pete learned that Winthrup wasn't married and lived alone. He had lots of friends, but Vernon didn't know any of their names, and there weren't any records to provide them.

Vernon did know, however, that for several days after Winthrup was last seen, at least a dozen people came looking for him, and some of them didn't look very wholesome. "They weren't the kind of guys I'd seen with him," Vernon said.

Unfortunately, none left contact information.

As Pete completed the call, Sergeant Zimmerman returned with a sheet containing the requested list of possible names, addresses, and phone numbers of the boys.

Pete hung up, smiled, said, "Thanks," and asked, "One more favor?"

There weren't many women at headquarters, at least not single women, capable of denying the sweet, pleading look he flashed her.

"Sure," she shrugged. "I'll make the calls."

Pete doubted he'd get any answers from Winthrup's former employer on a Sunday evening. Just the same, he wondered what would happen if he dialed Winthrup's work number. When he did, the voicemail message said, "Brad Winthrup's calls are being taken by an associate," and provided the phone number.

He tried that number and was transferred to Frank Baxter's voicemail, which instructed him to leave a message or press "0" to reach the receptionist. When he did the latter, he was connected to someone else's voicemail.

Next he flipped through the Minneapolis and St. Paul phone books. He found eight Winthrups listed between the two cities and their suburbs, but not a single Lori, Laurie, Laura, or L. Winthrup, nor a Bradford, Brad, or Wilson Winthrup.

Pete had hoped for a senior Bradford Winthrup or, using the middle name on the license, a Wilson Winthrup. But that might have made things too easy. With unusual names like those, there would almost have to be a connection between that person and the victim.

Next he did a statewide search for Winthrups via the Internet, but he failed to find any additional listings.

Without a positive ID on the body, he wouldn't do anything with his list of Winthrups. Notifying the wrong family about the death of a loved one had to be the ultimate *faux pas*.

Zimmerman hadn't yet reappeared. Pete thought it shouldn't be taking this long to contact the number of families on her list. Had she located one or both of the families? Before he went to check, he contacted Carney to get his best guesstimate of when the ME's provisional report would be ready. Carney said it would be at least a few hours.

Pete was amazed to find Zimmerman peering at her computer monitor, rather than speaking on the phone.

"What's up?" he asked.

"I struck out on the Browns and Greys—both spellings. So, I'm looking for Blacks and Greens. I'm even looking for Blues, Navys, Sands, and every other color that I can think of that seems feasible. I'm still putting the list together."

"I understand the colors, but Sand?" Pete raised an eyebrow.

"Sure," Zimmerman said, stretching. "Sand is brown. I know it seems farfetched, but I thought he might've come up with it. And that raises the question of why these kids were lying to you about who they are. What did you do to scare them?"

"Are they scared of me? Or the killer?"

"Or both," Zimmerman proposed.

"Yeah, that's comforting. I put out a BOLO. Once you finish what you're doing and we call all of those people, I don't know anything else I can do tonight. Any ideas?"

"No, but who's working this case with you?"

"Martin, but he's got his hands full. At least for now, the kids are my mission."

"Strange, since he's the one with a kid. You look exhausted. Why don't you head out? I'll make the calls and let you know if I come up with anything."

Pete knew she was at least as resourceful as he when it came to searching electronically and by phone, so he agreed. "But when you've finished, please let me know either way, okay?"

"Sure. Give me another hour."

Pete shut down his computer and headed home, but he didn't stop thinking about the case. With Zimmerman taking on the boys, he allowed himself to think about other aspects, including the victim's connection to Minnesota.

THREE

MARTIN SAUNTERED INTO HEADQUARTERS Monday morning, wearing a grin. It was 7:10, and he was confident he'd get a jump on Pete. That made this a rare occasion and would make up for his early exit yesterday. Even better than that, last night he devised a methodology he believed would assist them in their search for this and future suspects.

When he saw Pete sitting at his desk with his phone in one hand and a pen in the other, his enthusiasm wilted. However, he forced himself to concentrate on the positive. He still had his new tool, and for the first time since he became an investigator, he'd teach Pete something. He was pumped!

Pete raised a hand in greeting and smiled.

While Pete wrapped up the phone call, Martin shuffled and re-arranged the neatly stacked piles of paper on his desk, looking for anything new or requiring attention. Carelessly thrown on top, he found faxed copies of personal property sheets and wondered why they were on his desk. After paging through them and finding nothing of interest, he shrugged and put them aside.

He checked his email, typically responding only when the failure to do so threatened his career. The boatload of department-wide messages, most of which were irrelevant to him, wasted a lot of time and irritated him. Finally, he reached into his suit coat pocket, retrieved the sheet of paper on which he'd slaved last night, unfolded it and set it ceremoniously on the middle of his desk.

Martin hoped that Pete would observe this and ask what he had. His desk was in Pete's field of vision, and Martin figured it would be hard to miss. He was wrong. Pete wrote notes rapidly in the three-by-five spiral notebook he always carried. The letters, although penned with haste, were as meticulously formed as the output from any typewriter or laser printer.

Martin prolonged the ceremonial unveiling of his creation by getting up from his desk, hanging his suit coat on a coat rack, returning to his desk and smoothing out the wrinkles in the all-important sheet of paper.

Pete continued his note taking and appeared oblivious to Martin's tactics. However, as soon as Martin stopped the commotion, Pete retrieved a document from his desk and held it out to him without a break in his telephone conversation.

It was the provisional medical examiner's report. According to the report, the victim died of a gunshot wound. No surprise. The bullet entered through his back on a downward trajectory and broke a rib that punctured his left lung. The bullet passed through the right atrium and lodged in the left ventricle of his heart, which caused it to cease pumping. The St. Paul Crime Lab now possessed the bullet.

The ME was doing lab analyses on cut downs from the scrapes and contusions on the victim's forehead, left eyebrow, and left cheek. He and Pete had discussed those marks on the victim's face with Walker, Carney, and Houston at the scene. They all agreed that initial indications were that some or all were caused by a ring worn on the hand of a person who struck him. Gunshot residue was found on the victim's shirt and right hand.

It would be at least another week before the toxicology was completed.

With nothing better to do while waiting for Pete to get off the phone, Martin decided to get a cup of coffee and see if anyone brought goodies today. Some comfort food would taste terrific about now. Removing his coffee mug from the bottom desk drawer, he noticed something furry growing in the cloudy leftovers. Resolving to fix that problem, he walked down the hall towards the lunch room.

When he returned several minutes later, he carried two brownies and a cup of warm brew he'd enhanced with cream and three sugars.

Raising an index finger, Pete signaled that he was wrapping up his telephone conversation.

"Want a brownie?" Martin offered as Pete hung up.

He wasn't surprised when Pete declined. He couldn't remember the last time he saw the other man eat anything he deemed unhealthy. Now he'd have to eat both. That broke his heart—or at least the diet his wife had him on.

Pete had information to share with Martin. He'd just gotten a positive identification on the body. The man's fingerprints were on file, thanks to an arrest for DUI eight years ago, on his twenty-first birthday. The victim's name matched that on his driver's license. He was, indeed, Bradford Wilson Winthrup.

"But what do you suppose happened to his gun?" Pete asked, referring to the gunshot residue on Winthrup's hands and shirt, as noted in the ME's report.

"Got me," Martin said, accentuating it with a hands-up shrug.

"And what was he shooting at?" Pete added. "He might've been the one taking target practice. Ordinarily, my first guess would be that he was shooting at his attacker, but that doesn't make sense. He was shot in the back. Maybe he thought he killed the guy and was walking away when he was shot.

"The Crime Lab reported that Winthrup was hit by a fully jacketed bullet from a .45 caliber handgun," Pete continued. "The shell casings found in the vicinity where the person was likely taking target practice are also from a .45, raising the question of whether the victim or the murderer was doing the practicing. The lab's doing the DNA analysis of the epithelial cells found on the victim's ring, as well as some hairs found on his shirt that don't match his.

"I'll bet my bottom dollar he was shot where he was found," Pete continued. "And the boys who reported the body took off before I got back to them. We have to find them."

"Dammit! I should've taken them home right away. This won't look good on the reports."

"Don't waste your time second-guessing yourself. We were both busy. There were plenty of other things demanding our attention, and they told you they'd wait."

"Yeah," Martin sighed, "that's comforting."

"Zimmerman helped me last night. Unfortunately, all we determined for sure is that they were lying about their addresses, their home phone numbers, and probably their last names."

"You asked Zimmerman for help?" Martin asked, coming forward in his chair, out of his previously relaxed position. He had an empty feeling, and the two brownies he enjoyed moments earlier didn't compensate.

Pete read Martin's mind. "I told her you were working other angles. I didn't tell her they were family-based. She didn't think anything of it."

"Oh, thanks," Martin said half-heartedly. He wasn't convinced.

"Last night I put out a BOLO," Pete continued. "I also arranged to have a patrol car keep an eye on the Upper Landing. We'll know immediately if anyone sees them. Right now we'd best locate and talk to Winthrup's family."

He told Martin about the eight Winthrups living in Minnesota. It was only 7:30, and he hoped some of them were family members and were home.

"Why don't we call them first?" Martin asked. "It'll save time, and this could be a wild-goose chase."

"It could be, but I don't want his parents or another family member to find out about his death over the phone. Besides, if one or more of them was involved, I want to see facial expressions when we tell them."

Both men retrieved their suit jackets. Martin refolded and reluctantly reinserted the paper displaying his new methodology in his pocket.

Last night the temperature never dipped below the mid-seventies. This morning, there wasn't a cloud to break the relentlessness of the sun's rays. Public safety officials advised people to check on their elderly relatives to insure they were withstanding the heat, and after a two-year-old child was found alone and near death in a car, news reports were replete with warnings about the danger and illegality of putting a child or a pet in this peril even for a few minutes.

As they made their way to the parking lot, once again Martin half-ran, trying to keep up with Pete's long, brisk stride.

"Do you want to drive or co-pilot today?" Pete asked.

The question surprised Martin. Did Pete ever drive when they worked together? Martin liked to drive. Pete knew that. And by driving, Martin also hoped to have Pete look at his all-important piece of paper, while he explained it.

They decided to start with the Winthrups living on St. Paul's East Side and work their way west, wrapping up with the two in Minneapolis.

Pete wondered if Winthrup was born in Minnesota. That might explain his appearance here, after he lost his job. If he was born here, and their efforts to locate the family failed, with his date of birth they could obtain his birth certificate from the Minnesota Department of Health. It would show his parents' names and thus, with a little luck and a lot of tenacity, they'd find them—he hoped.

Pete told Martin about this morning's conversations with Bradford Winthrup's former supervisor, Frank Baxter. Again Martin had to bide his time before introducing his baby, but at least this would be a good segue, and it provided some data for it.

"Baxter said Winthrup was fired three months ago," Pete said. "Getting the cause for termination was as frustrating as tying your shoes while wearing boxing gloves. After making a few threats that, if push came to shove, I'd be hard pressed to deliver on, and after he spoke with Human Resources, he said Winthrup was fired for threatening a VP. He had to check with HR again, before he'd tell me that the VP's name is Walter Linton. Conveniently enough, Linton's out of state on vacation for the next two weeks, and supposedly no one has any contact information for him. I suggested they had a way to reach someone as important as a company VP, and he said it would take some time to check with everyone. He's getting back to me."

"Hmm, don't you usually tie your shoes before putting on your boxing gloves?" Martin asked. "Anyway, it sounds like a first-class runaround to me. Do you suppose Linton's on vacation in Minnesota?"

"It's certainly crossed my mind. Baxter claimed not to know where he went."

"A company vice-president is out of the office for two weeks, and no one knows how to reach him?" Martin asked. "He must be an integral cog in the organization's wheel. And Winthrup threatened Linton? What kind of crap is that? Who in their right mind threatens a VP?"

"Good question, Martin. And what was the threat? He could've been blowing off steam or threatening to go over Linton's head. If Linton's as inept as Baxter seems, I can understand Winthrup getting exasperated with him. If we're looking for something that would motivate Linton to kill Winthrup, it seems it would have to be more significant than that kind of threat."

"By the way, how was Marty's game yesterday?"

"He did pretty well, but he still has problems with the double-play turn I've been struggling to teach him." Martin appreciated Pete's interest in his son, but right now he wanted to tell Pete about his concept, not discuss Little League baseball. Even so, he bit his lip and resolved to wait for the right opening.

"And how many ten-year-olds have a double-play turn?" Pete asked.

"I know, you're right. It's just that there's a couple of kids who I swear play like they were born wearing a golden glove."

"If they're on Marty's team, all the better. Either way, the real question is whether they, and Marty, enjoy the game. Sometimes the kids with loads of natural talent are under incredible pressure from Mom and Dad. That can take all of the fun out of it."

"Speaking from experience?" Martin asked.

"No. I was blessed with loving parents, who did their best to give me every advantage. They never got on my back about trying hard enough. I think they were more concerned about me going overboard."

The two investigators made their way north on Arcade Street in St. Paul's East Side. Along this street was a blending, although not always a harmonious one, of housing and commerce. A variety of stores fought for every inch of retail space. Bars were well represented, and restaurants came in second with a photo finish. A corner drugstore fought a noble battle, attempting to survive within sneezing distance of two national chains. A butcher shop waged a similar battle with the down-scale grocery warehouses. A mortuary with a manicured lawn and bushes stood in stark contrast with the cement and tar landscape of the neighboring businesses.

The other streets in the area rarely sported anything but houses; however, a smattering of schools and churches provided some variety. Most of the houses, built in the thirties and forties, were two-story wooden structures with detached garages accessed off alleys.

Judging from the majority of homes, the residents preferred the natural colors: the browns, beiges, grays, and white. But, on rare occasions, a robin's-egg blue, violet, or lime green provided variety or disruption, or tested the neighborhood's tolerance for diversity. Or maybe it simply demonstrated the difficulty of envisioning the way a whole house would look, based on a one-inch square of color.

With rare exceptions, houses and yards were well maintained. Trees, bushes, and flowers alleviated the boredom otherwise linked to the uniform construction. Unlike the toothpick trees in the newer housing developments, most of these stood taller than the houses they shaded with their broad, lush canopies.

Pete began telling Martin about the personal property sheets he got from Minneapolis, and how glad he was he didn't work over there. His cell phone vibrated, and he checked the caller ID as he pulled it from his pocket. It was dispatch.

"Hope I'm not calling at a bad time, Lieutenant. I thought you'd want to know that a squad over near Cherokee Park just reported an abandoned silver mountain bike. It's a . . . hang on a second . . . let me check . . . It's a Jeep Rubicon. I guess that's the kind you're looking for?"

Pete closed his eyes, slid down in the seat and took a deep breath. He felt like he'd been punched in the stomach by a prizefighter. "Can you tell me who found it and if they're still in the vicinity?"

"What's up?" Martin asked. He knew from Pete's face that it wasn't good.

"Hang on," Pete said, holding up a finger, as the dispatcher returned.

"Okay, Lieutenant. Morris called it in. He's still there, with the bike. He's just north of where West Stevens runs into the park."

Rather than work through an intermediary, Pete asked the dispatcher to have Morris contact him. While waiting on Morris, he had Martin pull over and shared the details.

"Not good, huh?" Martin asked. "If it was a secondhand bike, no big deal. But you'd have to be crazy, or scared to death, to leave that bike in the grass. Bill Brown, or whatever the kid's name is, was really proud of that bike. But he can't own the only Jeep Rubicon, not even the only silver one. Right?"

"Yes, but I'm concerned for several reasons. First, like you said, that someone would leave a bike like that out of their sight. If my bike cost half as much, I wouldn't trust it to the most expensive locking system money can buy. The temptation to nab it is too great. Second is the proximity of Cherokee Park to the Upper Landing. East Stevens is only a stone's throw from the High Bridge, and the Upper Landing is only a moderate workout from there—if you're on a thousand-dollar bike."

By the time Morris contacted him, Pete was getting testy. Morris didn't help anything, when he said that it was obvious the bike was in prize condition—just like Bill's, the chrome was polished—just like Bill's, it wasn't licensed. And it looked like whomever was riding it dropped it and took off with little regard for it, because one of the pedals had dug into the grass.

Rationality prevailed over Pete's knee jerk reaction to turn around and head for the High Bridge. He arranged for Morris to coordinate a stakeout of the area and scour the park for the two boys.

"Look, Pete, there's nothing more we can do about the kids right now, right?"

"Not that I know of. And I've been racking my brain, trying to come up with something. Unless . . ." He tried the two phone numbers they had for the boys, again—the cell number and the home number that hadn't been proven erroneous. There was no answer, times two.

The subject Martin wanted to discuss with Pete took a backseat to everything else happening this morning. The way things were going, it might move from there into the trunk. He'd about resigned himself to shelving the topic when he realized it might provide the distraction they needed. Even more important, he believed it provided valuable direction for attacking problems like the one they now faced. Taking a deep breath, he dove into his spiel.

"Unless you have some other news," he said, "I want to tell you about something I developed last night."

Pete nodded.

Martin reached into his pocket for the paper, handed it to Pete and said, "Open it up, and I'll explain it.

"On the rows of the matrix," Martin said, reaching over and tapping the place, "is space for listing all of the suspects. They can be grouped, for example, as family, friends, work contacts, strangers, et cetera. We can use the columns to list motives," he continued, pointing to the relevant place. "For each suspect, we put an 'X' in the columns for applicable motives, adding new motives as needed. If we discount them as a suspect, we make a heavy line through their entire row. We can even create a matrix to look at what's going on with the boys. I mean, what motivated them to lie to us? They might be getting their kicks that way, but I think we both agree that's not likely."

Pete paid close attention, and that pleased Martin.

He explained how the matrix organized and tracked all of the facts they uncovered, and how it could be expanded as needed. He ended by asking, "So, what do you think?"

"I might've laid it out differently, but anything that helps is good."

"What would you do differently?" Martin tried not to sound de-flated. He thought Pete would be more enthused.

"There isn't one right way, Martin; but this is the way my mind works. I picture it as a time line. For example, the first point on the time line is the Upper Landing. There's a vertical line going up from that point. Along the vertical line, thus far, are two points. One is the boys who found the body. The second is the victim."

Pete explained how he'd show the information gathered about the boys and the victim, as well as the questions surrounding each, such as why the boys took off and how a homeless man had a ring with a sizeable diamond. The second point on his time line would be ACS Marketing. He'd list both Baxter and Linton on the line ex-tending from that point.

"Your system sounds a lot like what they use in one of the crime shows on TV," Martin said. "I can't remember which one it is, but they use a time line and insert all of the developments."

"I'm not familiar with it, Martin. I don't watch crime shows on TV. I get enough of it on the job."

"So what you're saying is, 'Nice try,' but you don't see anything to be gained from it?"

"No, I'm not saying that. I'm impressed that you worked on this last night, and I think you should use anything that helps you organ-ize the facts and flesh out areas requiring follow-up."

"But it wouldn't help you?"

"If it helps you, of course it helps me. We're a team. Whatever you do to insure we're not overlooking anything benefits us both."

As they turned the final corner, Pete pointed out the first house on their list—the residence of Casey Winthrup. Martin parked a half-block away.

The front porch of the Winthrup house was as littered by toys as the yard was tidy. It provided signs that at least one child lived there or visited frequently.

When Pete knocked on the screen door, the woman who responded had a toddler in her arms and a harried look on her face.

He identified himself and Martin, and they flipped their badges.

She said she was Gloria Winthrup, only after Pete asked for her name, and that she was Casey's wife.

Pete apologized for their interruption and said they needed only a few minutes. That elicited a frown and an irritated sigh. He showed her a copy of the photo from Bradford Winthrup's driver's license, explained they were looking for his family and asked if she knew him.

Shuffling the tot from one hip to the other, she said, "I'm running late. Come back this evening. Then I can answer any questions you have without getting in trouble at work."

Her nervousness was as obvious to Pete as the second child she carried, but he didn't know if her lateness or the picture was behind her anxiety.

The tot seemed as attuned to her displeasure as Pete, because he chose this moment to exercise his lungs—lungs which sounded as though they'd had plenty of practice. Gloria shot Pete a now-see-what-you've-done look. She cooed in the baby's ear and stroked his back, trying to console him.

"We'll return this evening, whatever time you like," Pete said. "However, we can't leave until we get a few answers. Again, do you recognize this man?"

"That photo's very small, and I don't have my glasses."

"No problem. We'll wait for you to get them," Martin said. "We realize you're in a hurry, so the quicker you answer our questions, the quicker you can leave."

"I'll be back as soon as I find them. I never know where they are, so it may take several minutes. But why can't you wait until this evening?"

"Because that man's family would appreciate hearing from us sooner, rather than later," Pete said. He sympathized with her predicament, but not enough to delay their investigation and, if his suspicions were correct, certainly not enough to allow her to preempt their efforts.

Gloria's face showed no reaction to the statement about the man in the photo's family. Turning, son in arms, she left the two men standing on the porch and closed the door in their faces.

Martin didn't say a word. He turned and hurried down the steps, around the corner of the house and into the backyard. Once there, he found a spot near the alley that provided a view of the back and both sides of the Winthrup house.

The drapes were open in an upstairs window, and Martin saw Gloria put down the child and raise a phone to her ear. He called Pete's cell and reported this.

While Martin watched for a fleeing woman, Pete stayed put on the porch. It didn't surprise him when she returned, *sans* spectacles.

"No luck?" he asked.

She looked confused, but recovered quickly and said, "No, but I have a pair at the office. I'll have them when you come back this evening."

"That's okay." Pete said, pausing long enough to draw a look of relief. It faded when he added, "We'll follow you to your place of employment. You can get your glasses and look at it there."

She put the child on the floor and asked to see the picture again. After moving it towards and away from her face a half dozen times, still squinting, she looked at Pete and said, "Is that Brad?"

Martin arrived in time to hear her question and answered with one of his own. "Brad who?"

"Brad Winthrup, my brother-in-law. I can't tell for sure. That must be an old picture."

"What's Brad's full name?" Martin asked.

"Bradford Wilson Winthrup. Now that's a million-dollar name, isn't it?"

"Is it a misnomer?" Pete asked, keying on the note of disdain in her voice.

"What do you mean?"

"I mean, does the name fit the man?"

"Oh, I don't know," Gloria said, possibly wishing to undo the cavalier remark. "I'm really late now. I've gotta go. Come back tonight if you have more questions. My husband will be here. He can help you. By the way, what's this about?"

"I'm sorry to have to inform you that Bradford's body was found yesterday, and we're trying to locate his family," Pete said. "Are his parents living? Does he have a wife, children, or other siblings?"

Gloria looked stunned, and for a moment Pete feared she was going to drop the baby.

He reached out, reflexively, just in case.

"No wife or kids. He has another brother and a sister, and his mother. His father died two years ago."

"We need their names, addresses, and phone numbers," Pete said.

As she rushed through the requested information, Pete circled each name she mentioned on his list of Winthrups, checked what she said against the addresses and phone numbers he'd gathered and added the sister, as well as the mother's first name next to the listing for Alexander Winthrup.

They accounted for half of the Winthrups on Pete's list. When he asked about the other four, she claimed not to know any of them.

He asked for the place of employment for each family member, learned she hadn't seen Brad in more than a week. Martin set the time for the return visit.

Gloria descended the porch steps on Pete and Martin's heels. As they walked to their car, she hurried to a rust-eaten Honda Civic and sped away.

FOUR

AFTER STRUGGLING THROUGH the required math and physics classes, Brad Winthrup's younger brother had attained his life-long dream—assuming his life began when he was seventeen. Casey had done this by obtaining a degree in engineering. His high school guidance counselor assured him he was well-suited to the work and that it would be a rewarding and profitable career for him. During his junior and senior years in college, when a few of the required classes became overwhelming, he refused to give up. Instead, he found a tutor and did little else but study, attend classes and sleep. The party that began at graduation ended a short time after he found a job. When he believed he could finally reap the benefits of his efforts, reality hit, and his life and dreams headed in opposite directions.

He discovered that getting ahead wasn't his destiny, regardless of what he did. As a civil engineer with the Minnesota Department of Transportation, Casey earned just enough to keep the wolves at bay and his small family sheltered, clothed and fed.

Now he spent much of his time worrying about the next catastrophe. What affliction would next send his wife or son to the emergency room? How much would health insurance, gasoline, and real estate taxes go up next year? Which appliance would bite the dust next? It felt like his life amounted to a series of panic attacks from events over which he had little control.

But all of that was prior to Brad's return to Minnesota. When that occurred, his concern for what might happen next crossed a critical threshold. Apprehension about the future still seemed to rule his life, but the threats posed by unknown future events were now totally out of control. He did things that in his wildest dreams he would never have imagined, and now he sought ways to dodge the consequences.

This morning at 6:50, like every weekday, Casey reported for work at the Transportation Building—a part of the Capital complex. That's where he was when his wife called much later.

Gloria said there were two cops at the door and, after finding a way to get out of their hearing range, she only had a minute to give him a head's up. All she knew was that they had a picture of Brad and wanted her to identify him.

That sent Casey into a tailspin. He was scared. No, he was panic-stricken. He felt the walls closing in, and his throat tightening around his windpipe. He had to get outside where he could breathe and, hopefully, think. He didn't have much time.

"Don't worry. I'm sure it's nothing," he lied, hoping she wouldn't pick up on it.

After signing out, he ran down the stairs and exited the building, via the back door. Crossing Rice Street, he hurried to the east door of Sears and found it locked. "Terrific," he murmured, dropping his arms to his sides and slouching in exasperation.

Finally, regaining control, he dashed around to the opposite side of the store. Hidden from the view of his co-workers by the two-story building, he felt some measure of comfort.

Masking emotions wasn't his strong suit, and he wasn't in the mood to field the questions of anyone nosing into his business. Right now, he just wanted to run. But that wasn't an option, at least not yet. Backed into a corner, he had to reach the rest of his family before the cops did.

Casey paced in ever-shrinking circles, staying in the shadows of the building. As soon as he stopped hyperventilating, brought his heart rate down to double digits and succeeded in steadying his hands enough to hit only one button at a time, he dialed the first number—his brother.

"Eric, this is Casey."

"No kidding? Like I wouldn't have recognized your voice?"

"Shut up. I need your help and I'm in a hurry. The police were at my house this morning. I was already at work, but Gloria was home. They were questioning her. I don't know what it's all about but, regardless, I need you to do something for me. I . . ."

"Wait a minute," Eric interrupted. "If you don't know why they were there, what makes you think you need help?"

"Okay, tell me you wouldn't be nervous if you heard the cops were at *your* door. All I know is that it has something to do with Brad, and that can't be good. Now would you please let me finish?"

Casey continued before his brother could answer. "You have to hide out until I get more information, Eric. If they go to your house and you're home, or if they call and you answer the phone, you'll be questioned. I may need an alibi. Please, until I get back to you, don't go home. Don't even answer your personal cell, unless you recognize the number. On second thought, don't answer it unless it's me. They could get Mom or Megan to call you. I'll get back to you as soon as I can. I promise."

"Wait a minute, Casey. Did you get into it again with Brad?"

"No. It's a matter of what the police might think I did. It's a matter of protecting myself."

"But if you didn't do anything, so what are you worried about?"

"I'm worried about joining the ranks of the falsely accused and convicted in our nation's prisons. Please, Eric, I'm just asking you to make yourself scarce until I know more. You know I'd do it for you in a heartbeat."

"You must have some idea what it's all about, Casey. What did the cops tell Gloria?"

"All I know is that they were asking about Brad. Trust me, Eric. As soon as I know more, I'll tell you everything, but for now I've gotta go. I've gotta call Mom."

"All right, Casey, but if I don't hear from you by eight o'clock tonight, I'll be pissed."

Casey had one last request. "Will you call Megan and convince her not to tell the cops about what happened between me and Brad? I can't deal with her right now."

"What makes you think she'll listen to me, Casey? She was furious with both of us."

"She may not listen, but you stand a much better chance than anyone else."

"I'll do what I can, but I'm tired of being the middleman between you and Megan. Our lives have gotten way too volatile, thanks to Brad. I hope this'll be the end of it."

Cringing at that remark, Casey thanked Eric. Eric had always been his ally and now might be his only hope. He wished he could tell Eric about everything on his mind and in his heart, but he couldn't, at least not yet. For now, he had to keep it locked inside.

After disconnecting, Casey spent a few minutes calming down, preparing for the second call.

He figured he had a good ten minutes before the police arrived at his mother's door. Eric lived closer to Casey's home than his mother did, so they'd stop at Eric's before working their way to his mother . . . wouldn't they?

He felt sweat trickling down his back, and the underarms of his T-shirt clung to his armpits. This profusion of perspiration was not due to the air temperature, nor was it due to his body mass.

"Hi, Mom, this is Casey. How are you feeling this morning?"

Mother and son exchanged an abbreviated series of niceties before Casey got down to the reason for his call. He was trying to get on her good side to gain her cooperation.

"Mom, I really need your help," he began. "Two police officers were at our house this morning. Gloria was very upset when she called to tell me. She said they were asking about Brad. They were still there when I talked to her, so I don't know what this is all about, but I still need your help. I know things got really ugly between Brad and me, but please don't tell the police. They don't need to know. You know I'd never really hurt him, don't you? What happened the last time he and I were at your house occurred only because I was trying to protect you."

"I would like to believe that, Casey."

"Please, Mom. If you love me, don't tell them there were hard feelings between Brad and me. What purpose would that serve?"

"But what purpose would it serve to lie to them? 'Oh what a tangled web we weave when . . .'"

"I know. I know, Mom," Casey interrupted. He hated it when she got sanctimonious. It bothered him almost as much as Brad's superior standing in the family.

"It hurts me to see you boys fighting," she continued.

"I know, Mom, but he makes me crazy sometimes. Things always come so easy for Brad and look what he's done with his life. And, Mom, he wears the diamond ring even though he's sleeping in the streets. I offered to buy it, even though that meant I'd have to borrow the money. We'll all be lucky if it isn't stolen. It'll break my heart if that happens. Dad . . ."

"Sorry, Casey, I have to go. Someone's at the door."

Before Casey uttered another syllable, she hung up.

"Damn it! I should've called her first," he muttered, kicking the curb with enough ferocity to send a wave of pain through his toes and into his foot. He limped as he hit the redial button. The phone rang and rang. He begged his mother to answer it before she went to the door. His future was in her hands. Why didn't she understand?

When the answering machine picked up, he snapped his phone shut. He couldn't leave a message. The last thing he wanted to do was let the jerkwater cops know he talked to his mother before they arrived. That would ice it for him.

FIVE

N ROUTE TO THE HOME OF THE next family member, Pete told
Martin about the personal property sheets for the four homeless
men who died in Minneapolis in the last several weeks. "My goal is
to find out if any of them had jewelry or anything else that might
make them targets," he explained. "I wonder if someone is preying
on the homeless, stealing their valuables."

"What did you find out?"

"According to their sheets, none of them had anything of value
in their possession at the time of death, and none of their families
claimed they should have."

"So you're giving up on that as a possible motive?" Martin asked.

"Not yet. The absence of valuables on the inventories supports the
theory. The families might not be knowledgeable or reliable when it
comes to their possessions. It's also possible they suspected items were
missing, but didn't make an issue of it. I think other homeless folks
would be better sources of that information. We don't know why
Winthrup was living on the streets, when he has family here. There
may have been problems between him and someone or everyone in the
family. If there were, does that explain why he was homeless? Otherwise, why wouldn't they help him? It seems rather cold to me."

"Are you kidding?" Martin asked. "It's already in the high seven-
ties, and the mercury's rising." A smile worked its way across Martin's
face. He was pleased with himself.

Pete acknowledged his partner's comeback with a smile and shake
of his head. The first time he was paired up with Martin, Pete resolved
to get the other man to take life less seriously, even if it killed him,
and there were undeniable signs of progress.

Bradford's mother was next on their list of contacts. She lived in a newer, circa 1980s, upscale part of White Bear Lake. The two investigators speculated over whether her answers would be less convoluted than the streets Martin drove to reach her house.

After their dealings with Gloria, fairly or not, they were suspicious of the family. They were also convinced that Gloria had called the others, who now awaited their impending visits. In cases like this, family headed the list of suspects. If their suspicions were correct, the best they could hope for was a few straight answers before the family huddled to create their version of reality.

The nagging question was whether the whole family was trying to hide something or if they'd find an ally—someone who was either outside the loop or brave enough to break ranks. Timing was everything, and time wasn't on their side.

The woman who answered their knock was as well-kept as her meticulously trimmed shrubs and lush green lawn. She looked to be in her early fifties. Her blond hair was short and stylish, her nails freshly polished. She wore khaki shorts and a lemon-colored knit blouse. Her clothes, intentionally or not, showed off her trim figure. Her posture exuded self-confidence—not mourning.

Again, Pete took the lead, introducing Martin and himself, as they showed their badges and IDs. She introduced herself as Ellen Winthrup. Pete explained that they had some questions. Unlike her daughter-in-law, she invited them in.

This seemed like a good sign. Pete felt a wave of optimism. Perhaps he shouldn't have allowed Gloria to raise his suspicions about all of the Winthrups.

He and Martin followed her down a half-dozen steps to the family room. It was packed with leather furniture, a big-screen TV, a half-dozen speakers, and shelves overflowing with DVDs.

Ms. Winthrop motioned them to sit in a couple of chairs that faced the fireplace. She sat opposite them and crossed her legs. Immediately, one flip-flopped foot began vigorously fanning the air.

"We're here about your son, Bradford," Pete said.

The woman waited for him to continue. Her smile remained, unaltered.

Watching her, Pete decided she either didn't know her son was dead or had recovered quickly from the news. He waited for her to tip her hand.

After several seconds, Martin grew nervous, thinking he'd missed a cue and was supposed to ask the next question. He looked at Pete, trying to read his partner. He tried to surreptitiously signal him, but Pete's eyes were locked on the woman.

When the lapse in conversation grew uncomfortable, she asked, "What about Brad?"

Pete spent years looking for ways to soften the delivery of the words, only to decide it was best to just say them. After all, he'd realized, it wasn't the words that hurt. It was their meaning. And the meaning was different for each person. It was shaped by how the person who died fit into a person's universe. That had never been as clear to him as when his wife had died, and he discovered Andrea meant something different to each of the people to whom she was closest.

Leaning forward, diminishing ever so slightly the distance between them and formalizing his previously casual posture, Pete said, "I'm sorry to have to tell you that his body was found yesterday on the Upper Landing."

"That can't be right!" Ellen Winthrop jolted in alarm. "You must be mistaken."

"I'm afraid it's true," Pete confirmed. "I thought perhaps you'd already heard."

Tears streamed down her cheeks. With a broken voice, she excused herself to get some tissues.

Pete figured she either deserved an Oscar, or the lines of communication in her family were slower than in the most bloated bureaucratic agency.

"Why would you think I already knew?" she asked, through sobs, as she returned to the room. She carried a box of tissues in her left hand and dabbed at her eyes and cheeks with the tissue she held in the other.

"We spoke with your daughter-in-law, Gloria," Pete said. "She was reluctant to answer our questions. Why would she be?"

Pete watched her closely. She seemed to be waiting for him to expand on the list of who knew. When he didn't, he saw a glimmer of relief in her eyes.

She said she didn't understand why Gloria wasn't forthcoming. "How did he die?" Tears continued welling up and streaming down her cheeks.

"He died from a gunshot wound," Martin said.

"Do you know who did it?"

"No, that's why we're here," Martin explained. "We're trying to get some leads." It made him uncomfortable that she was taking over the questioning, so he followed that immediately with another question. "We understand he'd been working in Chicago but lost his job. Can you tell us what happened?"

"He wouldn't talk about it, other than to say he was railroaded," she answered through tears.

"Your son had some bruises on his face that may date back as far as ten days," Pete said. "Do you have any idea how he got them?"

Ellen Winthrop's gaze fixed on her knees, and she said. "All I can think of is that my three sons were wrestling the day Brad moved out."

"How many children do you have, Ms. Winthrup?" Pete asked.

"Four. Brad's the oldest."

"Tell us about the others and their families," Pete asked.

"Well, where do I begin? Brad is, was," sob, "a good person. I recently learned that he'd been paying for all of the prescriptions for my husband's mother. Even with Medicare Part D, the costs are high. How he found out when I didn't know is beyond me, except they were very close. Brad always had a special place in his heart for the elderly and for kids. Months after my husband died, Mom's furnace needed replacing and he paid for that, too. He showered gifts on his nephew Kenny, and tried to help his brother Casey, but Casey's too proud to accept help.

"Everything came easy for Brad. Sometimes too easy, and that worried me. I was afraid he'd drift through life the way he floated through school, Little League, the Boy Scouts, everything. For him, life was a game—until he got the job at ACS Marketing. He loved that job and the company. He gave it all he had. He worked twelve-hour days and was married to his Blackberry. He came home on vacation a year ago and spent hours sending and receiving messages with other ACS employees and clients.

"Nothing comes easy for Casey, my second son. While he worshipped Brad, Brad grew impatient when Casey couldn't understand or do things as quickly as he did. That drove a wedge between them, and the less time Brad spent with him, the more Casey craved his attention. Try as I might, I couldn't change that. Finally, I decided they had to outgrow it. Well, Brad did, but a decade ago Casey's admiration for Brad changed to a persistent loathing. Don't get me wrong. I'm not blaming either of them. I know they'd have worked through it over time." Sob. "But now they won't have a chance and I don't know what this will do to Casey.

"I'm sorry. This is far more information than you want or need. I'll try to . . ."

"No, not at all, Ms. Winthrup. Please continue," Pete said.

"Casey has fought and struggled for every inch of progress he's ever made. It doesn't seem fair. It seems like every time he gains an inch, something happens to knock him down. Ever since his dad died, he seems less capable of picking himself up and moving on. About the time Brad lost his job, Gloria found out she was pregnant with their second child. That news sent Casey into a tailspin. He's a worrier. He doesn't know how they'll get by without Gloria's salary for the six weeks she's on maternity leave. She gets the time, but she's only paid if she has the vacation or sick leave hours to cover that time.

Unfortunately, ever since their first child, she's been off frequently, due to the never-ending stream of childhood illnesses and germs Kenny picks up in daycare.

"Don't get me wrong," she continued. "It isn't that Casey doesn't want another child. It's just that he's scared it could put them over the edge, financially. I told him I'll do what I can to help, but my husband's unexpected and untimely death has me handcuffed. And Casey's always been financially independent. We paid for his college education. Since then, he hasn't taken a penny from us."

She paused before continuing. "I said my sons were wrestling the day Brad moved out. That's not exactly true. They were fighting tooth and nail. Brad took some money off my dresser, and I made the mistake of telling Casey. He went ballistic—probably because he's in a financial bind. When he insisted that Brad move out, I capitulated. I couldn't argue with him at that point, but I was sure he'd cool down and have a change of heart in a day or two. Then Brad would move back in, and everything would be fine. I was wrong!" Sob. "Please don't get me wrong," she continued. "Casey isn't a bad person. He's a victim of all of this also."

"Tell us about Casey's wife," Martin asked.

"She's as loyal as the day is long and very protective of Casey. She'd do anything for him. Casey and their son, Kenny, mean the world to her. Since high school, she's barely spoken to her parents. They find fault with everything she does, including marrying Casey.

"How about your other children and their families?" Martin asked.

"Megan, my daughter, came next. She and Brad have always been close. Although she had to work a little harder than Brad, things came easy for her as well. I don't know if that was the reason, but it seems that they were forever pitted against Casey and Eric, my youngest."

Sniff. "That was rarely apparent until Brad was thrown out of my home ten days ago. Megan went wild. I walked away when the boys began fighting. I had to. It was unbearable. I felt so guilty but, as crazy as it now sounds, at the time I was more worried about Casey than

Brad. I thought Brad would be okay in the meantime and, once Casey cooled down, Brad could come back. I thought he'd contact one of his many friends for help. Brad always landed on his feet."

"I understand," Pete said. "But why didn't Megan take Brad in?"

"Because of her husband. Their marriage is on the rocks. They've been trying to address a lot of issues—one of which is Brad. It seems that Megan's husband, Gerald, is threatened by Brad—or jealous of him."

"Why would he be jealous of Brad?" Martin asked.

"I think he's jealous of the closeness between Megan and Brad, and the way she has him on a pedestal, both intellectually and achievement-wise. I think she sometimes, unintentionally, holds him out as a model for Gerald. Surprisingly enough, Gerald and Casey are quite close."

"Why is that surprising?" Pete asked.

"Because they have little to nothing in common, both economically and interest-wise."

"What were Brad's interests?" Pete asked.

"People, and his job. Everything was ACS this and ACS that. And he was very fond of people. His brothers never knew, but I know of many occasions when he went out of his way to help his friends. As I mentioned, he was good to my husband's mother. He's also done lots of things to brighten the lives of my parents. He never misses a birthday. He's quick to offer assistance—anything from making a phone call to resolving a problem, to doing repairs on their home. He's very handy and can fix anything. He was so thoughtful." Sniff.

"Tell us about your son-in-law, Gerald," Pete said.

"According to Megan, he'd spend a nickel for every penny they earned, if she didn't stop him. That's another reason for their problems."

"Was there animosity between Brad and Gerald?" Pete asked.

"Not that I'm aware of, but Gerald sided with Casey when Brad was thrown out of my home."

"Tell us about your other son, Eric," Martin went on.

"Eric is sweet, quiet, unassuming, and painfully shy. He'd give his life for any of my other children, especially Casey. When Eric was small, Casey defended him when the neighborhood bully picked on him, and Casey often included him in many of the things he did with his friends. Eric's single, and rarely dates. He's too shy to ask anyone out. When he does, making conversation is difficult."

"Do you know of anyone who had a bone to pick with Brad or might want to hurt him?" Pete asked.

"You mean murder him?" Ellen Winthrop's tears returned with renewed strength.

When Pete nodded, she said, "Absolutely not! Brad had a lot of friends. People gravitated towards him."

She didn't change that stance, not even when Pete pointed out that a person inevitably made a few enemies over a lifetime.

When Pete asked if Brad mentioned any problems with one of his former company's vice-presidents, she said he hadn't. Brad had come to Minnesota a couple of months after he lost his job, because he'd been unable to find another in Chicago. "The job market is tight," she continued, "at least for jobs paying significantly more than minimum wage. The fact that he had trouble finding a job isn't a reflection on Brad. His death is my fault," she moaned. "If he'd stayed with me, he'd still be alive."

Her head dropped into her hands, and her shoulders shook with sobs.

"If you didn't kill him, you can't blame yourself," Pete said. "It's unlikely that living on the streets precipitated this."

"What do you mean 'if' I didn't kill him?" she asked. Pete saw anger temporarily edging out pain, allowing her to regain her composure. "Do you actually think I did it?"

"Not at this time, Ms. Winthrup," Pete said, "but for now we can't eliminate anyone from consideration."

Ellen Winthrup's features hardened, and she shot a cold stare Pete's way.

He asked her to contact them if any enemies of Brad came to mind, explaining it could be critical to finding "the person who did this." He ended by saying, "I'm sure you want us to find him or her, don't you?"

"What kind of question is that?" she asked indignantly. "Of course I do!"

SIX

BRADFORD'S SISTER, MEGAN ALDEN, worked in the Highlander College alumni office. Highlander College was located a few miles west of downtown St. Paul. Founded in the second half of the nineteenth century, it was sandwiched between a commercial area and a historic neighborhood. The financial interests of the owners of both the businesses and the houses were dependent, at least in part, upon the college and its students.

In the alumni office, the alignment of the receptionist's desk permitted her to welcome the desirables and block the passage of everyone else. The woman sitting behind the desk looked up to the challenge. Pete thought it an appropriate arrangement for the office of a politician but a curious one for an alumni office. Did outraged alumni come flailing their maroon-and-gray pennants if their contributions weren't duly noted in the newsletter? If so, the receptionist must receive, or at least deserve, hazardous-duty pay.

She assumed a pit-bull countenance when Pete, followed by Martin, invaded her zone and asked to see Megan Alden. Pete wondered if she reacted so negatively because she was pounding feverishly on her keyboard and didn't want to be interrupted, or if the pounding was a tip-off that something else in her life or in the office irritated her.

"Do you have an appointment?" she growled. "I don't show any appointments on Ms. Alden's calendar for this time slot. We prefer to have visitors make appointments. That allows us to schedule our days more effectively and efficiently. It can save you time as well. Have a seat and let me see what I can do. You are?"

Would Bradford's sister be cooperative, Pete wondered as he and Martin introduced themselves.

The receptionist's left eyebrow shot up, and she gave them the once over. "Are you here on official business?"

Pete considered some of the alternatives. Unofficial business? Monkey business? He answered with a polite, "We are."

Pushing back from her desk, she spun on a heel and marched down the hall. In a matter of seconds, a more compact woman, who appeared to be about a decade older than Brad, made her way to the reception area, with the pit bull in tow.

"I'm Laura Brice, Megan Alden's administrative assistant." She extended a hand to Pete, then Martin, and flashed a smile. "Ms. Alden left about an hour and a half ago. She's on her way to Omaha to speak at a conference. May I help you?"

"Thanks, but Ms. Alden's the only one who can help us," Martin said. "When will she be back?"

"Thursday night. Would you like to leave a message for her?"

Pete remained optimistic. "Do you have her flight and hotel information?" he asked. He wasn't about to wait three or four days to speak to her.

Ms. Brice retraced her steps and returned posthaste, handing Martin, who was closer, a slip of paper. Her attention was concentrated on Pete when she said, "I wrote down the name of the hotel, but I don't have the phone number. If you like, I'll get it for you. It'll only take a minute or two."

"No, thanks, we can get it," Pete said as he looked over Martin's shoulder and read the information she'd provided. "It looks like her flight leaves in about fifteen minutes," he continued. "Do you have her cell phone number?"

Ms. Brice took the slip of paper she'd given Martin, wrote down the number and, this time, handed it to Pete.

The two men thanked her and the receptionist, and left the alumni office. Hurrying to the nearest exit in an attempt to reach the elusive Ms. Alden before she left town, Martin said, "I think she likes you, Pete, and she's rather pretty, don't you think?"

"The receptionist? I don't think she's my type. I like the shy, silent type—just like me." Pete tilted his head and smiled innocently.

Martin snorted.

They exited the building, in search of a private spot and found one under an ancient oak in the campus quadrangle. It provided some welcome shade and a break from the heat of the morning sun.

"Thank God for summer break," Martin said, seeing the campus was nearly deserted. All else being equal there wouldn't be any difficulty in speaking with Ms. Alden.

Pete dialed the number. After three rings he began wondering if the best he could hope for was leaving a message in her voicemail.

"Hello," came the harried response to the fourth ring.

"Ms. Alden?"

"Yes, may I help you? I'm in a bit of a rush. I'm on an airplane. I was searching for my phone, to turn it off, when I heard it ringing. They're about to close the cabin door, so I don't have long."

It was taking her so long to tell him she didn't have long to talk that Pete feared she'd be out of time before she finished. But, being at her mercy, he waited politely for an opening.

"My name's Peter Culnane. I'm with the St. Paul Police Department."

"Yes?" Her voice was laced with anticipation.

"Have you spoken to your mother or any of your brothers today?"

"Why?"

On an airplane and about to leave town is a bad time to learn about your brother's death, but she had a right to know, and this might be his only chance to speak with her before her family tainted her answers. So Pete delivered the news about Bradford.

"No, that can't be," she gasped. "Are you positive it's Brad you found?"

"Yes, and . . ."

"Do you know who did it?" she cut in.

"No, not yet. I spoke with your mother and your sister-in-law Gloria and . . ."

"And I bet they did little to help," she sobbed.

"I'm surprised no one called you."

"We aren't on speaking terms these days."

"Why's that?"

"Be . . . because . . . I . . . I side . . . I sided with B . . . Brad." After several seconds, she continued, "I'm sorry. Brad and I are . . . were very close—always have been."

Pete shared the scant information they had and hurried to get some answers. "I understand your brother was homeless," he said. "Can you tell me what happened?"

"Yes."

Pete heard her blow her nose.

"He was staying with Mom, but . . ." Sniff. "Oh, I have to go. A cabin attendant just said to turn off my phone immediately or deplane. She isn't happy."

"Will you call me as soon as you arrive in Omaha?"

"I can't," Megan whispered.

It sounded like she was doing her best to surreptitiously get in a few last words before being bodily thrown off the plane. Pete admired her spunk.

"I can't speak to an auditorium full of people right after talking to you," she explained. "I'm not sure I'll be able to now anyway. But I do want you to find whoever did this. I'll call as soon as I can."

SEVEN

I T WAS EARLY IN THE INVESTIGATION, but progress was coming at a painfully slow pace for Pete. He'd be at a loss if asked to list any accomplishments so far.

Martin, on the other hand, would list each detail gathered, the people they'd questioned, and each of the suspicions those meetings raised. For him, they were at least as far as they could hope to be after less than a day. Even as a new kid on the investigators' block, he realized that wheel spinning was often the nature of this business.

Pete was a realist, but an impatient one, particularly at a time like this, when the lives of two kids might be in danger. He couldn't get them out of his mind. His concern for them provided all the incentive he needed to review their tactics for ways to accelerate the pace.

His first solution was for Martin and him to temporarily head in separate directions, allowing them to do two things at once. He had Martin drop him off in downtown St. Paul, where he would talk to the victim's second brother. During that time, Martin, who was less pleased with the plan than Pete, feeling he drew the short straw, would return to headquarters and search for contact information for Bradford Winthrup's friends from school and work.

At 11:20 on a weekday morning, the St. Paul skyways were teaming with shoppers and downtown workers on their way to lunch, visiting the library, shopping, doing their banking, stretching their legs and doing whatever else it is that people did on their lunch breaks. Caught up in the throng, Pete breathed a sigh of relief that he wasn't a part of this scene on a daily basis.

On his way to get the lowdown from Eric Winthrup, he noticed a woman weaving smoothly through the barrage. Her fast clip and graceful dodging of laggards drew his attention. Her movements re-minded him of the way his wife, Andrea, had skied a mogul field, carefully picking a path and executing her moves with the grace and assurance of a ballet dancer. "Had" was the operative word. Andrea had died two years ago when a drunk driver broadsided her car.

But it wasn't only this woman's grace or pace that drew Pete's at-tention. He knew her. No, that was stretching things. He knew of her and some things about her, but he didn't really know her—at least not as well as he wanted to.

On the tall side of average, she came in just over five-foot-eight. She had the build of a runner, but wasn't. Her sun-bleached, brown hair was thick and short. She had small features but few, other than the occasional man who'd fallen for her, would describe her as more than pretty.

She was the intended victim in a case he and another investigator solved last January. He'd been attracted to her, but protocol dictated that he keep his distance. She'd been far too vulnerable for him to take a chance on preying on her emotions.

However, a lapse of seven months seemed reasonable and, in the last several weeks, on a half-dozen occasions when he was home alone and his house felt a little too big and a little too empty, he'd tried to contact her.

Each time, he'd gotten as close as her answering machine, and each time he hung up without leaving a message. Although he re-solved time and again to leave one, when the moment of reckoning came, his thumb shot out, hitting the disconnect button as soon as the message began. That thumb seemed to have its own ideas about how to approach a woman—or was more chicken than he cared to envision himself.

Pete hoped she'd see him. He wanted to say, "Hi," but soon knew it wouldn't happen. Her attention focused on whomever and what-ever might impede her forward progress and the pace she appeared committed to. He was too far to her left to be included in that screening process. As she approached on the far side of a crowd, he decided to go for it and called out.

Hearing her name, she pulled up short, smiled and looked in his direction. That surprised the man who followed close on her heels, benefiting from the openings she wove through the dawdlers—those who thought a lunch break was meant for relaxation. Pete warmed at the smile, but didn't have time to enjoy it. He saw an impending collision, silently cursed himself for the role he played in it and impulsively tried to minimize the repercussions. He wanted to get her attention, but not like this.

With a few agile moves of his own, he darted in front of her, as the man following her collided with a glancing blow that sent her pitching forward. It happened so fast, she wasn't able to get her feet out to catch herself. She only succeeded in raising her hands waist-high, when Pete caught her and scooped her up.

"Thanks!" she gasped, as he returned her to her not-so-steady feet. "I had visions of . . . Pete!"

Catching sight of her rescuer, a smile displaced her look of humiliation and embarrassment.

"You had visions of me?" Pete returned the smile. "Does that mean you're psychic?" They stood face to face, close enough to kiss, and he liked it.

Her face reddened. "No, I had visions of my face skidding across this carpet. I'm so embarrassed. I'm not usually this klutzy, really."

"Are you sure? It seems every time I come into contact with you, you're running into something. First an SUV, and this time it was almost the skyway floor."

Katie shrugged self-consciously and seemed to be indicating she'd like to be anywhere but here, as she turned her attention from Pete's face to the floor.

"I'm sorry, Katie." Pete bent down and looked into her eyes. "Don't be embarrassed. I was teasing. I know you're not a klutz. I saw you moving through this crowd. You must be in a hurry."

"Not really. I'm trying to log a few miles during my lunch break."

"Isn't that a dangerous business with all these people in the sky-way?" He considered telling her it would be safer to go running around one of St. Paul's lakes with him, but decided that was premature.

"Even more than I realized." Katie explained that she usually waited until 1:00 or 1:30, but had meetings all afternoon and wanted to get her daily walk out of the way beforehand.

Sorry to have put her on the defensive, Pete tried to make up for it, saying, "Your near-fall was my fault, Katie. It wouldn't have happened if I hadn't called your name." Testing the water, he asked, "Are you sorry I did?"

"No!" Her answer came out so fast it startled both of them. She released the grip she had on his biceps ever since he caught her. He waited a few seconds before removing his hands, which had migrated, respectfully, from her armpits to her shoulders after he returned her to her feet.

"Judging from the way you're moving, your injuries from January have healed," Pete said, still smiling at her last response. "How are you feeling?"

"I'm doing great, thanks."

His mission and the boys began encroaching on this unexpected bright spot, so he felt compelled to cut it short. "Wish I had more time," he said, "but I'm running late and have to hustle."

"It was nice seeing you, Pete."

"Likewise. I'll call." He knew he should ask her out now. It was a perfect opportunity, but he didn't want to put her on the spot.

The smile remained on Pete's face as he continued on to his meeting first with Cliff Lyon, who was a friend of his and also Eric Winthrup's boss, and then with Eric himself. A dozen steps later, he turned to catch one last look at the departing Katie Benton. He was surprised to see her standing where he left her and pleased to see that her smile lingered.

EIGHT

W HEN PETE REACHED THE OFFICE of the director of security for
the St. Paul skyways, Cliff Lyon told him what little he knew
about Eric Winthrup, the victim's youngest brother.

"He's a curious guy. I'd like to promote him, but every time I mention it, he balks. I know he has what it takes. He has to know it, too. If
I had to describe him in one word, it might be insecure—either that
or shy. Painfully shy is more accurate. Sullen would also be right on.
He's very private and very much an introvert. Based on the way he in-
teracts with the other guards, you'd think he was mute. I usually get
one-word responses when I speak to him. He has all of us mystified."

"Why do you keep him?" Pete asked.

"Because he's good at what he does and he works hard. He isn't
lacking in initiative or motivation. I like him. I think he's loyal and a
good person. I also feel sorry for him. I think he's very lonely."

"Isn't he friends with any of his co-workers?" Pete asked.

"Not that I know of."

"Does he ever meet anyone in the skyways?"

Lyon said he'd seen him with another man a couple of times, and
that the other person might be his brother. They had similar hair
color, blond, and something about the other man's features made him
think they were related. He didn't, however, know anything about
Eric's family or personal life, except that he's single.

When Pete asked if he remembered the last time he saw Eric
with the other man, Lyon thought it was a couple of weeks ago, but
he wasn't certain.

While Lyon retrieved Eric Winthrup's emergency contact information, Pete wondered if the name would be a Laurie Winthrup

whose address was the state capitol and whose phone number was the one for the Governor's Office. Remembering Brad used that contact information, Pete couldn't help but smile.

Eric was either less creative or less evasive than his brother Bradford. The contact he listed was his other brother, Casey, and the address was the one he and Martin visited earlier today.

He knew that Bradford and his sister were very close. Did that make it inevitable that Eric and Casey were close, and did that make them outsiders? If so, was it significant?

Cliff contacted Eric, obtained his location and arranged for him to meet Pete at the security desk in the Fifth Street Center.

After thanking his friend, Pete went in search of Eric. With Cliff's description, the uniform, and the man's painfully slow pace, Pete had no problem identifying the approaching Eric Winthrup. There was lean, and there was skinny. Eric was definitely the latter. If he had any muscle, the loose-fitting uniform camouflaged it. In fact, his physique made Barney Fife look like a Chippendale. Pete also noticed Eric's hair. It was closer in color to Bradford's dishwater blond than their mother's yellow blond.

Pete introduced himself, and Eric asked how he could help, adding he was surprised that an investigator wanted to speak with him.

"I have a few questions," Pete said. "It shouldn't take long."

"This is a bad time. I'm on duty, so there's likely to be a lot of interruptions. You'd be amazed at all of the things that require our attention, and talking to you will be a distraction. I'll be off a little after three o'clock. How about getting together then?"

After hearing Cliff's description of the shy, introverted young man, it surprised Pete when Eric strung that many words together.

Eric wore his nervousness like a wetsuit. It was all over him, tight fitting and readily apparent to even the most casual observer.

"I don't think this will take long," Pete said, "and now that I'm here, we may as well go for it."

"Okay, but if anything breaks, I've got to do my job. Let's walk. I have to keep an eye on things while we talk."

"Understood."

Pete estimated Eric was probably an inch or two taller than he appeared. His shoulders were rounded, and from the position of his head, he seemed to take great interest in the flooring. With that posture, and Pete standing six-four, Eric didn't come up much higher than his chin. He wondered if Eric's stance was the result of some physical ailment or if it was indicative of someone who'd been beaten down.

Without bothering to look, Pete knew that the underarms of Eric's uniform shirt were transitioning from slate gray to charcoal. The smell was a dead giveaway.

"Any chance someone could relieve you, allowing you to take a ten- or fifteen-minute break? That'll make it possible for us to find a private place to talk. I'll even buy you a cup of coffee or a Coke."

"No sir. That's not possible. I have to take over at a security desk in a few minutes."

As they walked, Eric appeared thoroughly engrossed in the passersby. That didn't stop him from talking, perhaps to delay the inevitable.

"Did you know that the original Twin Cities' skyways were constructed in 1962?" He recited like a conscientious tour guide. "They crossed Sixth Street and the Nicollet Mall in Minneapolis. Now seventy-two blocks in Minneapolis and thirty in St. Paul are linked by skyways."

"Have you heard about your brother?" Pete asked.

"Yes."

Pete noted he didn't have to explain which brother or what happened to him, and that Eric switched to his characteristic one-word-answer mode the first time he asked a relevant question.

While walking a few St. Paul skyways, Eric lifted his concentration from the floor, busying himself by looking into and around a bank, photo shop, leather repair shop, florist, and card shop. Anything and everything they passed got the once-over.

"What did you hear?" Pete asked. "I don't want to repeat what you already know."

"I heard Brad's dead. That his body was found yesterday."

Pete detected a break in the other man's voice.

Eric claimed he didn't know where Brad went after he moved out of their mother's house. He said he couldn't recall the last time he saw Brad or where he was at the time.

"Was your brother Casey there the last time you saw Brad?"

"I don't know. I don't remember. You should ask him. He has a better memory than me."

"Have the two of you discussed Brad in the last ten days?"

"I'm not sure. We talk a lot and about lots of things."

"What did Brad do for a living?"

"He sold promotional products."

"What are promotional products?"

"Things like shirts, water bottles, key chains, or anything else that a company can put its logo on."

"Why did he stop selling promotional products?"

"I don't know."

"If you were to hazard a guess, what would it be?"

Eric raised his eyebrows, shrugged and said, "I have no idea." He did all of that while looking off to his right, continuing to avoid eye contact with Pete. He also claimed to be unaware of a problem between Brad and a company vice-president.

When asked if he spoke with Casey today, Eric said no. His face told another story.

"Who told you about Brad?"

"My mother."

"What time did she call?"

"I don't know. I was busy. My phone rang. It was her, so I answered. She's taking this very hard, you know. We all are."

"Did you see Brad yesterday?"

"No!"

"The day before yesterday?"

"No."

"Did Casey see him last weekend?"

"I don't know."

"When was the last time you saw Casey?"

"Last weekend."

"When last weekend?"

"Saturday and Sunday."

"What time on Saturday and on Sunday?"

"I'm not sure. I never pay much attention to time between the time I leave here on Friday and the time I return on Monday."

"Do you have an alibi for last weekend?"

"Do I need one?"

"You tell me."

"I don't, and I don't really have one—other than Casey, I mean. I was mostly just hanging around home."

When Pete asked for the names of Brad's friends, Eric said he was due at the security desk in Town Square. Pete said it was good timing, because Eric could write more easily while sitting at a desk.

After relieving the other guard and settling in behind the desk and monitors, Eric found a ragged scrap of paper and wrote down several names. When he gave the list to Pete, Pete went through it, asking name by name if they were Twin Cities or Chicago friends. They all fit into the first group.

Eric said he'd met a few of the Chicago friends, but didn't remember any of their names—at least not their last names.

Like his mother, he had no idea where any of the friends live now.

"You don't have any friends in common?"

Without taking his eyes off the monitors, Eric said, "No, I'm five years younger. Brad and his buddies were too busy to babysit me."

The catch in Eric's voice didn't escape Pete. Hoping to get more reliable information by knocking a hole in the other man's facade, he said, "There was no love lost between you and Brad, huh?"

"I didn't say that. He's my big brother. I love him." For the first time since they arrived at the security desk, Eric looked at Pete. It was an icy stare.

"You loved him, but from a distance?" Pete hounded.

"What's that supposed to mean?" Eric concentrated so intently on the monitors that it seemed his future depended on counting the steps taken by each person who came into the view of the cameras.

"You loved him, yet you know little about his friends, and he was forced to live in the streets?"

"That's right," Eric said bitterly.

"On all counts?"

"Yes."

"Do you know if he ever got a meal at any of the soup kitchens?"

"I heard he sometimes went to the one on the western edge of downtown St. Paul. Do you know the one I mean?"

Pete knew of more than one that qualified, but with Eric's help he narrowed it down to Reaching Out. He asked if Bradford spent all or most of his time in St. Paul.

"As opposed to?"

"As opposed to Minneapolis, or did he go back to Chicago?"

"Don't know."

When Pete asked whether Brad had any girlfriends, the way Eric said, "Yeah," hinted at a lot of respect and a bit of amazement. He wasn't surprised that Eric couldn't recall any of their names.

"Was he seeing anyone in particular in the recent past?"

"You mean anyone special?"

"Yes."

"How recent?"

"Let's say the last year."

"Again, I can't remember any names. He may have brought one or two home to meet Mom. You should ask her—or Megan, my sister."

Pulling out a business card, Pete handed it to Eric and said, "Call anytime, if you happen to remember something that might help us find the person who murdered Brad."

"You bet. I'll do that," Eric told the monitors.

NINE

"ANY LUCK?" PETE ASKED as he slid into the unmarked car.

"I think so," Martin said. "I have all but one of the addresses for the Minnesota friends, thanks to the records that schools maintain on former students, and I have two lunches." Martin smiled. "That's a darn sight better than one of each or even all of the addresses and one lunch. You see, the other Minnesota friend has an unspecified, permanent address—in some cemetery."

"When did that friend die?" Pete asked.

"Oh, I don't know. Guess I should've asked, huh?"

Pete nodded.

"So, before I tell you the rest, how about if I drive over to Kellogg Boulevard?" Martin suggested. "We can find a shady spot and eat there, where it overlooks the river. You can tell me about the other brother, and we'll figure out what's next."

Pete agreed, and on the way Martin told him about the search for the victim's Chicago friends. It wasn't as productive, but he had all the phone numbers. Actually, there was only one phone number, but the list of friends was extensive.

"I was treated to my turn with Bradford's former supervisor, Tim Baxter," Martin said, shaking his head. "He told me all of Winthrup's former co-workers are his friends. I made the mistake of laughing. He heard me and went into a spiel about ACS Marketing being a model for teamwork. I refrained from asking how a member of this model team got fired. I'm saving that one for Vice-President Walter Linton.

"When I asked about his progress with getting a number for Linton's cell," Martin continued, "he said it hadn't been long since the last time we asked, and he's waiting for a reply to an email he sent about it. Unbelievable! If this is par for the course for the company, I'd be crazy after working there for about one day. I didn't have enough time to contact any of the friends."

Developing a useful list of the co-workers might require numerous phone calls, and Pete said that discussing it with the victim's sister would probably be much more fruitful. He also wanted her to get them a list of Bradford's Minnesota friends and compare it with Eric's and the mother's lists.

At the mention of Bradford's sister, Pete checked his watch. He shook his head and said, "I sure thought we'd hear from her by now."

"How long was her speech or presentation or class or whatever supposed to last?" Martin asked.

"I don't know. I didn't have time to ask."

"One of us could call her assistant and find out," Martin offered.

"True, but it wouldn't speed her up. It would only have me checking the time even more often once she should've finished, and I'd be wondering why she hadn't called. There could be a lot of things keeping her. I'm sure she'll call when she can. I'm sure we don't have to worry about her forgetting us."

"No problem with your self-esteem, Pete."

"You've lost me."

"You speak with a woman once and are confident she won't forget you. I wish I was that self-assured," Martin chuckled.

Lunch was a ten-minute affair. While Martin ate a Reuben sandwich and fries, Pete picked at his turkey sandwich and tried the two phone numbers he hadn't yet disqualified for the boys. The results didn't surprise him. No answer. He hoped Bill was getting tired of his incessant attempts to reach him via his cell and would, out of exasperation, answer, so he could tell Pete to give it up or get a life.

"I'd hoped to hear something about the bicycle or the boys before now," Pete said. "We're scheduled back at Casey Winthrup's in just over three hours and I want to find a way to make some connections with the homeless. But for now I prefer to return to the Upper Landing."

"Why? You said there's a BOLO for the kids."

Pete explained that they'd more readily recognize the boys than someone who hadn't seen them. He also suggested that they get another look at the area and talk to the construction workers.

Rather than a suggestion, Martin thought it sounded like Pete's mind was made up. *And a tornado sounds like a train, but you wouldn't want to confuse the two.* Besides, far be it for him to challenge Pete's instincts. Few investigators in the department were that foolish or that arrogant, and Pete's reputation extended far beyond the boundaries of St. Paul. Just the same, he hoped Pete was overestimating the threat to the boys.

When they arrived at the Landing, Martin parked on the hill overlooking the crime scene. Both men got out of the car and began searching for any sign of the boys or anything indicating they'd returned.

Pacing off the area, hands in pockets and eyes straining, Pete caught a glimpse of something behind a distant shrub. He walked over and found the remnants of snack-sized bags of Old Dutch potato chips and Coca Cola cans. The early afternoon sun reflected off the silvery, metallic surfaces of the packaging. He thanked Coca Cola and Old Dutch Foods for making these color selections. For preteen and teenaged boys, potato chips and Coke were a good match, even though the boys he sought didn't necessarily leave this trash.

The debris had to be new. The Homicide Unit wouldn't have left it behind. Pete smiled, encouraged.

His optimism rose, when his phone vibrated and he saw the number on the caller ID.

TEN

FINALLY, BRADFORD'S SISTER, Megan Alden, was getting back to Pete.

"With your help," Pete told her, "I hope to focus our efforts and concentrate on the key issues."

She asked, "Do you have any idea who did this?"

Pete explained that he couldn't share that information at this time and, changing the subject, asked Megan about the diamond ring her brother was wearing when they found him. Happy to hear he still had it, she explained it was their father's, and probably Brad's most prized possession.

Their conversation moved to Brad's living situation. Megan said Brad lived with their mother for about a month. Then, one day, Casey orchestrated a family meeting. Brad had taken some money off their mother's dresser, and Casey said Brad couldn't be trusted and had to move along—move out of her house—immediately. He decided it would be better for their mother. Megan didn't know if Casey discussed this with her mother before the altercation or not.

Casey wouldn't tell Megan how much money Brad took from their mother but, in Megan's opinion, it wasn't that much and no amount justified the way Brad had been treated.

Pete asked Megan if she knew when or how Brad got the cuts and bruises on his face.

"When I defended Brad," she said, "Casey went crazy and screamed at me. Brad told him he couldn't speak to me that way, and Casey started throwing punches. Brad mostly just blocked them, but he hit Casey once, and his nose started bleeding. Mom made a fuss and took Casey into the house to clean him up. Brad looked worse than Casey.

"While they were in the house," Megan continued, "I tried to help Brad. He just turned away from me and said he was fine. He told me he only borrowed the money from Mom, because he wanted to buy a bus card. He said he was looking for a job and an attorney. He had to have bus fare. He said he would have asked Mom, had she been home. He'd left a note on her dresser, telling her he'd taken the money and promising to repay it."

"Why was he looking for an attorney?"

"It had to do with his job. The only other time we discussed it, he said he found one and things were starting to happen. A set of inter-rogatories was delivered to ACS Marketing."

"Do you know the attorney's name?"

"No, sorry. I didn't ask, and he never said."

"Where did Brad go, after leaving your mother's?"

"All I know is that he ended up on the streets. I wanted him to come home with me, but my husband, Gerald, backed Casey and Eric in their treatment of Brad. I knew there was no sense in bringing up the subject. All I'd have accomplished was to start a fight. The situation between me and my husband is already dicey. As angry as I was with what was happening, I was afraid to do more than I'd already done when I took Brad's side."

Pete asked if she'd spoken with Brad after that day.

"Two days later, he called me at work," Megan said and began to sob.

Pete waited, wanting to give her as much time as she needed. He was all too familiar with the kind of pain that goes along with the loss of someone so close.

"I'm sorry," she said after a minute.

"There's no reason to apologize."

"Just one second," Megan said.

Pete heard her blow her nose.

"Do you believe the money your brother borrowed from your mother was really the reason for Casey's fury?"

"I know it doesn't make much sense. Brad tried to help me understand. Well, I can't. 'Casey's Casey.' That's what Brad always said."

Her voice told Pete that she was crying, and the faucets were wide open.

"Any idea what might've set him off?" Pete asked.

"The first thing that came to mind was my dad's ring—the one Brad was wearing. It's a sore point with Casey. He thought he should get it after Dad died. Don't ask me why. Brad's the oldest, so I wasn't surprised."

"What did Brad say when he called you two days after the ordeal with Casey?"

"What a delicate way of putting it," Megan said, causing Pete to smile. "He said he wanted me to know he was fine, and that I shouldn't worry about him. He also told me to give Casey the benefit of the doubt and to put myself in his shoes. He said it never pays to react in haste, or out of anger or hurt. I said it seemed Casey was most guilty of that. Brad said we'd both been guilty of short-changing Casey. He insisted it would all work out if I backed off and let Casey work through this at his own pace."

"I was so glad to hear from Brad. I told him to come to my office and I'd give him a key to my house and a bus card. I said he should go to my house anytime between nine and five on weekdays, when my husband's at work. I offered to buy him a prepaid cell phone, but he said a calling card wasn't as likely to be stolen. He met me and picked up the stuff. I knew he went to my house for the first three days, then he stopped."

"The first three days would've been last week: Monday, Tuesday, and Wednesday, correct?"

"That's right."

"How do you know when he went there and when he stopped?"

"He left notes in the laundry hamper. I told him it was a safe place. My husband leaves everything on the floor. Every day when I got home, the first thing I did was check the hamper, and every day there was a message. The notes said how much he appreciated what I was doing, and each one reminisced about an event from our childhood. I kept all of them."

After giving her a minute to compose herself, Pete asked, "What did he do while at your house?"

Megan said that Brad showered, shaved and got something to eat. He kept his good clothes there, in a wardrobe in the basement, and she washed and ironed them.

"Why did he stop going to your house?" Pete asked.

"My husband came home unexpectedly and caught him. Brad wouldn't tell me what happened, but that ended it. My husband's been on a rampage ever since."

"Why was he so angry about finding Brad in your house?"

"I guess because he agreed with Casey—that Brad couldn't be trusted."

Megan told Pete she'd had no way to contact Brad, but he called her every few days. The last time was last Friday. That was when he told her about having found an attorney and the interrogatories. She didn't know when the interrogatories were delivered.

Asked how Brad could afford an attorney, Megan said he found someone he could hire on a contingency. She gave him the upfront money. She also gave him two hundred dollars, and deposited two thousand dollars in an account that Brad could access through a cash card.

Pete asked if her husband knew about the money she gave Brad, and she said she didn't tell him. She knew he'd be furious. He was against, in his words, "funding losers."

Trying to verify what Eric told him, Pete asked if Brad got some of his meals at a homeless shelter.

Megan thought he made the circuit and often went to a place in St. Paul called Reaching Out.

When he asked if Brad stayed at a homeless shelter, she said he usually slept in one of the parks during the day and tried to stay awake all night. He said he felt safer that way. It meant he didn't have to worry as much about being rolled for the little he had.

"What little he had, other than the ring?" Pete asked.

"He told me that the ring fit so tightly, not even he could get it off."

"Is Casey right- or left-handed?"

"Right."

"Does he wear a ring on that hand?"

"I don't think so. I think he only wears his wedding band."

"How about your husband? Is he right- or left-handed?"

"He's right handed also. In addition to his wedding ring, he wears his college ring on his right hand."

Nearing the end of his list of questions, Pete asked about Brad's friends.

Megan gave him the names of two of Brad's closest friends in Chicago and of the local friends he contacted whenever in town— until this last time.

"Eric told me that Brad dated a lot," Pete said. "Can you tell me if he'd been serious about anyone, and if anyone was serious about him but not vice versa?"

Megan said she had to think about it, in order to come up with the names. She said this wasn't a good time. She had to get back to the conference. She hadn't planned to duck out for so long.

Pete asked her to bear with him. He was almost finished. He asked, "Were Brad and Eric rivals?"

"No. That was more the case with Brad and Casey."

Pete concluded by asking, "Do you know of anyone who might want to harm Brad?"

"If you mean 'kill' him, the answer's no."

Eleven

Pete snapped his phone shut and spent a silent moment, contemplating. He and Martin were leaning against the passenger side of Martin's Crown Victoria. They had been parked ever since he returned from the spot where he found the Coke and potato chip litter.

Growing impatient, Martin asked, "So, are you going to tell me what Alden said or are you just going to stand there, smiling?"

By the time Pete finished, they decided they had an attorney to find, and two friends and a brother-in-law to add to Martin's matrix.

While Pete made his way down the hill to speak with the construction workers, Martin waited up top, arms crossed, feet planted, eyes roving for any sign of the boys, as unlikely as he thought it was he'd see them.

The occasional sandy patch on the side of the hill gave way to Pete's weight and long strides, and he half-slid and half-walked down the hill.

He caught a whiff of green pine and treated lumber, and he noticed that today's construction sounds—the whining of table and radial arm saws, the *ka-chunk, ka-chunk* and smacking of nail guns and the disharmony blaring out of a couple of boom boxes—all but drowned out the river sounds.

Two men and a woman, all wearing hard hats, huddled outside a building in the early phases of construction. One man jabbed an index finger at something on the roof, and all three stood, necks craned, looking where he pointed.

As he drew near, Pete felt his eyes pulled in the designated direction. When he spoke, all three heads snapped around in unison, and three pairs of eyes fixed, suspiciously, on him.

"Sorry to interrupt," he said and asked if any of them had seen two boys, probably between eleven and fourteen, possibly with bicycles, hanging around the area.

The woman said she'd seen two boys riding bikes and spending time on the hill, and pointed to where Martin and the car were parked. She said she saw them there on a regular basis, but never down in the construction area. She didn't recall seeing them today.

When she described the boys, Pete was convinced they were his quarry. He gave one of his cards to each of them and asked them to call immediately if they saw the boys.

Some members of the construction crew must have heard about the body found there, for one of the men asked Pete if that was why he was there.

He said it was, and that was also why he was looking for the boys.

Hiking back up the hill, still scanning for any sign of the kids, Pete's spirits were sinking. It seemed he wouldn't reach them, using either of the phone numbers still in question. Nothing was happening with the bike found in Cherokee park, otherwise he'd have heard about it. The BOLO hadn't resulted in any sightings. They had vanished—with the possible exception of the Coke cans and potato chip packages.

That meant he now had to hope to succeed by going the school-resource-officer route. He doubted it would solve their problem. Only some middle schools had SROs, and the private and charter schools didn't have them. Would a kid with a thousand-dollar bike attend a public school? They hadn't a clue where the boys went to school. Complicating things further, he didn't know if they went to the same school. Whereas Bill and Tim might be their names, it was almost as likely, based on the fake last names, that they weren't. Hence, the police officers assigned to schools would have only his and Martin's descriptions to work from. He'd hoped for a more expeditious and assured way of finding them.

Nearing Martin, whose demeanor implied he'd given up on spotting them from this location, Pete saw a small, shiny speck in the sand.

There was something imbedded in one of the footprints he left on his trip down the hill. It must have surfaced when the sand shifted as he stepped there. Just the same, he was surprised that the metal detectors wielded by the Homicide Unit hadn't picked up on it. Extracting a plastic bag with a zipper closure from his suit coat, he plucked it up.

"So?" Martin asked when Pete reached his side.

Pete held out his hand, permitting Martin to see the contents of the bag.

"Do you think it belongs to the victim?" Martin asked.

"I don't know. Why'd you think of him?"

"Just that he had a diamond ring and it's a diamond tie tack."

"I don't think it would go all that well with the T-shirts he was wearing, Martin."

"And the ring did?"

"More so than the tie tack. We can ask the family, but there are lots of other possibilities."

"Yes, but those other possibilities probably don't have anything to do with this case, unless the killer wore a suit and tie, and that's not likely. You think?"

"I try to for a few minutes each day." Pete said, adding, "Look at the other possibilities connected to the case."

"I give up."

"Not so fast. Who'd we see in this vicinity yesterday?"

"No one but the boys."

"Exactly."

"You're dreaming, Pete. What would two kids be doing with a diamond tie tack? Why would you even consider them?"

"They were busy moving the sand around with the toes of their shoes. It may have been nerves, but it seemed they were looking for something. They were watching the crime scene, but they were at least as busy examining the dirt at their feet. If they dropped it, I'm sure they'd have tried desperately to find it. The eternal optimist in me wants to believe that, if they lost it, they'll come back to find it."

"So they'll come back to the Landing." Martin added.

"Right! And how do we maximize our chances of catching them?"

"Become invisible?" Martin asked.

"Well, in a manner of speaking. Can we find a place where they can't see us, but we can see them?"

"How about from the High Bridge?"

Pete looked over his shoulder and up at the structure and its ornamental ironwork towering 160 feet above the river, hence the name. "It would meet the requirements," he said, "but if we see them from there, then jump in the car and drive back, they'll be out of sight for several minutes. If they take off during that time, we won't know where to look. We'll be right back where we are now. I'd like to find a place where we'd be able to see them on our way back."

That would have been ideal, but they couldn't see or think of a place meeting those criteria. So Martin drove from the Upper Landing on a path that took them away from the High Bridge, towards downtown St. Paul. It was the only way to get to the bridge from the Upper Landing. Then he took West Seventh Street back around to Smith Avenue and the bridge.

He planned to drop off Pete on the far side of the bridge, come back across the river and park on the north side. This gave each a slightly different perspective on the Landing, and should enable them to see the boys approaching the Landing from further out and every possible route.

It was a good plan, given the constraints the terrain and human limitations imposed. However, its shortcomings were soon revealed.

TWELVE

A S THE TWO INVESTIGATORS NEARED the High Bridge, Pete caught sight of the Uppertown sign in a small park on the northeast edge of the bridge. It marked a historic and eclectic neighborhood in which a few of the homes were pre-Civil War era. Seeing this spot, he realized it was exactly what he'd been looking for. Standing alongside the fence, they could see the Landing, as well as Shepherd Road and the railroad tracks that lay between the park and the Landing.

From the front seat of Martin's car it was impossible to know for sure, but Pete suspected he'd be able to go over the fence, down a steep embankment and make tracks for the Landing, while keeping the area in view. At least he could if he was willing to trash the suit he was wearing. Unfortunately, by the time he conveyed the change in plans to Martin, they'd missed the last opportunity to opt out of crossing the bridge.

The High Bridge, four-tenths of a mile long, ran downhill from the southern side to the northern one, and curved to the west on its southern edge.

The problem with that curve wasn't apparent until they neared the far end of the bridge, and the median separating north and southbound lanes resumed. That's when Pete realized he should've gotten out of the car the instant he changed the plan. That's when his heart sank as two boys on bicycles came around the curve and onto the bridge.

How could he be so unlucky? What were the chances of this happening? "Let me out and turn around!" he yelled.

Martin jumped, surprised by the unpredictable change in the other man's characteristically calm persona.

Unwilling to waste a nanosecond, Pete hopped out before Martin could stop the car.

Bill was on the lead bike and must have recognized Pete. Or did seeing a man get out of a car, a moving car, in the middle of the bridge tip him off? After turning, probably to warn Tim, he crouched over his handlebars and frantically pumped the pedals.

By stopping the car, Martin halted the traffic behind them, giving Pete an opportunity to cross to the median. But a string of northbound cars still separated Pete from the boys. He tried to time a break that was sufficient to let him across, but the cars were moving too fast and distances between them were too tight. He considered diving onto the hood of a car, rolling across and jumping off the other side. If his actions were the only consideration, he'd have risked it. But he had no control over the actions of the driver. Realizing the driver might freak out and cause an accident, and the accident might injure or kill someone, forced him to abandon that plan. He was willing to sacrifice a suit for the boys. The life of an innocent bystander was another matter.

It was hard to miss the looks on the boys' faces, a combination of determination and fear. Seeing that, Pete figured the only way they'd stop was if he got a grip on one or both bikes, pulling them up short.

He was so close, but too far away to succeed. If they escaped now, how long would it take to find them? He knew he'd never have another opportunity like this one, and seeing it evaporate as the seconds ticked away increased his frustration. Frustration with himself for not getting out of the car before Martin crossed the bridge. Frustration with the boys for thinking they were protecting themselves by escaping. And frustration with all of the cars that kept him from reaching the boys.

Judging from the speed of the bikes, he knew he was running out of time. Soon they'd be unreachable. He tried to slow them down by yelling, "Guys, I just have a couple of questions."

He knew he only had an outside chance of getting through to them or at least causing them to slow down to consider his words. He didn't know if they heard him. If so, the words were as ineffectual as he'd feared.

The boys kept pedaling. They neither slowed nor ceased the motion, and they picked up an alarming amount of speed due to the downhill slant in the roadway. This gave him another reason to fear for their lives. What if they got reckless trying to escape and crashed? At their current speeds, being thrown off their bikes, even wearing helmets, could result in serious or fatal injuries. And what if one of them fell in front of a car?

A car slowed, probably in response to his location and facial expression. Taking advantage of the break, he sprinted across to the bike lane. The boys were already fifty feet past him, but he poured on every ounce of speed. For a few moments, he gained on them, but the trend soon reversed itself. He saw the distance between them increase at a hopeless rate, despite his best effort. Even so, he continued putting everything he had into it, and then some.

Meanwhile, Martin was more than a little put out when he reached the end of the bridge and had to go beyond the first intersection, Cherokee Avenue, because it wasn't a through street. The median continued for another half block. By the time he reached the end of it, he had the lights in the grill flashing and the siren screaming. They worked in his favor when approaching cars pulled to the side of the road.

The boys didn't show Pete the kind of courtesy the cars afforded Martin. As a result of daily runs, he was capable of a lot of speed, but not as much as a kid on a bike, not even a heavy kid, especially with the slope of this bridge. Running a four-minute mile is a major feat, but running downhill is more difficult than running on the flat. And riding a bike fifteen miles per hour downhill is nothing special.

Back on the south side of the river, Martin watched carefully to avoid any distracted driver who might ignore, or be oblivious to, the cars pulled over to the side of the road, or miss his lights and siren, and the look in his eye. Ready for the break he needed, he had the steering wheel cranked as far as it would go to the left. He found the opportunity he needed and stomped on the accelerator. Doing a tire spin and squealing 180 just beyond the median, he headed back across the bridge.

Once he got around the curve, he saw Pete running down the bike path, but he didn't see the boys. "Hell!" he yelled, slamming the steering wheel with the heels of both hands.

Despite the lights and siren, there was nowhere for the cars he caught up with to go. They had to continue crossing the bridge.

Tracking Martin's progress, through the sound of the approaching siren, Pete continued running and was near the Uppertown sign when Martin pulled alongside him.

Pete dove into the car, panting.

"Where'd they go?" Martin asked.

"Wish I knew. I lost 'em when they reached the point where Smith curves east. The last I saw of them, they were speeding away, hell bent for election."

THIRTEEN

As THEY CLOSED IN ON THE CURVE on Smith Avenue, still in pursuit of the boys, tension in the Crown Victoria hung as heavy as a side of beef in a butcher shop. Martin's hands clasped the steering wheel so tightly they ached. He tried to read Pete's thoughts, but the other man's silence contributed nothing to his efforts.

Martin hoped they weren't as negative as his. Repeatedly, he concluded it was his fault that the kids escaped. *If only I'd remembered the park when we were looking for a place to view the Landing . . . if only I'd stopped immediately and maneuvered onto the median when Pete saw the park . . . if I'd turned around and gotten back to Pete faster . . .*

On the passenger side, Pete sat with his chin propped on both fists and forehead furrowed. He was trying to coax a victory out of looming defeat. He felt the boys slipping through his fingers. Minutes ago, he was so close, and now they were out of sight. But he wasn't giving up. Around the curve, they might again catch sight of them. If not, well, for now, all he could do was wait and see what was around the curve.

NOT FAR AWAY AS THE CROW FLIES, the lead, lean biker, Bill, pedaled and searched desperately for any possible hiding place. He knew Tim couldn't keep this up much longer. His face was scarlet and he hung over his handlebars, mouth wide open, gasping. Tim had to rest.

The shrubs and flowers alongside the houses they passed wouldn't do the job, especially when they had their bikes. The cops might decide to go down the alleys, so hiding behind a house wasn't safe. All he could do was pedal and hope Tim kept up.

Bill knew the cops were gaining on them. He'd slowed down so he wouldn't lose Tim. Making matters even worse, he didn't know how fast the cop drove or how far they went on Smith before turning. Bottom line, he had no idea where they were. That meant every time they approached a street crossing the one they were on, he had to slow down to look both ways for the enemy vehicle.

Suddenly, Bill found himself empathizing with any criminal on the lam. He knew exactly how one felt.

Sighting an opportunity for deliverance, he frantically signaled his next move, pointing to the selected spot. Swinging his bike in an arc that took him out in the middle of the street, he positioned himself for a straight shot at the curb. At the last second he gripped the handlebars tightly and came up hard and fast off the seat, jumping into the air and assisting his bike over the curb in a sleek, smooth motion.

He was so pleased with himself that an involuntary smile pulled up the corners of his mouth. But concern for Tim quickly eliminated it. Realizing Tim was so exhausted he might not be able to navigate the curb, Bill pulled up short and turned to check.

Gratefully, he'd underestimated his friend's capabilities, or desire, or both. Tim pulled up and stopped alongside him, panting. Bill broke into a second, broader smile. This one too was short-lived, as he felt himself yanked back to the moment and their plight. He pointed to their destination, and the two boys ran their bikes over to what they hoped would be the perfect place to conceal themselves and, almost as important, their bikes.

ROUNDING THE CURVE ON SMITH AVENUE, Pete saw exactly what he'd feared ever since they'd outmaneuvered him on the bridge. Nada, zilch, nothing. No boys, no bikes.

He heard Martin's sigh. It matched his. At least there was some consolation in knowing the boys made it across the bridge and around the curve without mishap, despite their reckless bike riding. Now, on flat ground, they'd lose some of the speed they'd gathered on the bridge. He hoped that improved his and Martin's batting average.

It was now obvious that the layout of the streets wouldn't work in their favor. Most of them were short, running only two or three blocks. West Seventh, the street they took to Smith on their first trip across the bridge, was the exception. The boys had to be familiar with the area, so the straight-line shot afforded by West Seventh seemed an unlikely route for their escape. They'd be too visible for too long.

Pete supposed they could have been hiding, watching Martin and him take the curve on Smith so that they could cross to the west side, but he doubted it. He doubted their adrenaline pumped any less frantically than his. He doubted they'd collected their wits sufficiently to think of that before passing the point of no return—the point at which turning back became too risky.

That left this series of short streets as their most likely route. Here they could take advantage of the layout, following a jagged path, to lose Martin and him.

These were hunches, but all they could do for now was play those hunches.

The uncomfortable silence in the car was broken when dispatch came back with a response to Pete's request for support from squads in the vicinity. They were sending two.

Consulting with the dispatcher, Pete, Martin, and the third man quickly sorted through the options, looking for the best places for spotting the boys. They decided on the corner of Chestnut and West Seventh Street for the first. It provided a view of two of the longest streets on an outer edge of the area, in case the boys' path took them across or down one or the other.

They positioned the second officer at the High Bridge, and Pete instructed that squad to watch from a place where the boys couldn't see her, until they'd committed to crossing. Goodrich, west of Smith, was selected.

With the help of the dispatcher, Pete enlisted two additional squads in downtown St. Paul. He asked them to watch the Wabasha and Robert Street bridges, in case the boys took an alternate route back across the Mississippi River.

After all they'd been through in the last few minutes Pete didn't believe the kids were desperate or crazy enough to return to the Landing this afternoon. So, with too few resources to cover all the most likely routes, he decided against sending someone there. Before ending their conversation, he told the dispatcher to notify the squad in Cherokee Park to drop the stakeout there.

Looking for a break, Pete and Martin continued a sweep of the streets and alleys in Uppertown. They went from Smith to Forbes to Exchange, and that's when Pete saw the gazebo in Irvine Park. He knew right away it was the sort of place he'd select if he was a kid, found himself in their shoes and had no better means of escape. Although small, the pergola, which was often used for wedding ceremonies, could easily block their view of two boys with bikes. If the boys assumed he and Martin would stay in the car during their search, they'd also assume they could easily move around the structure to maintain their cover.

Pete pointed at it and motioned Martin to the side of the road. Possibly being overly cautious, they got out of the car and quietly closed the doors. Halfway from the car to their destination, they split up, blocking two of the three paths that two fleeing boys might take.

Martin continued on his path, while Pete ran to and around the pergola. It became his second futile run of the afternoon. However, this time he was less discouraged.

Making his way around the structure, which took no time flat, he realized that behind the wooden latticework at the base was a perfect hiding place. The latticework was old, and it was conceivable that one or more sections could be readily moved, allowing the boys to crawl behind it and underneath the pergola. The boys should have had more than enough time to accomplish this, especially if they worked on the side facing Smith Avenue, using the structure to hide their actions as he and Martin approached.

There weren't any telltale signs of the dragging that might be required to move the latticework and get their bikes underneath, but the boys were probably smart enough, even under duress, to take reasonable steps to leave the area looking as undisturbed as possible. The lush grass throughout the park would have aided their effort.

Hoping for a miracle of sorts, Pete squatted down and peered through the wooden web into the darkness on which the floor of the gazebo rested.

FOURTEEN

DESPITE THE WEB OF OPENINGS in the latticework, the shadows under the pergola, particularly near its center, stood in stark contrast with the bright sunshine of a cloud-free afternoon. Hence, it took a second for Pete's eyes to adjust. On the other hand, it took no time for his nose, working uninterruptedly at peak performance, to do its part. Reminiscent of a compost heap, the odor was hard to miss this close to the wooden structure.

When his eyes adjusted, he saw rotting leaves and twigs. He saw a few scraps of paper and similar rubbish. He didn't see anything resembling a boy or a bike.

MEANWHILE, CAUTIOUSLY WATCHING FOR ANY SIGN of cops or interfering residents, the two fugitives approached the hiding place Bill had sighted from the street. It was a dome tent, set up in a backyard. Bill knew it wasn't perfect, but it was all he could do under the circumstances. He was reaching for the zipper when a voice piped up behind them.

"Hey, what do ya think you're doin'?" a disheveled boy who looked to be their age asked.

"We were just admiring your tent. It's awesome! My parents have been looking at tents. This one's perfect." Bill said all that rapidly, while trying to inconspicuously withdraw his hand.

Using his bicycle to support his exhausted body, Tim worked to control his coughing and slow his breathing and racing heart. In spite of all that, he rolled his eyes when Bill looked at him, hoping for approval of his creative lying.

Bill saw him and knew it meant his friend wished he'd stop with the nonsense and find a place to sit down.

"What's with him?" The kid pointed at Tim.

"We're playing a game with some friends," Bill said. "I'll give you ten bucks if you let us sit in your tent with our bikes."

"You can use it, but you can't take your bikes in. It's new, and I can't take a chance on getting grease on it. My brother'd kill me."

Too winded to speak, but not to see, Tim pointed at the garage.

Again Bill understood. "How about if we and our bikes use your garage?" he asked.

The kid found that arrangement more acceptable, so he left them in the yard and went in the house to find the key.

"Can you hurry?" Bill asked the kid's back. "If we don't get inside right away, it'll be too late."

Waiting impatiently for the kid to return, Bill watched the street and the alley for any sign of the enemy. Sure that the cops drew closer by the second, his nerves unraveled, as evidenced by the way he danced around his bike, and played incessantly with the gears and the brakes.

Without interrupting his furtive looks down the street and alley, Bill prayed for all he was worth. He prayed they'd escape. He wanted to cross the High Bridge. He knew of an ideal hiding place on the other side of the river. But the distance across the bridge was too great. It was all uphill, and Tim was too slow. They'd never make it across without being seen, and if they were seen, they were screwed. He knew Tim needed to sit down, and they needed to find a place where they were less visible. They needed to do all of that right now.

MOVING AT A PAINSTAKINGLY SLOW PACE through the streets and alleys of Uppertown, the eyes of both investigators sought any sign of movement, anything out of place or newly disturbed, anyone who could point them in the direction of two kids trying for all they were worth to escape.

After the failed bridge attempt and a cursory examination of many of the streets and alleys in Uppertown, they might have given up. But they held on a while longer. They had little to lose and much to gain, and they wanted to be in the vicinity if one of the squads spotted the boys.

Pete's concern for the kids weighed heavily on his mind.

Doubting they were involved in the murder, he wondered if they'd had any run-ins with the police. If not, why were they so afraid of Martin and him? It always returned to the man with the gun. They could be afraid of that person, which meant they'd probably seen, and perhaps been threatened by, him or her—or them.

He'd bet his favorite running shoes that the boys knew something. Something critical to their investigation. Something they were going out of their way to conceal.

While passing the five-story, brick home for the aged, run by the Little Sisters of the Poor, Martin reported that there was a path behind the building, running along the edge of the bluffs.

"How do you know that?" Pete asked. "Were you working a case there? Did they have a problem with the nuns aiding the residents with the move to their eternal rewards?"

"If so, I haven't heard about it," Martin smiled. "I found out while visiting a former neighbor who now lives there."

The two men hastily covered the benefits and drawbacks of diverting their attention from the streets and alleys to this path. They decided against it, doubting the kids were aware of it. And knowing if they weren't there, the delay it entailed would probably eliminate any chance of finding them today.

ALTHOUGH IT SEEMED TO TAKE FOREVER, the kid soon returned with the key—one key. He started around to the overhead door.

Bill stopped him, asking if they could use the less visible side door—just in case their friends were close. He didn't mention the friends were in a Crown Victoria.

His concerns were well-founded. Pete and Martin were frightfully close to where he stood and where Tim hung over his bike. With a few correct turns, men and boys would be within each other's field of vision.

The kid shrugged. "Whatever," he said, "but I'll have to get a different key. I always use the overhead door, but for ten dollars I can use whatever door you want." Smiling, he turned and started back to the house before Bill stopped him.

"Wait," he said. He didn't want to waste any more time. He didn't want to stand there in the yard any longer than necessary. They'd already been there, far too visible for far too long. "We'll do it your way," he relented.

Their laid-back, to-be host played with the lock on the overhead door, and Bill and Tim found a marginally less apparent spot in the yard, huddled against the house-side of the garage. Less conspicuous than the other boy, they were by no means invisible. Other than inside the tent, there wasn't a place in the yard that was hidden from both the street and the alley.

They'd already lost precious time, and Bill worried he'd made a horrible mistake when he selected this hiding place. But he feared it was too late to search for an alternate. If it was as bad a move as he now suspected, the price would be mighty high for a couple of guys as young as he and Tim. In fact, for the last two days he'd been on an unprecedented streak of bad luck, even for him.

Bill began wondering if the other kid was yanking his chain, because it took him so long to unlock the door. It occurred to him that the kid might have called the police when he was in the house. He was thinking about telling Tim they had to take off, when he decided that the kid couldn't possibly know the cops were after them.

He considered going over to see if he could help. They would have been in the garage by now if the kid had just gone back in the house for the other key.

Exasperated, Bill leaned over to his friend and asked, "Hey, man, do you think we should go? Do you think you can ride your bike?"

Tim shrugged, then nodded.

As Bill swung his leg over his bike, the other kid called out, "Got it! This key needs graphite. My mom and dad have the good ones, but no problem. I don't see any kids looking for you. They're on bikes, right?"

"Yeah," Bill lied. "Can you just go in the garage, close that door and open the side door for us—in case they come down the alley any second?"

The other kid did half of what he requested.

As soon as Bill got his bike inside, he looked to his left and saw that the overhead door was wide open.

"Hey, man," he said, pointing at the door, "I thought you were going to close it. If we're found, you're out ten bucks."

Their host laughed, but walked through the garage and closed the door.

Reaching into a pocket, Bill extracted the ten dollars and handed it over, thinking things would now be okay in spite of the other kid's stupidity.

Their host tucked it in the pocket of his shorts and told Bill to make sure that all the doors were locked before they left. "Let me know the next time you want to use a garage," he snorted before taking off.

"Smartass," Bill muttered, letting out a long held breath. They were finally out of danger—he thought. Before he could worry about anything else, he double-checked the overhead and side doors. Both were locked.

"Sit here, man," Bill said.

Tim was no more a man than a chrysalis was a butterfly, but that didn't stop this tag that the boys used often in their exchanges.

Bill assisted his friend, whose face was bright red and who recovered from one fit of coughing, only to be caught in the grip of another onslaught. Propping Tim's bike against a wall, he helped him settle in a spot on the concrete floor that provided a wall as a back-rest.

Sweat rolled off Tim, but that wasn't the worst of it. The coughing persisted with too few breaks, and Bill was scared—so scared that he'd have given his iPod for a bottle of water.

He considered dashing out of the garage to get water from an outdoor spigot. His concern for Tim was mushrooming. But he didn't see a faucet while they waited to get in the garage, and the idea of leaving the perceived safety of this spot petrified him. Had he known it would take the kid a day and a half to let them in, he would have gotten Tim some water while they waited.

He should have asked the kid for a bottle of water. He'd gladly have paid for it. Why didn't he think of it while the kid was still around? He knew why. He'd been so scared that he wasn't thinking. Well, that wasn't really true. A single thought, namely what would happen if the police found them, hammered the inside of his skull. In the process, that thought dulled other considerations. Overcome with fear, he was unable to assess their situation or think of alternatives. Wouldn't his dad be proud?

Maybe now, in a safe place, he could think. He still had a lot to figure out.

MARTIN AND PETE PASSED THE END of the alley that provided a view of the interior of the boys' sanctuary, and Pete saw a kid closing a garage door.

"Pull over, Martin!" he exclaimed. "I want to check out a garage back there."

FIFTEEN

P UT YOUR HEAD BETWEEN YOUR KNEES and take some deep breaths. I think that'll help," Bill whispered in Tim's ear, striving to sound confident. He rubbed his best friend's back to help him relax and stop coughing. That's what his mother would do.

"You'll be okay in a minute, man," he continued. "Try to be as quiet as you can, in case they come down the alley looking for us. I don't think they will. I know it's hard, but do the best you can, just in case."

Acting on an inspiration that he hoped was a good omen, Bill pulled his T-shirt over his head and held it out to Tim. He whispered, "Take this, man. I know it reeks, but if you hold it tight to your face, I don't think anyone will be able to hear you."

Tim did as instructed, balling the shirt up to muffle his coughing. Although still breathing heavily, the coughing was less intense and less frequent.

Ideas raced through Bill's head. He didn't want to talk any more than absolutely necessary. He thought about the money he had paid the kid whose garage they were using, and hoped that ten dollars was enough to keep him quiet if the cops questioned him. He didn't seem like the kind of kid who'd tell the cops—unless he had to.

He was glad he'd made sure both doors were locked. The cops wouldn't be able to get in if they decided to look in all of the garages. He'd seen plenty of cop shows on TV and was sure, or pretty sure, they couldn't start breaking down doors.

The layout of the garage reassured him. There was only one window, and it was in the side door. Had there been windows in the overhead door, there'd be no place to hide. They'd be screwed. They were safe as long as they stayed here, he told himself. But that was followed by thoughts of the kid's parents or brother or someone coming home anytime soon. It tightened the knots in his stomach.

"How long do we have to stay here, Billy?" Tim whispered, muffling it with the shirt.

"At least an hour, maybe two. Got any food?"

"Nerds." Tim wheezed into the T-shirt. "Want some?" He reached for a Velcro-fastened pocket on his cargo shorts. Bill stopped him just in time.

As unlikely as it might be, Bill feared that someone might hear the ripping sound.

"Thanks for getting us away from them, Billy. I owe you one."

"It's okay. I was just lucky. Sorry I got you into this mess, man."

Sitting next to Tim, he continued massaging his friend's back and was relieved to see that, even without water, Tim was coming around.

"WHAT DID YOU SEE?" Martin asked, wondering why Pete had him pull over.

"I saw someone closing a garage door."

"And?"

"That's all, but I'm curious. The kids could be in there."

"But you didn't see them?"

"No."

"And they could be in any garage in the area or no garage at all, couldn't they?" Martin asked.

"They could be in any garage as long as the door was unlocked or someone let them in or their talents exceed my expectations."

"But we don't have a search warrant," Martin protested.

"I prefer to first find out if we need one, oh ye of little faith. This could be every bit as successful as our other efforts this afternoon, but I'd like to think it's our turn to win one." Pete smiled.

Martin turned off the ignition and pocketed the keys.

The garage was halfway down the alley, and Pete used that distance to explain his strategy. Secrecy was critical, so he conveyed the details in a whisper that had Martin straining to hear.

There was plenty of time to share the information. They moved slowly, carefully stepping from foot to foot, trying to eliminate any indication of their approach. The neighborhood seemed quiet for a summer afternoon and, assuming the boys were in that garage, they'd be struggling to hear anything suspicious.

When they reached the garage, Martin positioned himself at the corner that gave him views of the overhead and side doors. He wanted to cover both exits, in case Pete was right.

Pete continued through the yard to the front door. The back door was more convenient, but he didn't want the boys to hear him. He preferred cornering them in the garage to chasing them down the alley, assuming he found a cooperative resident.

After knocking, he waited a minute and knocked again. He rang the doorbell and waited some more. Deciding he'd given anyone in the house more than enough time, he concluded that the kid he saw was the only one home, and he'd left.

Returning to the garage, Pete informed Martin of the outcome, using a thumbs-down gesture. He went to the alley-side of the garage and positioned himself against the garage. It was the second time this afternoon he found himself kissing up to a wooden structure, and he hoped it wasn't indicative of the path his life was taking.

Going to and from the house, he viewed three of the four sides of the garage. The only window was in a door that faced the house. Enticing though it be, he didn't look through it. Just as important, he was sure the kids, if they were inside, positioned themselves so they couldn't be seen through that window.

He hoped the kids would think they were safely stowed away and talk or make some other noise—any noise an empty garage couldn't emit. If he succeeded in getting anything to confirm his suspicions, he'd try to get a search warrant. He knew he'd be challenged, but felt confident he'd succeed.

"Hey, mister, whatcha doing?" a small girl on a pint-sized pastel bicycle, complete with training wheels, called out as she rode down the alley towards Pete. The kid was as cute as a bug's ear, with big blue eyes, red pigtails, and freckles, but she had horrible timing.

This was a perfect demonstration of why the other side of the garage was preferable. It wasn't as visible from the alley or neighboring yards. Pete wondered how Martin was reacting, but wasn't about to call attention to the other man by taking a few steps so he could see. He only hoped Martin wouldn't do anything to reveal himself. Having the little girl disclose more than she already had was the last thing they needed.

Pete scrambled to think of a way to silence her.

TIM'S FACE SOUNDLESSLY SPRANG UP from Bill's T-shirt and his eyes locked on his friend's. The alarm they conveyed matched the reaction Bill fought to hide.

"Shhh," Bill whispered into Tim's ear, taking advantage of the ruckus created by the little girl. "If we don't make a sound, they'll move on. They can't know we're in here. You're doing great. Keep it up, man."

After silently thanking the little girl for the warning, Bill tried to concentrate on everything they'd done right. Panicking, he felt his gorge rise. Fighting it back, he worked to calm his stomach. If he heaved right now, they'd be done for. The cops would hear him. He tried to do what he'd told Tim. He tried taking some deep breaths, and he tried concentrating on believing they'd escape.

The cops couldn't stay here all afternoon. There must be more important things they had to do. After all, a man got murdered yesterday. Why would they bother with a couple of kids? Did the cops think they did it?

From the moment they got inside the garage, Bill knew they had to be quiet, in case the cops came looking. He was right. He couldn't imagine anyone else lurking outside. It couldn't be the kid who let them in. A little kid wouldn't call someone their age "mister." If it was someone who lived here or nearby, the little kid would know that person and not call him mister. It would be Mr. Jones or Mr. Whatever, not just mister. It was the cops all right.

Pete put his finger to his lips, hoping the little girl would abide by the signal.

"But whatcha doing?" she persisted.

He tried one more signal, raising an index finger.

This time she seemed more willing to play along, and Pete rapidly dialed the number for Bill's cell. While doing so, he reached in his pocket and felt what he was searching for—a quarter.

After holding it along its edges, between his thumb and index finger, giving the child an opportunity to get a good look at it, he tossed it as far as he could down the alley and into the grass. Simultaneously, he punched the talk button on his phone and pressed his ear against the side of the garage. Worst case, if the ringer was turned off, he hoped to hear the phone vibrate. The whole time, his gaze remained on the little girl, following her down the alley.

Bill felt the cell in his shorts pocket vibrate. With a shaky hand, he pressed the button that silenced it. It made a lot of noise before he succeeded, and he feared the cop heard it. He didn't say or do anything else, other than signal Tim, who'd also heard it. He knew that from the look on his friend's face when, for the second time in a minute, he lifted it out of the T-shirt and looked questioningly at him.

Trying to prevent another telltale signal of their location, should someone call the stupid thing again, he gripped it firmly in one hand.

Keeping a finger on the silencer button, he pulled it out of his pocket and, using both hands, pressed it tight against his stomach. His legs added a layer of insulation and he hoped this would, if necessary, block the sound until he silenced it. He wanted to turn it off, but the melody it played while shutting down ruled that out.

After it was silenced he peered at the bright screen to check the caller ID and see who it was. The cops again. It was a pretty safe bet, it was the same cop standing outside the garage. As he sat there, waiting for the worst to happen, Bill thought about poor Tim. He was in the middle of this thing, and none of it was his fault.

As SOON AS THE LITTLE GIRL collected her prize, she gripped it tightly in her fist, turned around, and giggled. She seemed to think this was great fun.

Pete was propped against the garage wall, and that piqued her interest. "Why are ya doin' that, mister?" she called out, louder than necessary.

He didn't know how long he could distract her with quarters, but one or two more failed attempts to scare a sound out of Bill's phone, and they'd have to give up anyway.

When he grasped another quarter and held it out, she quieted down. He took advantage of the silence and reconnected with Bill's phone. As soon as he heard it ring on his end, he tossed the quarter in the same general direction, but even deeper into the yard on the opposite side of the alley. In addition to diverting the little girl's attention, this kept her away from Martin. There wasn't a doubt in his mind that, if the boys were in the garage, the first thing they'd think was that the little girl was talking to the police. Right now, all he needed was another minute of near silence.

WITH HIS PHONE SO WELL SHIELDED and a finger on the silencer, Bill was physically, but not emotionally, ready for the next call. It shook him up, and he wondered how long this would continue. His stomach churned, and he was sure he was going to be sick.

Once again, he resorted to breathing deeply and concentrating on the positive. This time it proved less effective. The police must know they're in here. Otherwise, they wouldn't keep calling him. He wondered how long they'd wait before breaking down the door, regardless of what any laws might say.

CONNECTING AGAIN WITH VOICE MESSAGING, Pete hung up and immediately hit the talk button twice to reconnect. To his relief, the little girl enjoyed the game and played along with relative quiet, other than a series of giggles.

The boys, unlike the little girl, didn't play along, and his third attempt failed. Pete stroked his upper lip, frustrated and searching for another solution. He was about to throw in the towel, when an idea turned his frown into a grin.

SIXTEEN

K NOWING NOW THAT BILL WOULDN'T answer the phone, Pete resorted to texting. His message said, "Found your tie tack at Landing. Could be only opportunity to get it back."

It took about ten seconds for Bill to respond to this text message with one of his own. It said, "How?"

Pete answered that message, insisting they talk, not text. He'd barely disconnected, before his phone vibrated and a prepubescent voice said, "What do I have to do to get it back right now?"

"I think that can be arranged, assuming you cooperate."

After a protracted pause, the boy said, "Yessir."

"Then come outside, to the overhead door, and we'll talk."

"Yes, sir."

Pete and Martin heard the side door open, and the boys came around the corner, looking defeated.

"Glad we could work this out," Pete said. "Give me the phone numbers where I can reach your parents, and we'll get together with them."

Bill gasped and his face went white.

Tim gave him an understanding look.

"What will we talk about?" Bill asked.

"About what you saw at the Landing on Sunday."

"And you'll ask about the tie tack?"

"If it's a part of what happened," Pete said.

"Then we can't talk," Bill insisted.

"Do you understand that would be a crime?" Pete asked.

"My parents can't find out about the tie tack. I borrowed it to show it to Tim. My dad'll kill me if he finds out. Can't we talk without them, please?"

"My partner and I are concerned about the effects this murder is having on the two of you," Pete said. "That's why it's important we include your parents."

"We didn't see the murder. It's the tie tack and being chased by you that's stressing me out. How about you, Tim?"

Tim nodded feverishly.

"Hang on a minute, while my partner and I discuss this," Pete said.

He and Martin stepped back and talked in whispers about violating department policy. Pete didn't take this breech lightly, but was sure it would better serve the boys' needs and theirs. He believed Bill's assertion that their source of stress was the tie tack. *Sans* parents, he could use the tie tack to get answers. Without that edge, the boys seemed unlikely to tell the truth. It took a minute, but he convinced Martin to go along with him.

"Let's walk over to Irving Park," Pete concluded. "It's nearby and will give us the space we need to split up. I'll take Bill, and you take Tim. We'll head off in different directions. Divide and conquer. I don't want either of them to hear what the other says, in case they plan to continue playing games. If we get what we need, I'll give Bill the tie tack."

"But Pete, what about the chain of evidence?"

"If the tie tack belongs to the kid, it isn't really relevant to the case, unless the kids murdered Winthrup. Think they might have?"

"Of course not."

"Bill's sweating bullets over the tie tack. It's my best bet for getting him to level with me."

"I don't know, Pete. I don't like it."

"Don't worry. I picked it up, and I'll be the one to release it. Go easy on Tim, Martin. Forget the fact he lied to you. All we care about is why."

"Let's walk to Irving Park," Pete told the boys. "Then I'll speak with you, Bill, while my partner speaks with Tim."

Bill said, "Yessir," and Tim groaned.

During the short walk to the park, Pete attempted to relax the boys. "That was quite the display of bike riding and evasive moves you showed us today," he said. "You scared the hell out of me. I was afraid you were going to kill yourselves. I hope that's not the way you usually ride."

Silence.

Pete repeatedly adjusted his pace, keeping the boys and their bikes at his side.

In a couple of minutes, they reached the park. Pete and Bill left Martin and Tim behind at the periphery and continued on into the park.

Once out of the hearing range of Martin and the other boy, Pete stopped. He turned to Bill and looked deep into his eyes. His look was sympathetic, but firm.

"First, let's get the names straight," Pete said. "There's no sense lying about it. If you do, we have other ways to identify you. You'll accomplish nothing, other than making us angry. Got it?"

"Yes, sir."

"Good. So tell me your names and ages."

"Bill McGrath. I'm eleven."

"And your friend?"

"Isn't *my* name good enough? He's already in a lot of trouble because of me."

"What kind of trouble, Bill?"

Bill didn't respond, and his head hung so low that Pete couldn't see his face.

"It'll be harder to protect him if I don't know his name."

Bill looked up, pensively. After several seconds, he said his friend was Tim Hawley and he was almost twelve. It took a bit more prompting, but Pete finally got their addresses. He was right. They lived in Mendota Heights.

"Why's this tie tack so important to you?" Pete asked, retrieving the bag with the tie tack from his pants pocket.

Billy dove for it. He hoped to cut and run, but Pete was faster and extended his arm, complete with the bag, out of the boy's reach.

Billy's lower lip quavered.

"Let's sit down and talk. Is it okay if I call you Billy or do you prefer Bill?"

"Either's fine."

"I plan to give you the tie tack when we're finished, Billy, unless you make that impossible by refusing to answer my questions. I think you saw something on the Upper Landing yesterday, but for some reason you don't want to talk about it. If the circumstances were different, I might respect you for that. But it could mean the difference between solving the case and letting a killer walk. That killer might be planning to kill someone else. I can't risk it."

Billy flinched.

"Did someone threaten you, Billy?"

Silence.

"If that's why you're not talking, it doesn't work. If you were told you'd be hurt if you told anyone what you saw, keeping quiet won't protect you. It's probably the worst thing you can do. I've been in this business a long time, Billy, and I can guarantee that. If someone told you that, they might think you squealed when we hone in on them. And we're going to catch them. If they know how to find you, the only way we can help you is if you speak up and help us catch them. Tell me what you saw, Billy. Let me help you and Tim."

Billy looked like he might break down.

Pete searched for a way to reach him. After a long, silent minute he asked, "Do you want my help, Billy?"

"Yessir, but talking could kill Tim and me, and I don't think you can keep that from happening. I don't want to make you angry. That's just the way it is."

It was Pete's turn to deliver the silent treatment. He sat on the grass, with his hands behind his back, propping up his shoulders.

"Can't you just give me the tie tack?" Bill pleaded.

"Against the advice of my partner, I'm willing to put my neck on the chopping block to return it to you. But I can't do it if you aren't willing to trust me. Why don't you trust me, Billy?"

After an extended silence, Pete stood and brushed off his pants. "Okay, Billy, you have my phone number. Let me know if you change your mind." He turned and started walking towards Martin and Tim.

Stopping after several steps and turning back, he said, "Stay here. We'll send Tim over when we're finished with him."

Bill's head dropped as soon as Pete turned around, and it looked like he was crying.

Pete waited a few minutes, before going back and sitting next to the boy. "Tell me what you're afraid of, Billy. Let me help, please."

Billy sniffed, and Pete didn't rush him. He did his best to remember how it felt to be that age.

"Tell me about the tie tack, Billy."

Billy said his great-great grandfather wore it at his wedding. His dad just inherited it. Billy thought that the tie tack was awesome because the event of note happened more than a hundred years ago. "All I wanted to do was show it to Tim. Then I was going to put it right back."

"Something had to scare you pretty badly, for you to leave it behind, Billy."

Billy nodded.

"I'll bet that 'something' was the murderer. If I was you and saw a killer and he threatened me, I'd run as fast as my legs would carry me. When I couldn't run any further, I don't know what I'd do. What would you do, Billy?"

"Find a place to hide."

"Like in a garage?" Pete teased.

Billy couldn't help it. Hard as he tried, he couldn't keep from smiling.

"You and Tim are pretty good," Pete said. "With the two of you, working with my partner and me, we'll outsmart the guy you saw on the Landing. Tell me what he looked like, Billy. We're going to find him. We found the tie tack. With your help, we'll find him a lot faster."

Billy did his best to remember the man who threatened them. He described the man as average height and build. He wore a black do-rag and large sunglasses, so Billy couldn't see his hair, eyebrows or eyes. He wasn't sure, but he thought the man wore a dark-colored T-shirt and jeans.

"Did he talk to you?" Pete asked.

"Yeah. That's the problem. He told us to get the hell out of there. I looked around real quick, trying to see the tie tack, when he said, 'Right now or else!' He told us that if we told anyone anything about him he'd find us and he'd make short order of us. He had a really deep and a really mean voice. We knew he wasn't kidding."

When Pete asked why they had to look for the tie tack, Billy explained they were getting ready to leave, and he was showing it to Tim. The man who threatened them snuck up behind them, grabbed their shirts and spun them around. The tie tack went flying, and he was afraid to react. He didn't want the man to find it and steal it. His dad would never understand.

Pete asked if the man who was shot and the man who scared them were the only two people they saw at the Landing that day.

Billy told another segment of his story. "When we got there, two guys were down where they're building. One was the guy who got killed. They set up some sticks and cans, and the guy who got killed was taking target practice. I don't think they saw us. We lay on the ground, behind the hill, and looked over the top. One of them left, and the other, the one who got killed, stayed. He wandered around, like he was maybe waiting for someone."

Billy described the man who left as about the same size as the victim, and said they had the same hair color.

"Now can I have the tie tack?"

"In a minute. You've been very helpful, but I have a few more questions. First, do you have a deep pocket where it'll be safe, until you get home?"

"Yes, sir!" Billy seemed to relax, and his smile returned.

"Good. We're almost finished."

"Do you think the man you saw with the victim could have put on the do-rag and the sunglasses and come back?"

"I don't think so."

"Why's that?"

"Two reasons. That guy had long sideburns, and he'd have had to change shirts. He wore a T-shirt that's my favorite color. Kind of a sky blue. He wasn't carrying anything when he left, so I don't know how he could've changed, put on the do-rag and come all the way around behind us so fast. Besides, the do-rag couldn't cover his sideburns. One more thing. The guy who left him down there gave him a hug, a long hug, before he left. Would you do that if you were going to kill him?"

Pete asked why Billy was so sure that the man who chased him and Tim away was the man who killed the victim.

"After we left, we heard the same popping sound the gun made when the man was taking target practice. We got scared."

After what the man said to chase them away, he'd worried about what was going on. He doubted it was more target practice. If it was, it didn't make sense to him that the guy who chased them away was so angry and so nervous.

At that point, they took off for the High Bridge. Once there, they looked through the railing. They didn't look over the top, in case the man with the do-rag was still there. They didn't see him, but they saw the other man lying face down. Billy called 911, hoping the paramedics could save him. When the paramedics arrived, the boys hurried back to look for the tie tack. Neither wanted to go down there, but they had to find it. He didn't know what happened to the gun the victim used for target practice. He concluded by looking Pete in the eye and asking, "Are you sure you can keep that guy from finding us?"

"I'm sure I can do it better than I could have without your help, and I'm positive that what you've told me won't make things worse for you."

Pete handed him the plastic bag and said, "What do you think? Should we see how Tim and my partner are getting along?"

Billy laughed. He was sure they weren't getting along. Tim had insisted that talking to the police meant more trouble.

Billy hoped this cop, not Tim, was right. "Can we go soon?" he asked. "I want to put the tie tack back in my dad's drawer before he gets home. Then, I don't ever want to see it again. I wouldn't care if it was a thousand years old." Billy was getting antsy and kept checking the time on his cell phone.

Pete bit back a smile, as he and Billy walked over to Martin and Tim.

Both stood with their arms crossed, glaring at each other.

When Pete asked if Tim gave Martin a description of the man who threatened him and Billy, Tim's glower shifted first to Pete and then to Billy.

If this wasn't Martin's least productive questioning session, it was certainly in the top five, and he wondered how Pete could look so satisfied.

Getting details from Tim still took time. However, with Billy's help, the boy relented. He insisted all he remembered were the man's legs and feet. He was too scared to look at his face, but he knew the man wore jeans and hiking boots.

Pete worried how best to protect the boys. He asked about relatives living outside the Twin Cities. Both had family that qualified. He got, and through dispatch verified, their addresses and home phone numbers, and he said they'd speak with their parents tonight.

Tim didn't pull any punches. He didn't believe any of that would help.

"The man you described doesn't know you or your names, and he let you go yesterday," Pete said. "That means he didn't want to hurt you. That's important."

Pete and Martin gave their business cards to the boys and instructed them to call if they remembered anything more or if anything else scared them or made them suspicious.

SEVENTEEN

MARTIN WAS SULLEN DURING THE RETURN trip to headquarters. It was obvious from the way he sat, the way his head hung and the way his silence filled the car.

Pete knew why. "You know I had an unfair advantage, don't you?" he asked.

Martin's fingers were doing a dance on the steering wheel when he said, "How so?"

"Tim had everything to gain and nothing to lose by refusing to talk. Billy, on the other hand, was in a quandary. He had to get the tie tack or else face the music, and he knew the only way to get it was to talk."

He was glad Martin didn't ask why he got Tim and Pete got Bill. It wouldn't help to tell him that Pete had more confidence in his own powers of persuasion, regardless of whom his partner was. It sounded rather arrogant.

Nearing headquarters, they had an hour before the meeting with Casey Winthrup. Pete decided to use the time to contact the soup kitchen that Bradford Winthrup was said to have visited.

The man who answered at Reaching Out told Pete his name was Ray and he coordinated the meal service part of the operation.

Pete explained he wanted to speak to some of the people who frequented Reaching Out in hopes of getting information about Bradford Winthrup. He wanted suggestions on how to proceed.

"I think your best bet is to show up at a meal, be outgoing and try to gain their trust," Ray said. "It could take several visits. One thing, though. They don't fit in a nice little box. They're just as different as the rest of us."

"You needn't pretend to be homeless," he continued. "If some of them warm up to you, you can tell them the murdered man was a friend, and you're trying to find out who did it. I think that will work better than telling them you're a police officer. Some of them have had run-ins with the police. If they trust you, they might share what they know."

When Pete asked the best way to dress, considering his mission, Ray suggested, "Some of the people we serve have one set of clothes, and some of them dress better than I do. Don't get me wrong. That doesn't mean they shouldn't come here. We serve everyone seeking our assistance, and I'm sure you realize it isn't always possible to determine someone's status from their appearance."

Pete asked if it would be best to show up for a particular meal or more than one meal per day, and Ray said it probably didn't matter. He said some people are there for three meals a day, but most aren't. Unfortunately, he didn't know which meals Winthrup ate there, so Pete couldn't use that to decide.

"Many of the people we serve are the working poor," Ray said. "Even with jobs, they can't make enough to get by. Rents are high in the Twin Cities, and the minimum wage often doesn't cut it. Also alarming is that veterans make up a quarter of the adult male homeless population in this state. Besides that, about one-in-three homeless women experienced domestic abuse. Sorry, I guess that's not the type of information you're after. I'll get off my soapbox. It's just that some believe that people are homeless because they prefer that to working. It's ludicrous, but there I go again. Is there anything else I can do for you?"

There but for the grace of God go I, Pete believed. But what he said was, "Your organization is providing a wonderful service. If you have time, I have another question."

"Sure, go ahead."

"I feel guilty taking advantage of your services. I'm concerned it could mean someone goes without. Would it be best to mail a check to you or what do you suggest?"

"We always welcome contributions. Many of our meals are paid for and served by a variety of church groups. Some of the food they serve is purchased from, or donated by, food shelves. So, that gives you three possibilities."

After Pete thanked him for his help, Ray wished him Godspeed. He added, "Too often our folks are easy pickings for the predators of society. I'm glad the police are taking such an active interest in this case."

EIGHTEEN

PETE AND MARTIN HAD TO MAKE tracks to reach Casey Winthrup's home by the scheduled time, and it seemed they hit all of the lights wrong. That added a little color to Martin's vocabulary, causing Pete to laugh, despite his edginess.

They didn't want to give Casey an excuse for not being there. Both men suspected that arriving two minutes late was all the excuse the guy needed.

Pete decided to call and let him know they might be a few minutes late. Flipping through his trusty notebook, he found the number and dialed. After five rings, the answering machine picked up. He left a message, hoping Casey was within earshot.

Gloria had promised to double check the time they established for the meeting and get back to Pete if it had to be changed. She hadn't called.

Pete wondered if she made it early, in hopes he and Martin would be finished and out of the house before she returned. He, too, hoped they'd complete the questioning in short order. He wanted to get to Reaching Out before they opened the doors. Even so, he wouldn't cut short his time with Casey. There was no telling whose information was more critical—at least not yet.

Pete was peeved and his voice didn't mask it when he told Martin, "No answer. I hope this doesn't mean what I suspect it does."

"As in, he's avoiding us?"

"Exactly. I'd call Gloria's cell, but we're only a few minutes away. I don't want to alarm her if he's out in the yard and didn't hear the phone."

"So, does that mean you're losing your grip on reality?"

"That's a definite possibility."

They arrived at the Winthrup house with a minute to the good, and Pete congratulated Martin on getting through all the "orange" lights. "When you were on the street, what would you have done if you saw a guy driving that way?"

"Are you kidding? I plead the fifth," Martin laughed.

Their punctuality was the end of the good news. There was no activity in the Winthrup yard and no response to the doorbell or their knocking on the front door.

Martin stayed at that door while Pete went around to the back. There wasn't a vehicle in the garage, nor on the street in front of the house.

On the outside chance Casey was home but didn't hear the previous attempts, Pete knocked on the side door. While waiting for an answer, he entertained himself by listening for any sounds coming from within. After three failed attempts to rouse someone, he walked back to the front yard.

"So, is there a car out back?" Martin asked.

"Nope. I'll call Gloria." Pete tried her cell. When he reached voicemail, he called her office. The way things were going, he was amazed when she answered.

She acted surprised when he said Casey wasn't home. "I talked to him this morning, and he said four o'clock would be fine. He's always home by now. Maybe he had a flat tire. Maybe he was in an accident." Her voice rose an octave and a few decibels with the second "maybe." It sounded more like a question and conveyed concern.

After he promised to notify her immediately if there'd been an accident, Gloria told him the route Casey *always* took home from work. He called dispatch, while Martin knocked on neighbors' doors.

Before long, Martin returned. "A woman who lives next door saw Casey drive up at about two-thirty,'" he said. "She was weeding her flower beds, when he parked in the street and went into the house. She heard the door slam when he came out, carrying a suitcase. When she asked about it, Casey said he was going out of town, on business, for several days. She said he was unusually abrupt, and that 'he's such a nice young man.'" Martin shook his head and rolled his eyes.

Pacing on the sidewalk, Pete called dispatch, told them to cancel the check on Winthrup's route and redialed Gloria's office. Controlling his anger and trying to give her the benefit of the doubt, he told her what the neighbor had said.

Blubbering, she told him she didn't know Casey was planning this. She named every feasible reason, except the most obvious one— that he skipped town.

Pete asked where he might go, and she said the only people he'd go to were his mother and brother.

She described her husband as five-foot-ten and about 170 pounds, with blond hair.

"Did he go to the Upper Landing yesterday to meet with Bradford?" Pete asked.

"No. I can't imagine him doing that. But if he did, I'm positive he'd have told me. You're not suggesting that . . ."

"His disappearance raises a lot of questions," was all Pete would say.

In spite of that, she cooperated by telling him her husband drove a 2002 Dodge Neon. She didn't know the license number.

"Before I let you go," Pete said, "check and see if your car or Casey's is where you parked it."

Back in a minute, she reported it was hers.

He gave her Martin's cell number and instructed her to call immediately if she heard from Casey.

Pete closed his phone and turned to Martin, who was listening intently. "Okay," he said, "there's nothing more we can do around here, at least for now. Let's head back downtown, by way of my place. I want to change clothes."

They were at Pete's house for less than ten minutes. In that time, Pete changed into a broken-in pair of jeans, a polo shirt, and a retired pair of running shoes.

That gave Martin enough time to forage for sustenance.

Pete found him in the kitchen, slumped down in a chair, drinking a Coca Cola and munching on a handful of Sun Chips.

"Bring the Coke and the chips along, if you like," Pete offered.

Martin smiled. He was starving. After chugging the rest of the Coke, he grabbed the bag of chips and followed Pete out the door.

When he asked about accompanying Pete to the soup kitchen, Pete said, "That would be nice, but you're not dressed for it. The maitre d' will refuse to seat you. Besides, I'll have better luck gaining acceptance or being adopted if I'm alone."

"Do you think I should call Megan Alden and try to get a picture of Casey?" Martin asked. "She seems to be the most likely to cooperate without a hassle. I know she's out of town, but maybe she carries one with her and can have a copy faxed to us. She might even be carrying a laptop and have a jpeg of him on the hard drive. So, what do you think?"

"I didn't realize you're bilingual."

"What do you mean?"

"Jpeg, hard drive. Next thing you know you'll be talking about gigs and RAM. What's this world coming to?"

"Trust me, you don't want to know. Ignorance is bliss."

The words had barely escaped, before Martin regretted the utterance. They provided the perfect set up, if Pete wanted to zing him.

Ignoring it, Pete said, "If she doesn't have a photo, she might contact her husband and tell him where to find one. You could pick it up."

"Yeah, I've already got it on my to-do list. After that, I'll start contacting Bradford's friends."

Nineteen

H E'D DONE HIS SHARE OF ACTING. Nine times out of ten, it was essential for an effective interrogation. But tonight would be a radically different performance for Pete, and he was nervous.

Jogging from headquarters to Reaching Out, he considered how to melt into the background. That seemed like the best way to get what he needed. The mile-and-a-half run relieved a bit of the tension.

A block west of the Assumption Church, he slowed to a walk and checked his watch. Twenty minutes until the doors opened. Perfect. He had plenty of time to hang around and hope someone, better yet, several people, approached him.

After he turned the final corner, Reaching Out came into view. He scrutinized the building and the people in the vicinity, trying to get a feel for the interpersonal dynamics.

Aside from those who appeared to be families, the people seemed to gather primarily by gender—rather like at a high school dance. A group of guys stood by the entrance, possibly staking their claim to the head of the line. Pete couldn't tell whether there was any connection between them, besides proximity. Other than one man, who chewed a wad of gum in excess of the speed limit, their mouths were frozen in a variety of expressions.

He meandered up the sidewalk, stopping close enough to the door to read the signs. Taking his sweet time, he achieved his goal. He drew a comment.

"Wanna borrow my specs?" the man asked.

Pete looked in the direction of the voice and saw a man who looked to be in his thirties, smiling at him.

"Sorry, no. I think I've got it. I'd hate to threaten anyone's turf or make an enemy, so can you tell me where I should wait?"

"As long as you don't cut the line, you're cool. Most of us aren't territorial. Life's broken us of that."

"Thanks, but I can't tell if there's the beginning of a line. For example, the guys over there, to the left of the door," Pete motioned with his chin, "are they in line?"

"Not yet. Give it another ten minutes. When there's a line, you'll know." He smiled and walked away, joining the men waiting left of the door.

Pete claimed a solitary space to the right of the door, leaned against the wall and stared at his feet. It seemed like the best way for someone new to the system to fit in.

A few other men planted themselves in his vicinity. They kept enough of a distance to be considered standoffish, and they made a point of looking anywhere but at him.

Arriving twenty minutes early was looking like a bad idea. He passed the time planning the next steps in the investigation.

He developed an opening line he'd use with some of his fellow diners, given the chance. Then he revised it once, twice, three times. Next he wondered how Martin was doing with getting a picture and contacting the victim's friends.

His thoughts drifted to Casey. What was up with him? First his wife played games with them, and then he skipped out on their meeting. It all meant something, but what?

About the time he was going to have to change positions, he saw the guys on the other side of the door begin working their way towards the sidewalk and forming a sorry excuse for a line. Were they the daily trendsetters or was this a special occasion?

Taking his time, Pete pushed himself away from the wall and wandered over, getting in line.

There's a gaggle of geese, a pod of whales, and a rookery of penguins. He wondered what you would call a group of homeless people.

He decided it depended on the season. In the winter, way too cold. In the summer, often way too hot. And much of the time, hungry. This wasn't the first time the inequities in life bothered him.

As the line moved, Pete played Follow the Leader. When he turned the corner into the dining room, the process became less apparent, and he looked every bit as confused as he felt. The look served him well. A fiftyish man came up behind him and asked, "First time?"

"Yeah, 'fraid so."

"Don't worry 'bout it. I'll show ya the ropes."

"Thanks, I'd appreciate it."

"Let me slide 'round ya, here," he said. "Then do everything I do—'cept for flirting with the pretty girls." He winked at Pete and asked, "Ya got a name?"

"Yes. Pete. And you?"

"Just call me Stew." They shook hands.

They made their way down one side of an almost sneeze-proof counter, while their trays worked their way along the other side at nearly the same pace. In response to the questions of the volunteers, they accepted or rejected generous portions of the foods offered. It reminded Pete of his grade school cafeteria, only in grade school they had to take and eat at least a little of everything.

As they advanced, their trays accumulated the main course—chicken, mashed potatoes, and green beans. Bread and butter were piled on top. At the end of the counter, each person was given a handful of assorted homemade cookies. The final addition was a choice of milk, coffee, or both.

Throughout the process, Stew greeted the female volunteers. Calling them "darlin'" and "beautiful," he flashed a smile at each.

Without exception, they responded in kind.

After receiving his tray, Pete scanned the dining room for a place to sit. Round and rectangular tables filled the room. All were occupied, so it wasn't an easy task.

Once again he hesitated, for fear of alienating some of the other diners. He didn't know if there were rules about sitting at someone else's table. For all he knew, it was as inappropriate here as at any restaurant. Was he supposed to wait to be invited? And if no one invited him?

Stew recognized his uncertainty and pointed to a volunteer across the room, seating others in the same predicament.

Pete thanked him once again and walked over to the volunteer. She seated him with a couple of men who looked to be about his age. He wondered if she did that, thinking their shared ages might mean they had other things in common.

Before placing his tray on the table, Pete asked, "Do you mind?"

Both shook their heads, so he settled in. He took a shot at small talk, but gave up when their one- or two-word answers failed to expand, regardless of the topic.

Many of the patrons made short order of their meals, and within a half hour the crowd had thinned. Even so, after the first steady stream of diners, there was an occasional straggler, including what looked like a family. It consisted of a middle-aged man and woman and two small girls. Pete pegged the children as preschool age.

Dawdling, he continued hoping for another encounter or two. By 5:45 when there were more empty tables than occupied ones and he hadn't spoken to a soul, he bussed his tray and headed out.

A man who stood by the entrance, greeted him and asked how he was doing.

Pete gave him the stand-pat answer. Then he posed the same question.

The man smiled and gave him a thumbs-up.

"Didn't I see you sitting with Stew?" Pete asked.

"You did. Stew said he was explaining things to you. He does that a lot. He likes helping newcomers."

"He's a nice guy. I like him," Pete said.

"You're a good judge of character. I'd better be going," he continued. "I have miles to go before I sleep."

"You, me, and Robert Frost," Pete said. And, carrying Robert Frost's poem a step further, he knew that for someone like this man, undoubtedly the streets are "weary, dark and deep."

The man responded with a smile, but didn't speak.

With that last, failed attempt, Pete jogged back to headquarters. One trip to Reaching Out completed, and an untold number remaining before he either succeeded or gave up on this effort. Now he wanted to know what, if anything, Martin had uncovered.

TWENTY

MARTIN WAS ON THE PHONE when Pete returned from Reaching
Out. As he walked through the door, Martin held out a photo
of Brad's family.

When Martin hung up, Pete said, "Great job getting one. It's perfect. Did Ms. Alden email it?"

"Yes, and she gave me the lineup. From left to right, it's . . ."

"Hang on, Martin. Let me see if I can get it right. It's Eric, Ellen,
Casey, Megan, her husband, Gerald, and Bradford."

"You're correct on all counts, except you have Casey and Bradford
reversed. It's easy to do. I know twins who don't look that much alike."

"Did Ms. Alden tell you when it was taken?"

"She said about a year ago. You can tell from the grass and flowers
that it was taken in the summer. She still can't remember Brad's girlfriend's name. All she remembers is that the first name is very Irish,
like Shannon or Shawn, but the last name isn't. She said Brad's friends
from work should know and, before you ask, I haven't gotten to them
yet. I thought it would be best to start with those in Minnesota.

"When I told her Casey skipped out on our meeting and seems
to have disappeared," Martin continued, "she thought she could find
him. I asked how, and she said it might be better if I didn't know.
What do you make of that?"

"That she didn't want to tell you?"

"Thanks, that's insightful. She said she'll call back tomorrow
morning."

"You've been busy. Anything else happening?" Pete asked.

"I spoke with a couple of Bradford's friends. Both were from high
school. Both said they hadn't heard from him in at least six months.

They didn't even know he was back in Minnesota, and they were shocked to learn of his death."

"Did you hear from Frank Baxter, his former supervisor?"

"I sure did. He still doesn't have the phone number for Walter Linton. I asked if he knew how to spell obstruction of justice."

"You didn't!" Pete feigned shock.

"I did, and he said he'd get back to me tomorrow."

"Do you believe him?"

"I don't know. He might've been brushing me off. If I don't hear from him by late tomorrow afternoon, maybe I'll go over his head. What do you think, Pete?"

"Often the mere threat is more effective than the act."

"Good point. I've been there."

Pete told Martin about his dinner and his failure to make any detectable progress.

"You didn't really expect much more than that on your first trip, did you?"

"No, but it didn't stop me from hoping."

It was still early, so before going to see Billy's and Tim's parents, Martin and Pete split up the remaining Minnesota friends and made the calls.

They completed the process, speaking with as many answering machines as people, and the former were every bit as helpful as the latter. Calling the Chicago friends had to be delayed. The only phone number they had was the ACS switchboard, and the receptionist wouldn't be there this late.

"If you had no money and no place to live, wouldn't you call a friend?" Martin asked.

"I'm not sure, but I think it depends on a lot of things. For example, if I'd gone out of my way to help one or more of them, it might be more likely. But pride can get in the way. He was looking for an attorney. Do we know if any of his friends are attorneys? If one is, I can't imagine him not contacting that one either for help or for a referral."

Martin said he didn't know about an attorney friend, but he had another question. "Are you surprised that, other than one girlfriend, all of the friends the family named are men?"

"If he had female friends, maybe they're all in Chicago and the family doesn't know them."

"But, Pete, maybe they're intentionally steering us away from the female perspective."

TWENTY-ONE

WITH ASSISTANCE FROM THE INFORMATION technology staff, Pete extracted individual photos of Gerald Alden and Casey Winthrup from the family photo Megan provided. While he did that, Martin called the boys' parents and arranged to meet with them. He answered their questions about the reason for the meetings, by saying the boys weren't in trouble and he'd save the details until they arrived.

The parents were agreeable, possibly, in part, because the scant information piqued their interest.

Mendota Heights was a short trip, and on the way Pete and Martin decided to each take a family. Pete let Martin choose, and Martin had decided to stick with Tim. His meeting with Tim earlier had been an abject failure, so he hoped to have better luck with his parents. Just as important, if one of the boys was going to recognize one of the photos, it would be Billy. By leaving Billy to Pete, if the kid failed to recognize one or both photos, he'd forego being a party to that failure.

Martin dropped off Pete at Billy's and continued on.

Standing outside the front door, Pete caught a whiff of steaks on the grill, and his taste buds began doing back flips. There were few things he liked more than a grilled steak, and he hadn't had one in ages. Inviting Katie Benton, the woman he saw in the skyway today, to his home and grilling steaks might be a good start in getting to know her better.

Billy's mother answered the doorbell, and it was obvious from the potato peeler in her hand that she was in the middle of preparing dinner.

Pete apologized for the interruption and explained that he needed only about ten minutes of their time.

"Come on through the house and onto the deck. My husband's out there."

As they made their way from the foyer, through the living room and out the sliding door in the kitchen, Pete got a feel for the family's upper-middle-class lifestyle. Being a babe in the woods when it came to today's kids and their accoutrements, he couldn't tell if the house was in sync with a kid owning a thousand-dollar mountain bike.

With introductions out of the way, Pete's curiosity got the better of him. "That's quite the bike Billy's riding. Do you worry about it being stolen?"

"Not as much as we worried about the number of hours he played video and computer games," Billy's father said. "It's an addiction for a kid like Billy. He'd spend twenty-four hours a day playing them, if we allowed it. Often, when he's not playing one of the games, he's contemplating how he can reach the next level, or whatever they call it. The bike's our attempt to diversify his interests."

"Is it working?" Pete asked.

His father responded with a shrug and a side-to-side, so-so motion of his hand.

Changing the subject to the reason for his visit, Pete said, "Your son provides a great example for kids his age. Yesterday he saw a man in need and called 911."

When he felt he'd done a respectable job of adding Billy to the *Who's Who of Preteens in America*, he concluded by saying they must be very proud of their son. Then he worked his way into the potentially touchy idea of sending Billy away for a while, perhaps to visit relatives, "strictly as a precaution."

"How far away?" Billy's dad asked, frowning and rubbing the back of his neck.

"I think the operative word is 'away.' Anywhere out of the seven-county metro area should be good. Can you arrange that with family or friends?"

"Will that suffice? Shouldn't we do more than that?" Billy's mother asked.

"The man whose body they reported was shot. We're concerned that the person who shot him saw Billy and Tim. That's why I'm making this recommendation. I'd be surprised if the guilty party can identify them, but getting them out of the area for the time being makes sense, for the sake of their safety. It's also important to watch for any signs in Billy that the discovery is having an emotional impact on him."

"His emotional state is fine," Billy's dad said. "He didn't even mention it to us."

"He may not have because I said I'd be stopping in to talk to you. Nonetheless, please watch for signs of emotional distress, even subtle ones."

"I knew we shouldn't let him hang around the Landing," Billy's mother said, going wide-eyed and pressing both fists to her mouth.

"Don't blame yourself. In all of my years with the St. Paul P.D., this is the first incident down there."

"You said Billy should go away for a while," Billy's dad said. "Can you define 'a while?' That'll help us find a place or decide if we should move him around."

"I can't say just yet. I don't think more than a couple of weeks—three at the max. My goal is to wrap this up as quickly as possible. Please remember, the reason for asking you to do this is to increase the comfort zone of the boys, as well as my partner's and mine."

"Look, I don't want to be disagreeable, but what if you don't catch this person?" Billy's dad asked.

Trying to gloss over her husband's remark, Billy's mom said, "I have a sister in the Brainerd Lakes area. Her son and Billy are fast friends. If that doesn't work, I have other family around Rochester. I grew up there."

"Either one sounds like a good solution," Pete said. "As I'm sure you realize, a kid can develop a distaste for being a Good Samaritan, if it means he spends time having nightmares or fearing for his safety. I'd hate to have your son punished for his good deed."

Billy's parents agreed—his mother heartily. His father's endorsement was more reserved.

As an added assurance that the relocation occurred, Pete gave Billy's mother one of his cards. He asked her to call when she had a phone number where Billy could be reached, in case he had additional questions.

Before he left, Pete asked to speak with Billy and was told that he was at Tim's. Thanking them for their time and saying he hoped he hadn't spoiled their dinner, Pete left and began walking the half-mile to Tim's house. He took his time, not wanting to interfere with Martin's efforts.

Meanwhile, Martin's experience at Tim's paralleled Pete's, except this time dinner was over, they met in the living room and neither parent questioned or challenged his recommendations.

"I have the perfect solution," Tim's mother announced. "My sister and brother-in-law have a dairy farm near Belgrade. Do you know where that is?"

Martin didn't, so she explained. "It's not far from St. Cloud. Because of the dairy farm, they're always home. Tim and my nephew get along really well. He's always asking Tim to come for a visit. I'm sure Tim can help out, so he won't be a bother. I'm also sure my sister won't mind."

"Tim might mind," his father cautioned. "I don't know that he'll be very enthused about spending a week or three on a farm."

"I know what will fix that," Tim's mother said. "I'll check on having Billy go along. The two boys are almost inseparable, and Billy will get along fine with my family. He's an exceptionally easygoing boy."

After giving her his business card, Martin got the phone number at the farm. He also asked to be notified when the relocation occurred.

Tim's mother took the card and promised to arrange everything posthaste.

Martin had one last task—showing the pictures to Tim. When he asked to speak with him, Tim's mother said he and Billy were in the basement. She offered to have them come up, but Martin said he'd go downstairs.

After walking Martin to the basement door and calling down to Tim that someone wanted to see him, she smiled at Martin and walked back into the living room.

The stairs led down to a large family room. The only light came from the TV. When he reached the bottom step, Martin saw two boys sitting within a yard of a big-screen TV and oblivious to his arrival. They were too busy jerking controls from side to side, waving their arms and bouncing up and down on the cushions they occupied in lieu of chairs. They were playing what appeared to be a war-based video game.

"Hi, Tim. Hi, Bill," Martin said, loud enough, he assumed, to be heard over the TV.

Neither boy reacted. All they said was, "Oh, man" and "Yes, yes," interlaced with a heavy dose of expletives. There were also plenty of sounds coming from the TV—gunfire and war whoops being the mainstays.

Martin continued saying their names at top volume, as he edged in, amazed at the lifelike actions and gore on the screen. Failing to elicit a response from either boy, even when he was within a foot of them, he walked back to the stairs and flipped on a light.

"Oh, hi," Tim said, after he hit the pause button and spun around to see who it was.

"That looks like quite a game. What are you playing?"

"Call of Duty . . . on Play Station 2," Tim said. "Have you ever played it?"

"No, and much as I'd love to try it out, I'm in a bit of a hurry. My partner's meeting with your parents right now, Billy, and I just finished speaking with yours, Tim. They're arranging to have you visit family. I have some pictures I'd like both of you to look at. I want to know if either of the people looks like the man who told you to leave the Landing or the one who was with the victim, while he took target practice."

He pulled the pictures out of his suit jacket and handed them to Tim. Billy moved in close, so he could inspect the photos at the same time. Before either boy looked at the page, Tim asked, "Where are they sending me?"

Martin said he had to get that information from his parents.

Both boys winced and turned their attention from Martin to the piece of paper. As soon as he looked at the page, Billy said, "Woe! He's ..."

"Hang on, Billy!" Martin interrupted. "Take your time and look carefully at both photos. I want Tim to have a chance, before you influence him."

He watched as they checked the photos, each with his own ritual. Billy bit his lower lip, stared at the first, lifted his chin and raised his eyes, repositioning his stare on the ceiling for several seconds, raised his eyebrows and moved on to the second. Tim propped his head on one hand and transitioned from gazing at a photo to closing his eyes and scrunching his face in concentration. He finished several seconds before Billy and looked at Martin.

When Billy looked up, Tim said, "I recognize this one." He stabbed his finger at the photo of Casey.

"Me, too," Tim chimed in.

"Was he the man you saw with the victim or the one who threatened you?"

"He was with the man who was shot," Billy said. "It's really hard to know about the other guy. Like I said before, he wore a do-rag and sunglasses. So I didn't see much of his face."

Martin covered part of the forehead and the top of the head of Gerald Alden, using an index finger, and asked if that helped.

Billy frowned and said, "Sorry, I just don't know. I'm not sure. I think that man had big ears, like his, but I think his ears were bigger. Much bigger."

"A do-rag might make them look bigger, if it was tight against his head," Martin said. "And that man's hair might be making his ears look smaller."

"Yeah, true." Billy tried covering the hair on the sides of Alden's head, but the effort did little to help him visualize how he'd look wearing a do-rag. He gave up and said, "I just don't know."

All Tim said was, "Ditto about the one guy, and like I told you this afternoon, I didn't see the face of the man who threatened us."

Martin wore a broad smile as he exited the Hawley home. He was pleased with his performance with both the parents and the boys. Hearing the discussion between Billy and Tim, as he left Tim's home, would have put him on edge.

TWENTY-TWO

TUESDAY MORNING THE FIRST THING Pete did was call the switchboard at ACS Marketing. He was looking for the two men Bradford's sister identified as his best friends. When he asked for Alan Slayton, the receptionist said he was in a meeting. Expecting something similar, he asked for Joe Gaylord. When Martin arrived, he was still on hold.

Pete explained what he was doing and asked Martin to work on the list of St. Paul employment attorneys.

The words were barely out, when a chipper voice said, "Joe Gaylord, how may I help you?"

Pete said he was a member of the St. Paul P.D., investigating the murder of Bradford Winthrup."

"No way! When? What can I do to help?"

Tilting back in his chair, Pete stretched his legs and rested his feet on the desk. He hoped for a prolonged and enlightening conversation.

"How did you get my name?" Gaylord's voice was now muffled and barely audible.

"From Bradford's sister."

"Why didn't you call my direct number? Did you identify yourself to the receptionist?"

Pete explained that the only number he had was the switchboard and that he didn't give his name or title. "It's just like the military. Don't ask; don't tell."

"It's great hearing from you," Gaylord exclaimed loudly. Reverting to a whisper he said, "Loyalty to Brad is no longer a good idea, and these offices have ears. I mean Dumbo-sized ears. How about if I call you in twenty minutes, once I'm out of the building?"

Pete gave him his office and cell phone numbers.

Thirty minutes later, when Gaylord hadn't called, Pete thought he made a mistake by letting the man out of his grasp. He kept busy, going through the stacks of paper on his desk, but that didn't derail his impatience. Faith in his fellow man was restored when the phone finally rang. He simultaneously picked up the receiver and a pencil, and jotted down the number displayed on the caller ID.

"Hi, this is Joe Gaylord. I was on my way out, and my supervisor lassoed me. I thought I'd never get away from him. Sorry to have kept you waiting."

He said he was in a Dunn Brothers, drinking a latté and sitting in a corner, where he could keep an eye on all newcomers. He wanted to see any ACS employees before they saw or, worse yet, heard him. The only one he really trusted these days was Alan Slayton.

"What's happening at ACS to make you so jumpy?"

Gaylord explained that Brad was in the center of it. "The circumstances surrounding his being fired were hush-hush, but the rumor was he'd threatened someone. Brad was the golden boy. He was on his way up, and everyone, including Brad, knew it. It just doesn't make sense. Why would he do anything that stupid?"

"Did you talk to him after it happened?"

"Not about the firing. The day it happened, he was gone before I knew anything was going on. When I talked to him afterwards, he wouldn't discuss it. It was strange. It was like he was too embarrassed or didn't trust me. I don't know which."

"Did he have a lot of friends at ACS?"

"Quite a few, I'd say, but he's closest to Alan Slayton and me."

"I'm trying to find the name of Brad's current girlfriend," Pete said. "Can you help me?"

"Sure, it's Erin Felton."

"Do you know where she lives?"

"Yes, in the same apartment complex as Brad. Her brother came to the office, looking for him. He said she's pregnant, and Brad's the father. Had Brad been around, I think he might have started throwing punches. That's how angry he was. I tried to call Brad to tell him, but his phone was disconnected."

"Can you describe the brother, and do you know his name?"

"His name's Dan Felton. He's about thirty, average height and build, dark hair and eyes, baritone voice. That's all I remember about him. Maybe he should be a suspect. The day I saw him, he seemed capable of murder—and then some."

"Where does he live?" Pete asked.

"All I know is that it's someplace in or around Chicago."

"Have you spoken with Alan about Brad's departure from ACS?"

"Yes. He doesn't know any more than I do. After Brad lost his job, he treated Alan the same way he treated me."

"I understand that Walter Linton is gone for a couple of weeks," Pete said. "Do you know anything about that, such as where he went?"

"The word around here is he's sick. We aren't allowed to contact him. He was supposed to be in the office yesterday. Alan said they were supposed to meet, and it was cancelled at the last second."

Pete asked for Linton's ACS-provided cell phone number, and Gaylord refused to share it. "Much as I want to help, it would be the end of my career here. I'm not kidding."

"Do you have an office brochure, newsletter, or other document with staff pictures?"

"There's a brochure with pictures of the top management. Years ago, they talked about putting all of our pictures on the company website, but nothing ever came of it."

"Would you fax me a copy of the brochure or scan and email it to me? All I need are the pictures and names."

"I can do either, but only from home. I may be paranoid but, as the saying goes, 'Just because you're paranoid doesn't mean they're not out to get you.'"

"Could you send an email from your work computer to your Blackberry and forward it from there, so I don't have to wait so long? They don't have access to those emails, do they?"

"All I know is I'm not taking any chances. I'll send it when I get home."

They settled on faxing the information to Pete's office, and the estimated time it would happen was shortly after six o'clock. Before ending the call, Pete obtained Alan Slayton's office and cell phone numbers.

Martin wanted to talk, but Pete reined him in. He wanted to finish this round of ACS calls before he did anything else.

Slayton answered on the second ring. He seemed a little less fearful than Gaylord. Even so, he added little of value to the information provided by his co-worker. He didn't know why Brad lost his job, but said he heard Brad locked horns with a vice-president. He didn't know where Linton was or why he wasn't in the office. He spoke with Brad a few times after he was fired. Brad seemed distant and said little. The last time they spoke was about a month ago.

"So?" Martin asked as he hung up.

Pete told him about the two conversations and concluded saying, "It sounds like fear and secrecy are the corporate culture. And I thought we had problems around here."

"Well, I have good news and bad news," Martin said. "The good news is I got Linton's cell number from Baxter. The bad news is that the voice mailbox is full and won't accept any more messages."

"You haven't mentioned it," Pete said, "so I assume you haven't yet pulled Winthrup's attorney out of your hat."

"No, but there's still plenty of possibilities, and we have Minneapolis, if we don't find him in St. Paul."

"Or her."

"Huh?" Martin asked.

"Never mind."

TWENTY-THREE

I HAVE ANOTHER TIDBIT, courtesy of Joe Gaylord," Pete said. "You're going to love this. It means another column and another row for your matrix."

Pete told Martin about Winthrup's girlfriend and her brother.

Martin wanted to switch priorities, immediately contact both of them, but Pete convinced him they should stick with the current plan.

They were both on the phone involved in the attorney search when Martin's cell rang. Pete hung up first, and Martin motioned for him to take the call.

The familiar voice asked for Martin. When Pete identified himself, Megan Alden did likewise and said she'd reached Casey. She said he was on his way home. Although he should arrive that afternoon, she didn't know what time.

"Where was he when you reached him?"

"I don't know. He wouldn't say."

"But you're confident he's on his way back and will show up this afternoon?"

"I'm as sure as I can be. He's pretty broken up over Brad's death."

"Will he call me as soon as he gets back?"

"No. He said he'd call me when he arrives. I think he wants me to serve as an intermediary of sorts."

"But you won't be back until Thursday."

"That's right, but he'll meet with you before I return. First he wants to spend a little time with Gloria and his son, Kenny. You won't try to keep him from doing that by watching his house and barging in when he arrives, will you?"

"Much as I'd like to, I won't."

"Good. He'll get back to me when he's ready, and I'll call you. I don't think it'll be late, but just in case, how late can I call?"

Pete said to call anytime, but to call his cell rather than Martin's if it got late. After thanking her for her help, he asked if she told Gloria about Casey's return.

"I did. I knew she'd be frantic and don't think it's good for the baby. I might be a bit of an alarmist, but she had a lot of problems during her last pregnancy."

That provided a smooth segue for Pete to ask about Erin Felton's pregnancy. He asked if Megan remembered the name of Brad's girlfriend.

She said no, but admitted that Brad said the girlfriend was an ex and claimed to be pregnant with his child. "I didn't want to tell you about it, because it doesn't paint a very favorable picture of Brad. I know he wouldn't run out on her if the child was his."

"You said her first name was Irish. Does the name Erin . . ."

"Yes, that's it! Erin, Erin Felton."

"What did Brad say about Erin's pregnancy?"

"That when the baby's born, he'd prove, via DNA, that she's lying."

The Winthrups were an interesting group, and Pete wondered how Brad fit into the mix. A lot went on beneath the surface, and it might and might not have anything to do with their investigation.

After hanging up, he waited for Martin to return from wherever. Seconds later, Martin walked in with a welcome cup of full-strength coffee for each of them. That drew a smile from Pete.

"You aren't going to believe this, Pete. While you were talking on my cell, one of Winthrup's college buddies returned my call."

"That's shocking!"

"Would you shut up and let me finish?"

Pete's eyebrows and hands went up, but his smile quelled any misinterpretation.

"We killed two birds with one stone," Martin continued. "Winthrup was in contact with him. The guy's name is Ted Cook, and he's an attorney. You were right about Winthrup contacting a friend, if one was an attorney. Good call. Anyway, Winthrup met with him and asked for help."

"And?"

"And he isn't in the right field, but helped Winthrup find someone. He referred Bradford to an attorney named Amy Pennington. Is it worth meeting with her, what with attorney-client privilege?"

"There's no way of knowing. She's unlikely to share much, but it can't hurt, and it could be helpful, since we're getting so little from the people at ACS Marketing."

While Pete set up an appointment with Brad's attorney, Martin obtained Erin Felton's unlisted phone number from the manager at Winthrup's former apartment complex.

TWENTY-FOUR

MARTIN'S FIRST IMPRESSION OF Amy Pennington was that she ought to be able to make it in professional basketball should her career as an attorney not fly. She was taller than he, and only an inch or two shorter than Pete, even discounting the pumps she wore. If Pete had his heart set on tall kids, which was often more important to people his size than Pete's, Amy should be able to deliver. She was young enough, too.

Although it was readily apparent that she was slender, her suit concealed any curves that might be lurking. Her hair was pulled back tight in a ponytail and tied with a bright, print scarf. The scarf was the only colorful thing on her person, including her face. Either she'd conquered the natural look or she was make-up free, except for unnaturally shiny lips.

Ms. Pennington had her own firm, and her law office was in a St. Paul highrise office building. She seemed to be justifying her impressive office location when she told the two men she was "a new kid on the block" and believed a more prestigious location was critical until she was established.

Pete figured her cherry wood desk could easily serve as a table for a family of ten. If nothing else, he contemplated, walking around it to greet clients provided a great source of exercise. It appeared to serve as a file cabinet, at least for her active files, because more than a dozen piles of neatly stacked pages occupied its surface. With the matching client chairs and file cabinets, the furniture had to set her back almost as much as law school, he thought and smiled.

Amy Pennington invited the two investigators to make themselves comfortable. She settled into her high-backed chair, hands laced on the desk in front of her.

Pete told her about Brad's murder and having learned from his sister that Brad had seen an attorney. "The family is distraught over their loss. We're doing everything possible to find the killer, thus bringing them some peace of mind in the face of all this turmoil. Several things are pointing us in the direction of his former employer, ACS Marketing. Due to the lack of cooperation or even straight answers from ACS, we're hoping to get a little help from you to make sure we're on the right track."

"But you know I'm obligated to operate within the constraints of attorney-client privilege."

"We understand," Pete said. "We also realize that Brad would want nothing more than to have his murderer found and prosecuted. He was already seeking redress from ACS. If we're right and his murder was tied to his employment there, no doubt his desire for justice would override his desire for protection under attorney-client privilege."

"Tell me the information you're seeking," Pennington said.

"Who did Bradford name as the defendants?" Pete asked.

"I'm sorry. I understand about wanting to find this person, but I can't . . ."

"We understand. Did he have friends at ACS who weren't being named in his lawsuit?" Pete asked.

"I'm sorry . . ."

"Okay. Can you at least tell us the names of his friends at ACS?" Pete asked.

"No. I'm sorry. I'd like to help."

"Why did Brad lose his job?" Pete asked.

"Again, I can't . . ."

"Have it your way," Martin snarled.

"Much as I'd like to . . ."

"Yeah, yeah," Martin said. "Thanks for all your help." He pushed himself up and out of the chair, spun around and exited the office.

Pete shrugged, told Pennington "Thanks anyway," and followed Martin.

TWENTY-FIVE

WHILE PETE SPENT THE FIRST SEVERAL hours of the afternoon in court testifying on another case, Martin worked on the list of contacts and updated his matrix. Regardless of Pete's reaction, the matrix helped him organize the case and track the suspects.

When Pete returned, Martin lamented the growing likelihood of a trip to Chicago. Then, in a magnanimous moment, he offered to go to Reaching Out this evening, in place of Pete.

Pete turned down the offer. Despite the absence of detectable progress, he hoped he'd made headway.

Before getting Martin's update, Pete checked the fax machine and his personal email. He hoped that Gaylord either had a lapse in paranoia or, in a spirit of cooperation, decided to go home for lunch and send him the ACS photos. The fax tray was empty, and it took a minute to check the sender and subject of the emails delivered in the last several hours. There was nothing he needed to open. His personal email tended to be even less relevant than much of the office "spam."

When Pete's attention turned to Martin, the other man was more than ready for center stage. "Thanks to Vernon, your friend in Chicago," Martin said, "I reached Erin Felton on her cell. She didn't want to talk. She said she doesn't have any privacy at work. I told her she could either speak to me from her present location or find another, without hanging up. I said if she refused to do one or the other, or if we were accidentally disconnected, she should plan on a visit this afternoon from the Chicago P.D."

"Did you practice threat tactics this morning while shaving?"

"Yeah, and I think it's helping." Martin grinned. "Despite what Erin Felton told her brother, her baby isn't Brad's. She lied to her brother about it, because he was overly protective, and Brad had already left Chicago. Her brother kept pushing for the father's name and she decided it was best to say 'Brad,' because, and I quote, 'Dan would never find him.' She and Brad broke up shortly after he lost his job, but she didn't tell her brother."

"And she's sure Dan didn't find out that Brad's in Minnesota?" Pete asked.

"She said she never told him."

"As if she's the only way he'd find out," Pete said. "How did she react to the news about Brad's death?"

"Not well. She was shocked. I wonder if she'd have said as much about her brother if that was the first thing we talked about."

"Timing is everything," Pete acknowledged. "How about Baxter? Any news from him?"

"Of course. I'm on a roll. It's hard to know what worlds I'd have conquered, had you stayed away another hour or two." Martin tilted back in his chair and cracked his knuckles. He said he told Baxter it was impossible to reach Linton on his cell, and Baxter said he couldn't help that. "When I told him I understood Winthrup was a valued employee, he said Brad was a hero in his own mind.

"In the unlikely event we'll want access to Winthrup's old files, I asked who's doing his former job. He said the duties were split up and are being done by several people until they revise the job description and fill the job. So, your guess is as good as mine when it comes to what they did with his files, including the evidence he gathered.

"I asked where Linton is today, and Baxter said he answered that question yesterday. Testy, isn't he? He said nothing's changed since then. He also said he's too busy to keep answering the same questions. I said it was in his best interest to cooperate, and he said Linton must be at home, since he's sick. I reminded him that yesterday he told you Linton was on vacation. He said he must have talked to you before he got the update. He doesn't know when Linton will return to work but, for all it's worth, he said he's still assuming it'll be two weeks."

TWENTY-SIX

AS THINGS WERE PLAYING OUT, Pete's concerns over trying to fit both Casey Winthrup and Reaching Out into too small a time slot were overly optimistic. It was 4:20, and he'd yet to hear from Megan Alden.

He called her cell phone, hoping to find out if she'd heard from Casey and get an idea of when the meeting might occur. She didn't answer. He wondered if she checked the caller ID and let his call go to voicemail. At times like this, he hated the caller-ID feature on cell phones. Well, more accurately, on the cell phones belonging to other people. On his, it was a bonus.

Was Megan avoiding him? Did she make up a story about Casey's return to buy time?

She seemed distraught over Brad's death, and she seemed trustworthy. Did the former insure the latter? Family ties were often strange mechanisms—like when it was okay for you to beat the crap out of your brother, but not for anyone else to take a swing at him.

Pete gave Martin his cell phone and asked him to monitor it while he was at Reaching Out. Even though Megan was supposed to call Martin's cell if she didn't reach Pete, he didn't want to give her, or them, any excuse for again delaying the meeting with Casey.

"You as concerned as I am about not hearing from Ms. Alden?" Martin asked. "My money says that when she calls, she's going to be all upset because he conned her, no pun intended. In the unlikely event I hear from her before you return, what do you want me to do?"

Pete said not to wait for him if it would make Martin late, and he'd be back no later than 6:30. If Martin had to leave before he arrived, Pete asked him to call Ray's office at Reaching Out and ask whoever answered to give him a message, that there's been an emergency. He wrote the phone number on a slip of paper and gave it to Martin.

"They shouldn't have any trouble finding me," he continued. "They can use my first name. I've introduced myself to a couple of people, so it's okay. If you go ahead without me, leave a note on my desk and take my cell with you. Depending upon how things are going, I'll either leave there as soon as I hear from you or wait until the meal's over."

Martin wanted to accomplish several things while Pete enjoyed a relaxing dinner at the homeless shelter. For starters, he wanted to check for any Feltons in the Chicago area, whose first name began with D or Dan. He also wanted to reach Gerald Alden, the victim's brother-in-law. It was unusual, but this evening he was glad his and Pete's respective duties panned out the way they did.

The jog over Interstate 94 and through downtown St. Paul relaxed Pete and cleared his head for the first time today. Smiling, he slowed to a walk, turned the corner, and his destination came into view.

The first two people he recognized were Stew and the nameless man with whom he spoke after dinner last night. When each man caught sight of him, Pete held up a hand and returned their smiles. They'd both laid claim to the same turf as yesterday, and Pete followed suit, moving towards the opposite side of the door.

In response, Stew motioned him over.

Crossing the sidewalk, Pete joined him.

"How goes da battle?" Stew asked.

"Can't complain. How about with you, Stew?"

The man seemed pleased that Pete remembered his name and carried the discussion a step further. "Complainin's a waste a time."

"You're right there," Pete acknowledged, before assuming the silent wait common to most of those around him.

When the line began forming, Pete jockeyed for the place behind Stew. Stew seemed like his best link to the other folks. Nothing had changed with Stew's routine and, although it was a new group of volunteers, the women reacted exactly as they did last night.

Pete respected them for it. It seemed to take so little to make the day of a guy like Stew.

The volunteers weren't the only ones Stew treated the same. Once again, he offered Pete a helping hand. This time, however, it wasn't with the food line.

When he and Pete received their trays, he said, "Follow me, if ya like. My buddies over there'll make room for us."

Encouraged by this second step towards acceptance, Pete followed and they wove a path to one of the large, round tables at the far side of the room.

Along the way, Stew greeted several of the other diners, many by name. When they reached Stew's destination, he set down his tray and said, "Ya don't mind if ma friend here joins us, do ya?"

The group responded with a series of grunts, nods and other sounds and actions that Stew interpreted as unanimous acceptance.

"Great!" he said and grinned at Pete. "Benny, Hardy, Willie, Doc, this is ma friend. What did ya say yer name was?"

"Pete."

Once they'd settled in, Pete turned to Stew and said, "Thanks for your help last night and again tonight. You've made it much easier, and its great having someone to eat with."

Stew smiled and nodded. He looked pleased. "What're friends for?" he said. "Ya looked like ya needed a little help."

"That's where you're right," Pete agreed.

The man who greeted Pete after dinner last night was part of the group, but Pete still didn't know his name. When Stew rattled off all the names, it was impossible to tell if he went clockwise or counter clockwise around the table, or if there was any particular order. Most of the men did nothing to acknowledge their names as they were called out. Pete hoped to ask Stew later if the man's name didn't become apparent from the dinner discussions.

For the next thirty-five minutes, Pete said little and listened much. He wanted to get a feel for the things they discussed and the attitudes conveyed. There were times he'd have sworn he was with a bunch of cops, although, admittedly, this group tended to be less conservative about most issues.

They talked politics, debating who'd win the next election and what it would mean. They discussed gas prices and the effects of ethanol production on the price of diesel fuel and food. They were divided on the wisdom of building a new sports stadium and enlarging the Mall of America. As with any group, the weather provided fuel when the conversation lagged.

Their discussions typified those of the five million people in the state.

Most of the guys at Stew's table hung around waiting for him to finish eating. He went about the process rather painstakingly, and Pete wondered if he had problems with his teeth. After consuming less than thirty percent of the food on his tray, Stew wrapped his bread, butter, and cookies in his napkin and stood up.

The others took it as their cue. In unison, they stood, picked up their trays and made their way back across the room to the nook that housed the dishwashers—the machines and the people. Taking turns, they threw out the paper and placed their trays on the counter.

Pete was last in line. He followed the others out of the air-conditioned building. It struck him as curious that they didn't prolong their meal until the last minute. He knew that in their position, he would.

Once outside, he was surprised how much cooler it felt. A front must have moved through while they were eating. In addition to the drop in temperature, there was now a refreshing breeze out of the northwest.

Stew and one other man from their table hung around. The rest were off in every possible direction. The ever-faithful Stew watched him and seemed to interpret his hesitation as a sign that he didn't know what to do next.

"Got a place ta stay tanight?" he asked.

"I slept on a park bench last night. Thought I'd do it again tonight," Pete ad libbed.

"Yer pretty lucky. Unless ya want a cop disturbing ya about the time ya finally nod off, ya better look for somethin' else."

"Any suggestions?"

"The best places are under bridges. Some of us used to set up in Swede Hollow. Ya know where it is?"

"I've heard of it, but I'm not exactly sure."

"Over that way," Stew said, motioning eastward. "Some of my friends had a great little setup there, but had ta move. The city begun buggin' the livin' daylights out of 'em."

"Where do they go now?"

"They move 'round a lot. That's what most of us do—hafta do. Ya might find an outa-the-way place down by the river. Stay in the underbrush. Da skeeters may drive ya crazy, but they're less a problem than other things that might be nosin' around."

"It's hard sleeping outside. It's not just the air conditioning or a fan that's lacking. I'm nervous about falling asleep, when someone could sneak up and attack me. Are you nervous about that, Stew?"

"Jus' when I got money or somethin' of value, so not often. Ya know not to let anyone see if ya got stuff, right?"

"Oh, yeah," Pete nodded, "but not much danger of that. Just the same, thanks."

"Tomorrow, ya don't hafta wait to be asked. Just come on over an' join us when ya get here," Stew added.

It was obvious that, although Stew wanted to help, he wasn't going to share his domicile, if that term appropriately referenced wherever he slept.

Pete wanted to ask if anyone stayed at the Upper Landing, but decided to wait—in hopes of a better opportunity.

Stew walked away, and Pete looked for the man with whom he'd spoken last night. He was quite sure his name, or nickname, was Doc.

"Are you Pete?"

The voice from behind startled him. When he spun around, he didn't see anyone who'd know his name. Then it clicked.

TWENTY-SEVEN

PETE DIDN'T JOG BACK TO THE OFFICE. After hearing from Martin, who was leaving shortly for Casey's home, he ran his best marathon pace. The distance to the office was twenty-five miles shorter, so it was a decent clip, but nothing to write home about. Six minutes after leaving the soup kitchen, and a few minutes to the good, he cut across the parking lot to headquarters. If he had more time, he'd have taken a shower and changed back into his suit, but he didn't.

"How did you get here so fast?" Martin asked when he walked in and retrieved his cell phone. "I don't think you could've driven here that fast."

"Faster than a speeding bullet. More powerful than a locomotive. Able to . . ."

"Run on a full stomach," Martin interrupted, shaking his head and rolling his eyes. "Here," he continued. "This came for you, but in a slightly different form." Martin handed Pete two sheets of paper with two rows of photographs—three stacked on three, with head-shots of the directors of ACS. "The IT folks turned the brochure into a photo lineup for us."

"Are you bringing a copy along, just in case?" Pete asked.

"Got it right here," Martin said, patting a suit-coat pocket as he followed Pete to the parking lot.

In all the times they'd worked together, this was the first time Martin was better dressed than Pete. That fact didn't escape Martin.

"By the way, did you get dinner?" Pete asked.

"No, I thought you were bringing me a doggie bag."

"Oh, that's right." Pete smacked his forehead with the heel of his hand. "I left it on the table. Sorry."

"Not as sorry, however, as you are full of it. Don't worry. I had a spaghetti dinner from the Savoy."

"That explains the orange spots on your tie."

Martin's head snapped down to look for the dreaded stains.

Pete laughed and said, "Gotcha."

En route to the Winthrups' Martin told Pete about his accomplishments. He checked for Feltons and found a D. Felton and a Dan Felton in the Chicago area. He didn't reach Gerald Alden, but checked all of the Winthrups and Aldens. "Gerald is the only one with a registered gun. It's a .45 caliber Smith and Wesson, so it can't be disqualified as the murder weapon. I have one last bit of information you may find noteworthy. Megan Alden's on her way home."

That didn't surprise Pete. If someone murdered his brother, he'd catch the first flight home.

When they arrived at the Winthrups', they saw Casey's Dodge Neon and Gloria's Honda Civic parked out front. The sound of a wailing child escaped through the open second-story windows as the two investigators made their way up the porch steps. They heard a deeper voice than Gloria's say, "I'll take care of it, honey."

Ah, the benefits of open windows over air conditioning, Pete thought. *This way, so many private moments become so public.*

Casey appeared in the doorway a minute after Pete rang the doorbell. He was a mess. His blond hair was tousled. His five o'clock shadow had logged an additional twenty-five hours. There were dark circles under his eyes, and his clothes looked slept-in.

Pete decided those things made him look even more like Brad— at least the only way he'd ever seen Brad.

Casey stood inside the door, staring at them.

"Casey Winthrup, I assume," Pete said, helping him out.

"Oh, yes, I'm sorry. You're the detectives, right?" He didn't bother looking at the IDs they proffered.

Pete nodded.

Winthrup seemed slow on the uptake, so Pete asked, "May we come in?"

"Yes, yes, come in. I'm sorry," Casey shook his head and explained, "I'm running on empty, and my head's not screwed on. Let's go in the living room."

"The kitchen would be better," Pete said. "We'll sit around the table."

Casey led them through the living room and into the kitchen.

Pete smelled fried hamburgers and onions as soon as they walked in the front door, and the smell, a pleasant one, grew stronger as they worked their way back to the kitchen.

A box fan filled the window near the table. Before sitting, Casey turned it on, and Pete felt a significant improvement in the temperature.

The furnishings in the Winthrup home were modest, but neat and clean. Framed posters and photographs hung on the walls, and miniblinds, in lieu of drapes, decorated the windows and provided a measure of privacy.

Pete and Martin waited for Casey to select a seat at the square table. When he moved towards the chair that put the fan at his back, Pete took the seat across from his, providing the best view of Winthrup's face.

That left Martin with one of two chairs, each kitty-corner to Casey. He'd just selected one and sat down when Winthrup slumped in his chair and propped his head on one hand. Intentional or not, this blocked Martin's view of his face. So he got up, walked behind Pete, and sat on Winthrup's other side.

Pete placed his notepad and a pen on the table, clasped his hands and leaned in for the questioning. As soon as Martin sat down, ramrod straight with hands on knees, Pete began. "You were at the Upper Landing Sunday morning. What were you doing there?"

Judging from the look on his face, Casey didn't anticipate this kind of question. "What makes you think I was there?" he asked.

"We don't *think* it. We *know* it. Now, answer my question," Pete said, silently thanking Billy.

"I went to see Brad. He asked me to meet him there."

"Why did he want to meet you?" Pete asked. "I understand the two of you weren't particularly close."

Casey's eyes grew moist, and he looked ready to crumble.

"Brad was scared. He suspected someone was after him, and he needed my help."

"Did you help him?" Martin asked.

"Yes."

When it became apparent Casey wasn't going to continue, Martin asked, "How?"

Casey stared, wordlessly, at his hands. His fingernails looked like they'd served as a teething ring for the last several days if not longer.

"Tell us about the gun," Pete said.

Casey's eyes flew up and fixed on Pete's chin, avoiding his eyes. "I don't know what you're talking about," he said, but his face said he was lying.

"Look, you're tired and we're tired. Let's cut the crap and get down to facts," Pete said. "Otherwise, we'll just haul you in and let you spend the night thinking about it."

"How do you know about the gun?"

"We know a lot more than you think, Casey," Pete said. "So start at the beginning and tell us the whole story."

Casey took a deep breath, followed by a prolonged sigh. He concentrated on his hands and began. "Brad called me at work last Friday afternoon. One of the guys at Reaching Out gave him a note. There wasn't a name indicating who left it, but it said to meet him at the Upper Landing at ten o'clock Sunday morning."

"Did Brad think he knew who left the note?" Pete asked.

"No. He only knew it was a man. Brad asked me to get him a gun. Meeting an unknown someone at the Upper Landing made him nervous. He said 'the timing was too coincidental,' and he thought it might mean that someone was 'gunning' for him. Those were his exact words. I tried to find out what he meant about the timing, but he wouldn't give me any details. All he'd say was that he had this feeling, and the gun made him more comfortable about going there with so little information and so much suspicion.

"I don't own a gun, so I called around—called everyone I could think of—and then some friends of friends. I finally found one I could borrow. I left Saturday night to pick it up. I didn't get back until Sunday morning. I was running late, so I went right to the Landing, where I met him.

"I gave him the gun and the ammunition. He took some practice shots to get a feel for the gun. I tried to get him to come with me and avoid the whole situation. He said he couldn't. I think he had mixed emotions about it. I think he wanted to meet with the person in hopes it would help get his job back. At the same time, he didn't want to risk it. I also think he worried that leaving with me could put me or my family in danger.

"I begged him to forget the job." Casey sniffed and blotted his eyes on one shoulder, then the other. "I told him there were plenty of other jobs, and ACS wasn't worth it. He said we'd discuss it later. I could tell he was in a hurry to get rid of me.

"He told me to take the ring—Dad's ring. He tried to get it off his finger but couldn't, so he asked me to try. No matter how hard I pulled and twisted, I couldn't get it over his knuckle."

Pulling a hankie from his back pocket, Casey blew his nose and blotted his eyes. Tears had been flowing, but with that last statement he broke down. With a quavering voice, he continued. "I knew he wouldn't tell me to take the ring unless he was more than a little scared, and that scared me, too. That ring meant a lot to him. The hell with the ring, I told him. I told him he's more important. Again I begged him to come with me, but he said he couldn't. He looked at his watch and said I had to go, right away.

"I hugged him and told him to call me that night or Monday. As I walked away, he called out, 'I love you, Casey.' I felt closer than we've ever been. Walking away, I hoped it was a permanent change, that we'd turned a corner and could finally be friends. I've always looked up to him, even though I never admitted it.

"The next thing I heard, the police were here. I prayed it meant he was caught with the gun or shot someone in self-defense. You know the rest better than I do."

CASEY CROSSED HIS ARMS ON THE TABLE and rested his face on them. He wanted to ask some questions. He wanted to know if the cops had found the gun he gave Brad, and he wanted to know about Brad's ring, but for very different reasons. He didn't think the gun was traceable. If the guy who killed Brad took it, he'd have to replace it. That was doable.

The ring was a different story. Until yesterday, it was the ring his dad wore every day for decades, the thing he considered his father's trademark, the thing that cut him to the quick when it was left to Brad. Now it was symbolic not only of his father, but also of his older brother, his dead older brother. Unlike the gun, the ring couldn't be replaced. Even so, he couldn't ask about it. He hoped Brad was still wearing it when the police found him. And if he was, he hoped it didn't mysteriously disappear afterwards.

"THE GUN YOU GAVE CASEY, what was it?" Pete asked.

Lifting his face from his arms, Casey said, "A Glock, a .45 caliber. I don't know much about handguns. Maybe all Glocks are .45 caliber."

And Bradford was, per the ME's report, shot with a fully jacketed bullet fired by a .45 caliber handgun, Pete knew.

"What kind of bullets did you give him?" Pete asked.

"Like I said, I don't know much about handguns. I gave him what was given to me."

The last two questions registered, slowly, in Casey's brain. His eyes went wild, and his mouth dropped open. "Oh, my God, was Brad shot with a Glock? Did I provide the murder weapon?"

"We have no way of knowing at this time," Pete said. "All we know is the caliber of the gun. Did Brad have any idea who may have left the message to go to the Upper Landing?" he continued.

"No. Like I said, he thought it might have something to do with his job, but he wasn't sure. Do you think someone from ACS killed him?"

"We're looking at all the possibilities," Pete said. "Was Brad suspicious of anyone in particular at ACS?"

"I don't know. If he was, he didn't say."

"Did Brad mention anyone else who might be after him?" Pete asked.

"No." Casey closed his eyes and slowly massaged his temples.

"At what time did Brad tell you to leave the Landing?" Pete asked.

"I looked at the clock when I got back in my car. It was 9:51, and it only took me a couple of minutes to walk to the car."

"Where were you parked?" Martin asked.

"On the far eastern edge of the Landing, east of all the construction. That's where Brad and I met. We walked west from there to the western edge of the construction area. That's where we set up some debris for him to practice shooting."

"Did you see or hear anyone, in a car or walking, approaching the area as you left?" Pete asked.

"No, I went back to my car and took off. I shouldn't have left him there. I'm the only one who could've saved him, and I didn't." Casey's head hung over the table. He looked dejected, as he closed his eyes and shook his head slowly, grimacing.

"Did Brad tell you why he lost his job at ACS?" Pete asked.

"No, he didn't like talking about it. I asked again on Sunday. All he'd say was he hoped he'd be able to get it straightened out, and he'd tell me more then."

"Casey," Gloria called from the living room, "I have to go. That isn't a problem, is it?"

Casey explained that she was going to the airport to get Megan, and he was supposed to stay with Kenny. He asked Pete if that was okay.

Pete nodded.

"Megan's furious with her husband," Casey continued. "She's staying with us, at least for a while."

"Why did you take off yesterday?" Pete asked.

"Because I was with Brad right before he died. He and I had our differences. I knew once you talked to my family, I'd be the first one you suspected. All of the cards were stacked against me, and I had no way to prove I'm innocent."

"And why did you come back?" Pete asked.

"Megan convinced me it was the only way."

"The only way? What does that mean?" Pete asked.

"I guess she knew I'd been cleared."

Before Billy and Tim cleared Casey, Megan had been working on getting him to return to St. Paul, and Pete hadn't spoken with her before she accomplished that. Instead of mentioning any of that, Pete asked Casey if Brad was having problems with a girlfriend.

Looking at him quizzically, Casey said he didn't think so. He did not think Brad ever had problems with women. It seemed to him that women fell all over Brad. He didn't think Brad was ever turned down when asking for a date.

When Pete asked the name of the woman he was dating when he lost his job, Casey said he and Brad didn't discuss those things, but Megan would know.

Pete asked if Brad ever mentioned the name Dan Felton, and Casey said it sounded familiar, but he couldn't place it.

Twenty-Eight

WEDNESDAY MORNING, WHEN MARTIN checked his voicemail, there was a message from Gerald Alden. He threw up his hands in exasperation. Alden had ignored his request to call his cell phone if he didn't reach him at headquarters yesterday. This had all of the markings of a delay tactic and, after last night, he and Pete were anxious to meet with the guy.

It was 7:30 so, after conferring with Pete, Martin delayed his call to Alden until Pete reached Megan. They wanted a few answers from her before speaking with her husband.

She was walking out the door of Casey's house on her way to work when Pete reached her via her cell. Although she preferred answering his questions over the phone, she agreed, after Pete leaned on her, to stop at headquarters on her way to work.

With that meeting to work around, Martin had a target for arranging one with Gerald. He began by calling the Alden home.

A man answered. From the sound of his voice, either the phone woke him up or he hadn't been out of bed very long.

Martin found pleasure in the possibility that the first was true.

Alden balked at Martin's request for a meeting prior to 10:00, but Martin was like a dog with a bone. He knew Pete planned to have lunch at Reaching Out, and both investigators wanted to question Alden before then. They settled on 9:30 at Alden's house.

Martin was updating his matrix when Megan arrived. She looked exhausted, but smiled when Pete and Martin introduced themselves. If the way she incessantly twisted her long blond hair around a finger was any indication, she was more than a bit uncomfortable with this meeting.

Pete didn't know if it was because of the location or if she had a sense of the nature of the questions. He began by thanking her for her assistance in locating Casey and said they'd try to keep the meeting short. "I understand you're staying with Casey for a while. Why's that?"

"It doesn't have anything to do with the case." Megan smiled in an effort to compensate for failing to answer the question.

"We realize that some of our questions may seem irrelevant," Pete said, returning the smile. "But at this point we're trying to gather as much information as possible. Believe me, we have no interest, per se, in your personal life."

Megan looked perturbed as she explained, "Gerald found out I gave Brad some money. He's furious. He wants to take a cruise through the Panama Canal, and I've been adamant about waiting until we have enough cash to pay for it up-front. We've both been contributing to a travel fund, and the $2,200 I put in an account for Brad was supposed to go into that fund. Can you imagine letting your brother go without the bare necessities, while you save for a vacation? Gerald insisted that Brad needed a little tough love. That's also part of his and my problem. He thinks everyone has to pull himself up by his bootstraps, and intercession only weakens the down-and-out."

Pete saw tears pooling in her eyes and wondered if he'd be capable of "tough love." Judging from his interactions with family members, he doubted it. Both of his nieces had him wrapped around their pinkies. He admired anyone who could, under the right circumstances, muster the required discipline.

"How did he find out you gave Brad money?" Pete asked.

"I don't know. Good question. I never thought about it. How would he find out?"

"Did you open the account for Brad at the same bank you usually use?" Pete asked.

"Yes."

"Does your husband have friends at that bank? What I'm getting at is—might someone who works there have told him about it?" Pete asked.

"I don't know. I guess it's possible."

"Would he have been as upset if you'd given the money to Casey or Eric?" Martin asked.

"Probably not, but I can't be sure."

"Do you know how much money Brad withdrew from the account you established for him, and the amount and date of his last withdrawal?" Pete asked.

"No, but I'm sure I can find out with a phone call."

"Please check on that and let Martin or me know. Do you or your husband own a handgun?"

"You're not suggesting that . . ."

"I'm not suggesting anything. I'm gathering information, trying to solve this case."

"Well, it doesn't matter, because the answer's no."

"Where were you and your husband last Sunday morning?" Martin asked.

"I was home. Gerald went for a ride on his motorcycle. He said he crossed into Wisconsin and went north from Hudson."

"Do you believe him?" Martin asked.

Megan shrugged noncommittally.

"When did he leave and when did he return?" Martin asked.

"He was gone when I got up at eight o'clock, and he returned in the afternoon."

TWENTY-NINE

WHEN GERALD ALDEN ANSWERED the door, Pete noticed the whiskers and wondered if they reflected the current fashion or if he hadn't yet cleaned up for the day. The way he wore his dark-brown hair provided no hints, and his khakis and polo shirt likewise failed to clarify anything.

After hearing about Billy's comment, Pete's attention was drawn to Alden's ears. It wasn't so much that they were large as the way they stood out from his head. No doubt a tight-fitting do-rag would accentuate that. Furthermore, his sideburns were short enough to be concealed by a do-rag.

Alden looked less than enthused as he ushered Pete and Martin into his home. At Pete's urging, they bypassed the great room and settled at the dining room table. The great room chairs were too cushy, and the dining room table provided a firm writing surface for note taking. He and Martin sat across from Alden.

Martin jumped right into the Miranda warning. Pete decided Martin was being cautious because of the boys' description of the ears and voice of the man who threatened them, as well as the things Megan said.

Alden bristled at the implications and made forays into getting an attorney, before they continued. When they got beyond the to-do, Pete settled Alden down further by asking what he did for a living.

"I sell real estate."

"How's business?" Pete asked.

"Painfully slow."

"Do you think this trend will continue?" Pete asked.

"A lot of the old timers think it will until the foreclosure crisis is resolved. Want to sell yours while you can still get something for it?" he asked, looking from Pete to Martin. "I'd be happy to do the listings for you. It may sit on the market for an extended time but, if some of the economists I hear are right, the sooner you sell the better."

"Thanks for the sales pitch and the offer, but I'll stay where I am," Pete said. "My house suits me."

"Can't say I didn't try." Alden smiled.

Martin erased that smile when he asked if Alden owned a handgun.

Alden said he bought a gun for Megan to protect herself when he was away.

"When did you obtain it?" Pete asked.

"Around two months ago."

"About the time that Bradford lost his job?" Pete asked.

"I guess."

"What's the connection between the two?" Pete asked.

"None. The timing's strictly coincidental."

"And you bought it to protect yourself?" Pete asked.

"No." Alden added through clenched teeth, "I bought it so Megan could protect herself."

"Did you confer with her before you bought it?" Pete asked.

"No."

"What kind of gun is it?" Martin asked.

"It's a Smith and Wesson."

"What caliber?" Martin asked.

"Forty-five."

"Where do you keep it?" Martin asked.

"It's on the closet shelf in the bedroom that serves as my office."

"What does your wife think about the gun?" Pete asked.

"I haven't told her yet. I'm waiting until the time is right, because I know I'll meet up with some resistance."

"So you've had it for two months, and thus far your wife, who you bought it for has yet to hear about it?" Martin asked.

"That's right," Alden said, not bothering to mask his irritation with both the investigators and their line of questioning.

"Has the gun been fired?" Pete asked.

"Yes, I took it out for target practice. I have a friend who owns a farm."

"Let me make sure I have this correct," Pete said. "You bought a gun two months ago for your wife to protect herself, and so far you're the only one who's fired it."

"That's right."

"Have you spoken with your wife since you learned of Bradford's death?" Pete asked.

"Yes, she called me on Monday."

"Where were you last Sunday morning between nine and eleven?" Martin asked.

"I was riding my motorcycle."

"Can anyone attest to that?" Martin asked.

"Not between seven o'clock and eleven o'clock. I joined up with some friends for lunch and we rode together that afternoon."

"Let's see your handgun," Pete said.

"Do you have a search warrant?"

"Are you sure you want to play that game?" Pete asked.

"What I'm sure of is that I want to protect my rights. So, until you produce a search warrant, I'm not producing the gun."

"When did you say you took the gun for target practice?" Pete asked.

"I didn't say, but it was a week ago."

"Be more explicit," Pete said.

"Last Saturday."

"Did you see Bradford after he stopped living with his mother?" Martin asked.

Alden hesitated for several seconds. "Once."

"Where were you at the time?" Martin asked.

"I was here."

"You invited him over?" Pete asked.

"Not that I know of."

"Explain," Pete said.

Before answering, Alden's jaw tightened and he placed his hands on his lap, perhaps to hide them. "Brad was supposedly here to shower and change clothes."

"And what did you do?" Pete asked.

"I kicked him out and told him he'd better not return unless Megan was here!"

"Did it get physical?" Pete asked.

"I physically threw him out, if that's what you're asking."

"Yes, it is," Pete said.

"I didn't kill him!" Alden shouted, slamming a fist on the table, causing the centerpiece to jump.

"Any idea who had a motive?" Pete asked.

"No."

"Why were you so upset over finding him in your house?" Pete asked.

"He couldn't be trusted."

"Based on?" Pete asked.

"He stole money from Ellen—his mother."

"Stole or borrowed?" Pete asked.

"Definitely stole."

"Based on?" Martin asked.

"Based on what I heard."

"From?" Martin asked.

"From his family."

"Who in his family?" Martin asked.

"I don't remember. There was a lot of discussion. I don't know who said what."

"Did he steal anything from you?" Martin asked.

"Not that I know of, but I wouldn't be surprised."

"The day you found him here, was it the first time he came here?" Martin asked.

"I don't know."

"When did you find Bradford in your house?" Pete asked.

"About a week ago."

"Be more specific," Pete said.

"I can't. All I remember is that it was last week."

Pete pressed, but Alden insisted he couldn't narrow it down any further.

"And when did you take target practice with the Smith and Wesson?" Pete asked.

"I told you! Last Saturday."

"Then there was a connection between those two events," Pete said.

"No. There was no connection."

"So it was another coincidence?" Martin asked.

"No, I took target practice when my friend's schedule permitted ... the friend whose farm I took target practice at."

"Did you take target practice before or after you found Bradford in your house?" Pete asked.

"I'm not sure."

"What would be your first guess?" Pete asked.

Alden paused more than long enough to consider the implications of each alternative before saying, "Probably before, but I'm not sure."

"So what you're saying is that neither event was particularly memorable," Pete said.

Alden didn't respond.

"Does your friend with the farm have handguns?" Martin asked.

"Yes."

"Did he also take target practice that day?" Martin asked.

"Yes."

"What kinds of guns does he have?" Martin asked.

"I'm not sure. I didn't pay that much attention, but I think the one he used was a Smith and Wesson."

Pete asked, "Does he have any other guns?"

"I don't know. I didn't ask, and he didn't say." Alden now sounded annoyed.

"Where does this friend of yours live?" Pete asked.

"On a farm not far from St. Cloud."

"Give me his name and the exact location, including the mailing address," Pete said. "If you need to look it up, we'll wait."

A friend with guns who lives on a farm near St. Cloud wasn't something Pete wanted to hear. Per Martin's report, that placed him uncomfortably close to Billy and Tim's so-called "safe haven." *Great!*

THIRTY

I'M SO GLAD I REACHED YOU," the distraught voice gasped. "I got to the office, was going through my mail and found a letter from Brad." The last word came out as a wail.

"Megan?" Pete asked. It didn't sound like her. He and Martin were en route back to headquarters.

"Yes, it's me."

"Take your time. Tell me about it."

"Brad sent a letter to my office. He must have mailed it on Sunday, because it was postmarked Monday. It arrived while I was in Omaha. Do you want me to read it to you or fax it?"

"It might be easier for you to fax it, but tell me what you want to do," Pete said.

"You're right. I can't read it. I'll fax it."

Pete gave her the number, and it was there when they arrived. The letter said:

> Dear Megan,
> By the time you receive this, you'll know whether or not I was overreacting. When I found an attorney and began working to get my job back, I had no idea the whole situation would take on a life of its own. It appears that's what's happening. I'm supposed to meet someone at the Upper Landing today. The way I was told to be there, the whole situation, is steeped in intrigue. That's why I'm so nervous—okay, scared.
> Maybe it's my imagination. If so, you can stop reading here and give this to me the next time I see you. However, if something happens to me, please give this to the police.

It may help them figure out where I am and/or who done it.

Here are the facts:

I returned to the office at about 2:00 one Saturday morning. While on a date, I realized I didn't have my Blackberry and thought I must have left it on my desk. To get to my office, I had to pass the workroom. When I did, the high tech printers were humming away.

That was strange, so I checked the output. It was a major printing job—at least a thousand pages, and it was a brochure for some company I'd never heard of. Well, Megan, ACS doesn't do that kind of printing, so I was suspicious. I made a copy of the document being printed.

Monday I took it to my supervisor, and he sent me to Walter Linton, the vice-president who oversees computer support. I told him what happened, gave him the copy of the printing job I made for myself, and he thanked me.

After a month, when I hadn't heard a thing, I began gathering additional evidence by going into the office early two or three times a week. At least once a week, I found a large printing job underway. Each time, I made two copies—one for Linton and one for me.

The documents were always full color, and they were always for companies or groups I'd never heard of. There's no way ACS would be printing them—legitimately.

When I thought I had enough to prove what I suspected, I went back to Linton. He said an investigation was underway, and everything was under control. He told me to back off. When another month passed and the problem persisted, I told Linton that what was happening was a crime, and I was going up a level if he didn't take action. The next morning, I was fired.

Unfortunately, all of my evidence is, or was, locked in a file cabinet in my office. I kept it there, so it would be accessible when the time came to share it with the right people.

After I was fired, I tried contacting other VPs and members of the ACS director group. The receptionist refused to forward any of my calls, as did the administrative assistants. I mailed several letters. They weren't answered. I tried to get in to see members of the director group, and security kept me out. I even waited outside the office on several occasions, hoping to catch one of the directors on his or her way to lunch, but it seemed that security was warding off the people I wanted to see.

I thought about going to the home of one or more of the members of the director group, but was afraid that would make things worse. If they set up that kind of wall around themselves at work, they might be alarmed and call the police if I went to their homes or tried to call them there. I think Linton may have told them that I was dangerous. Otherwise, I don't know why no one would talk to me. I'd always gotten along famously with the higher-ups.

I don't know who was doing the printing or participating in it, so I didn't know whom I could trust. I was also concerned about getting my friends in trouble. You see, when I asked what was being said about my departure, they said there were lots of rumors, but no one could get the facts. I think they feared for their jobs. It looks like the company was making an example of the way they treated someone who did whatever it was they claimed I did. Megan, the only thing I did was try to stop whoever was stealing from ACS. It was going to hurt all of us, and I loved that company.

My attorney, Amy Pennington, recently spoke with the HR department, and interrogatories were delivered there on Thursday. I was sure that would make at least one person more than a little nervous. When a note was left for me at Reaching Out the very next day, the timing was too coincidental. Now I'm the one who's nervous. If I'm right, and I hope I'm not, you're going to need this information. On the other hand, it could be someone wanting to help me get my job back. That's why I can't miss the meeting on the Upper Landing. Then again, how would anyone at ACS know where I hang out?

Worst case, I want you to know how much I love you and appreciate everything you've done for me. You are the world's best sister, and you are and have always been one of my favorite people. Give my love to Mom, Casey, Gloria, Kenny, and Eric. Tell all of them, especially Casey, that I know they were doing what they thought was best, and none of this is their fault. Finally, please help Casey through this. I'm worried about him. He's a good person and deserves better than life seems willing to deliver to him.

Love,
Brad

THIRTY-ONE

PETE MADE TWO COPIES OF BRAD'S letter and gave one to Martin. Each investigator went through the letter several times, making notes in the margins and highlighting key sections.

When finished, Pete still had a little time before going to Reaching Out, and he used it to call the Chicago P.D. Having arrived at the point where the help of that department was vital to his and Martin's investigation, getting a contact there became a priority.

When the line was answered, he explained who he was and why he called. He was transferred to a detective named Edgar. After explaining, again, who he was, Pete said, "I'm looking for a little help with a murder case. The victim lived and worked in Chicago until a few months ago, but he was murdered in Minnesota. Some of the chief suspects are his former co-workers."

"I know. You guys in Minnesota think your hometown folks wouldn't hurt a fly. It's a part of what you like to call 'Minnesota nice,' isn't it?" Edgar chuckled.

"Close, but the summer heat's putting people on edge, making them cranky. However, that doesn't change the fact that some of our leads are pointing in your direction. That's why I'm calling."

"Sure, sure. So what do you want from me?"

Pete gave him a rundown of Winthrup's connection to ACS Marketing and the purported reason he was fired. "I have two people who saw a man we believe to be the murderer. I'd like your help in getting a photo of each ACS employee. No doubt the company has ID badges, so a copy of all of those photos, along with the names, should be perfect."

"Where's ACS Marketing located?" Edgar asked.

"Right downtown, on Wacker Drive. I can get the exact address if you like."

"No, don't bother. But I suppose you needed these pictures yesterday."

"You've got it. Any idea how quickly you can get at it?"

"Do you want the actual pictures or another format?" Edgar asked.

"I want whatever format I can get my hands on the quickest. I'll speak with our computer people, but I'd assume either individual computer files or one large file with all of the photos and names would be best. Can you call when you get to ACS, and I'll let our IT staff speak with theirs? My partner, Martin Tierney, will answer if I'm unavailable when you call back."

"Unavailable?"

"Yeah, I'm having lunch at a homeless shelter, and they might look askance if I'm carrying a cell phone."

"It sounds like you should look for a job with a larger department. I can afford both a phone and lunch on my salary. Any idea how many employees ACS has?"

"I could only take a wild guess."

"Hell, I could do that, and I don't know anything about them," Edgar sniggered.

Edgar said he should be able to get a disk with all of the photos either later today or early tomorrow if he leaned on them hard enough. He said his IT people could probably either transmit the information or print the photos and fax or overnight them.

Pete thanked him for getting right on it and asked him to call from ACS anyway, just in case the IT specialists, working together, could further expedite things.

"Oh, by the way, the man who either fired Winthrup or had him fired was the VP in charge of IT. Has a nice ring to it, doesn't it? Anyway, for that reason, they may want to play games with us. The VP's name is Walter Linton."

"No problem," Edgar said. "I'll talk to our IT people before I go and get some idea how long it should take to put it together. I'll also make sure they don't try to short me any photos, like Linton's."

"I have a couple of other requests," Pete said.

"Ask me if I'm surprised."

"I have two different stories about why Linton hasn't been to work since Winthrup's murder. Think you might have better luck in getting a straight answer about where he is, why he isn't reporting in for work and why his voicemail isn't accepting any more messages?"

"I'd like to think so. I'll get back to you on that as well."

Pete hung up and turned to Martin, who was working on his matrix. For a time, he sat patting his mouth with the palm of his hand. Next he imitated a bobblehead doll. From there he went to propping his chin on his fist, drumming the desktop with the fingertips of the other hand and sighing. Then he started the process all over again, as he rotated between adding to and erasing items from the matrix. Throughout the process, his feet tapped an erratic beat and his eyes stayed locked on the page.

"I thought you were going to cross out the people you eliminated from consideration," Pete said, referring to the erasures.

"I am, but I'm having trouble phrasing the motives, so they aren't too narrow."

Pete thought about suggesting he not worry so much about the semantics, as long as he knew what everything meant, but decided to let Martin work out the snags.

"When the time comes, I wonder if we can justify both of us going to Chicago," Pete thought out loud. "The order of the day is 'cut expenses.' Regardless, there's enough going on here that one of us should probably stay behind. I know you'd like to go, and the experience might prove valuable. Edgar seems helpful. I'm confident he'll do everything he can, within reason, to assist us. What do you think?"

Relieved to hear he had an opportunity to forego Chicago, Martin frowned and said, "As much as I'd like to go, I don't think it's appropriate. I don't mind staying, so you go. Is there any chance you won't have to?"

"I can't predict what will happen between now and then, but my best guess is no. If we somehow discount everyone connected with ACS, Winthrup's girlfriend, Erin Felton, and her brother are there. I'd like to meet with them."

"While you were on the phone, Megan Alden called," Martin said. "Bradford had withdrawn a total of $360 from the account she established for him, and he withdrew $200 last Saturday. I checked his personal property sheets. He had $4.67 on him when he was found. Also, I went online. Watkins is about thirty-five miles from Belgrade, right down Highway 55. Shouldn't we let Tim's mom know about Alden's farming friend, Bruce Kinney? Maybe she should check to see if her sister or brother-in-law knows him?"

"Yes, she might want to let her sister help her decide if Belgrade is now an undesirable location for Tim, or for Tim and Billy. I don't know if a farmer would know all of the farmers within a thirty-five-mile radius. I hope not," Pete said, running his hand through his hair.

THIRTY-TWO

CHANGING INTO WHAT HE'D DUBBED HIS "dining out at Reaching Out garb," Pete had an idea. He walked over to IT and asked the staff to isolate Bradford from the family photo and print two copies for him.

While inserting them in his wallet, something else occurred to him. His wallet might look too expensive for someone trying to pass himself off as down on his luck. So, he asked the IT guys to pull out their wallets. Although he liked to believe he wasn't a sexist, the men and women weren't equal this time.

The guys looked at him like he'd lost his mind, but they complied.

Pete saw what he wanted and said to the owner, "I'll trade you. How about it?"

"Lieutenant, you're kidding, right?"

Pete assured him he wasn't and smiled while he emptied the contents of his wallet, in preparation for the trade. The smile remained on Pete's face, and the look of astonishment changed to one of disbelief on the other man's, as they reloaded their wallets and Pete walked away.

Having kissed goodbye a perfectly good wallet, Pete now possessed one that was worn and held together by a wide rubber band. He didn't bother to smell it. He already knew it didn't have the fragrance of fine, Italian leather. Replacing his new acquisition, at the earliest opportunity, was added to his to-do list.

As he walked away, another of the guys from IT called after him, "I think we may be about the same size, if you have any suits or shoes you'd like to swap. In fact, I have just the tie for you."

Pete shook his head. "Sorry," he said over his shoulder. "I don't think I can afford to make a practice of this. If I have a change of heart, you'll be the first to know."

When did the world become overcrowded with wise guys? he wondered. But he couldn't wipe the smile off his face.

Reaching Out was becoming his most frequent dining spot. That reminded him that he had to get a contribution in the mail.

It surprised him that he enjoyed going there. He found the group that adopted him interesting and educational.

Although he'd always believed luck was an essential part of success, his understanding of one segment of those on one end of the spectrum, the homeless, was growing. He'd habitually shrugged and walked away when someone asked for his help with bus fare or for a few bucks. There'd been the looming suspicion that the requestor made a living this way or, worse yet, used the money for drugs or alcohol. He'd always known some of these people had legitimate needs, but the others dictated his response.

After spending a few hours at Reaching Out and speaking with the manager of the food service, he was rethinking that. He now worried about ignoring the needs of this segment of society, even if only one in a hundred—or one in five hundred—of the requests was legitimate. The way the others spent the money was a consideration, but did it override his obligation to those in genuine need? He no longer believed so, but he wanted to find ways to improve the chances the money went for the stated purposes.

That brought his thoughts back to Reaching Out. Added to Pete's original mission at the soup kitchen, thanks to Billy McGrath, was paying special attention to anyone with large ears. The larger the better, it seemed, because the ears, the do-rag and a deep voice were the things that stuck with Billy.

As planned, he arrived twenty minutes before the doors opened. The lunchtime crowd numbered close to sixty by then. As he'd learned to anticipate, they gathered in small groups. After all, why would something like that be contingent on the time of day or the meal? Didn't it go deeper than that? Was it a social norm? His next time around, if he had another chance, Pete decided he should be a social psychologist—maybe. He added that to the list that currently included being a fireman and joining the circus.

He saw the man he thought they called Doc, but didn't see Stew. Last night, Stew told him not to hold back, to join him and his group right away. Would the other men feel the same way about it, or would they be put off if he did so when Stew wasn't there? Pete tried to think about how he and his friends would react. He'd join the group, he decided, but not yet.

The man he thought was Doc seemed like his best bet for answers, assuming Stew was a no show. Second thought, if he read things correctly, regardless of Stew, he had to find a way for a private conversation with Doc.

He stood on the periphery, checking out everyone, while looking like he saw no one. Large ears were the subject of his search.

While caught up in this, someone tapped him on the back. He jumped and spun around, positioned to defend himself, scaring Stew.

Pete wasn't accustomed to being touched, at least not by a stranger, and especially when he didn't know it was coming. He hoped his reaction didn't set off a flashing, neon arrow that pointed at him and said "COP." The word around town was that cops moved, or carried themselves, in a characteristic way. He didn't believe it. He was convinced that his and Martin's styles were at opposite poles.

Stew responded to his startled move with a hoarse laugh, and Pete joined in.

"You are one quiet son-of-a-bitch," Pete said.

"Yeah, I know. Come on." Stew signaled Pete to follow.

As they joined a group, only a few of whose faces were familiar to Pete. Stew said, "Ain't seen ya here for lunch before."

It wasn't a question, but Pete had an opportunity to explain, if he wanted. He didn't.

Encouraged by Stew's friendliness, Pete decided to press his luck. "I've been looking for the guy who told me this was a good place to get a meal. We were supposed to meet here the night before last. If that didn't work out, he said he'd see me here for sure last night, but he still didn't show. I can't figure it out."

"What's his name?" Stew asked.

"Brad. Do you know a Brad?"

"No, but that don't mean much. Lots of us know people by the names we pin on 'em. We call ya Harry, 'cause of all that hair."

"How about him?" Pete asked, looking over at the man he assumed was Doc. "I know you said last night, but I'm not sure I got it right."

"That's Doc. He's our scholar."

Hearing his name, Doc joined them. Apparently he overheard the rest of the conversation as well, because he said, "I thought we should call you 'Rogue.' That name incorporates Rogaine, because of all that hair, of course, and it includes a reference to the fact you strike me as one—a rogue I mean."

"Ya mean like James Bond?" Stew asked.

"Something like that," Doc said.

He didn't mention the meaning Daniel Webster referenced, and Pete was glad. Wanting clarification, but afraid he knew, and not wanting to alert the others, he just shrugged. To keep the conversation moving and steer it away from himself, he asked, "Is your name Doc, as in PhD? After listening to you, I think the name I'd give you would be 'Professor.'"

Doc's hands were shoved deep in his pockets, and thinking back, it seemed to Pete that he was perpetually in that stance.

"Talked 'bout that one," Stew said. "But chose 'Doc.' He looks like Doc from Snow White."

Doc didn't look the least bit put off at that assessment. His smile remained, unaltered.

"I see what you mean," Pete said.

"With whom are you siding?" Doc asked.

"Why, with you, Doc," Pete said. "I was quick to see your talent. Does everyone around here have an assigned name?"

"I don't think so," Doc said. "As best I can tell, it's only this group."

Pete wanted to turn the discussion back to Brad, but hoped either Doc or Stew would do it for him. It took some time, but patience paid off.

"You said you was looking for a friend?" Stew asked.

"Yes, my friend Brad. Would it help if I describe him?"

"Can't hurt," Stew said.

"Shorter than me, maybe about your height, Stew, with a medium build. Late twenties, blond hair, blue eyes. Nice looking, but not as handsome as me." Pete grinned.

Both Stew and Doc laughed.

"That sure narrows the field," Doc said. "We all look better than you."

Pete was trying to decide whether he should mention Winthrup's ring or produce the photo. Why would he be carrying a picture of Brad? If he was family or his lover, it might fly. Otherwise it might seem contrived. He decided on the jewelry.

"Okay, he's better looking, but something else about him stands out."

"What's that?" Stew asked.

"He wears a ring that has a very large diamond. It reminds me of a ring worn by Elizabeth Taylor. I don't understand why he doesn't sell it and buy a condo."

"Do you spend a lot of time with Liz?" Doc asked.

"Not even in my dreams."

"I know why he keeps the ring," Doc said. "But I can't say."

Pete's mouth dropped open, figuratively speaking. There was no change in his expression, but he was dancing on the inside. *What else did Doc know?* "You know Brad?" he asked.

"I do," Doc said. "Nice young man. I, too, have wondered why he hasn't been around for several days."

"Can you remember the last time you saw him?" Pete asked.

"Last week. Friday."

"Any idea where he might have gone?" Pete continued. "It's important. I've been holding onto something for him."

"The last time I saw him," Doc said, "was after a man gave me a note to give him."

"Can you describe the guy who gave you the note?" Pete asked. "Did he look like Brad?"

"Only if they had different mothers . . . and different fathers. He didn't look anything like Flash. That's what we call Brad."

"And you gave Brad the note?" Pete asked.

"Yes. It was wrapped in a twenty-dollar bill. Wouldn't you have?"

"I would have if it was wrapped in a five," Pete smiled. "To me, money is money. Had you seen the guy with the twenty bucks around here before?"

"No. He showed up Friday afternoon and asked about Flash," Doc explained. "We call him Flash, because of the ring."

"How did you know he was talking about Brad, not someone else?" Pete asked.

"He called him Brad, and he had a picture. Flash looked flashier in the picture than he does around here, but I recognized him immediately."

"Did the man say why he wanted Flash?" Pete asked.

"No, just that he had an important message for him."

"Did anyone else see the guy who gave you the note?" Pete asked.

"I don't know. There weren't many people around at the time, but I have no way of knowing if anyone saw him or paid any attention. Why all the questions?"

"You've piqued my interest. This is the best information I've obtained thus far. Can you describe the guy with the twenty bucks, Doc? I might know him. If I do, maybe he'll help me find Brad."

Doc described the man as in his late twenties or early thirties. His hair was dark brown, and Doc thought he was a little taller than Brad, but shorter than Pete, with a medium build. He couldn't describe the man's eye color because of his oversized sunglasses. He didn't wear a do-rag, for what that was worth, but he wore a baseball cap.

Pete wanted to ask about the man's ears, but would have difficulty justifying the question, if Doc challenged him. He settled for asking, "Doc, did Brad read the note while he was with you? I'm wondering if he reacted to it or said anything about it."

"He read it and tucked it in his pocket. He reacted about the way you'd expect someone to if it said that Thanksgiving will be on a Thursday this year."

"In other words, ho-hum?" Pete asked.

"Precisely."

Thirty-Three

WHILE WAITING FOR LUNCH, the more the group talked the more questions Pete had. At the top of the list was whether Doc would work with the Bureau of Criminal Apprehension forensics artist. If he resisted, Pete knew there was no sense in forcing his hand. Doc might dig in his heels, go through the motions and the result would be worthless.

Pete was anxious to show Billy and Tim a picture of the man who gave the note to Doc. It could result in a breakthrough, and knowing that had him pumped. He had to create the opportunity, the sooner the better, for some private words with Doc.

When the doors opened, Stew's group, or was it Doc's, was near the head of the line, so they had their pick of the tables. The large, round one they occupied the last two evenings got the bid, but they didn't fill it. However, the chairs to Doc's right and left were occupied by the time Pete got there.

During lunch, Doc seemed uncharacteristically nervous. He arranged and rearranged the plates on his tray and the food on the plates, and he repeatedly repositioned himself on his chair and his chair at the table.

Pete wondered if Doc regretted saying as much as he did or if something else was going on. All he knew was that shortly after Doc answered his questions, his demeanor changed dramatically. He distanced himself from the rest of the group, became less talkative and his smile vanished.

Lunch was soup, a choice of sandwiches, chips, fruit, pudding, and the usual beverages. Doc was the first at their table to finish, and he hadn't eaten much. He excused himself, saying he was late for an appointment, asked Stew to take care of his tray and left.

That left Pete flatfooted. Explaining that he had to ask Doc something, he bussed his dishes and hurried outside.

Doc was gone. It didn't seem possible he'd moved that fast, so Pete went back inside and looked, unsuccessfully, for him.

When he reached headquarters, Martin was eating lunch, and his desk was littered with the remnants. With his mouth full, he said, "I almost missed your call from Edgar. The IT staff is making us four sets of the photo lineup of all the ACS staff. Two will have names below the pictures. Two won't. I also asked for a copy of Dan Felton's driver's license photo. Edgar says we're wearing him out and at this rate he'll soon need a vacation. He asked me to donate the hours to his account. I told him I'd submit the paperwork." Martin laughed and shook his head. If he had to go to Chicago, Edgar would make it bearable.

"I'm glad you asked for the photo of Felton. Good thinking, Martin. How many pictures in the lineup?"

"ACS has 127 employees. With the addition of Dan Felton, Gerald Alden, and the driver's license photo of Alden's friend, Bruce Kinney, and with six photos a page, that makes twenty-one complete pages and one partial. Winthrup's friends will make it twenty-three plus."

Pete settled in a chair and told Martin about Doc and Brad, the note, and the description of the man who gave it to Doc.

"Now you'll be able to ask Doc to check the photos for the guy who gave him the note."

"Do you have any idea when we'll have them?" Pete asked.

"They said by late afternoon, barring a catastrophe."

"I'd better make my dinner reservation." Pete said.

"Huh?"

"At Reaching Out. One of the ACS photos I'm particularly interested in showing Doc is Brad's. I hope ACS hasn't gotten around to deleting it from the file."

"Why? You said he knew Brad."

"Yes, and the man who came looking for Brad showed Doc his picture. If it's the same photo, that means . . ."

"Got it."

"Did you reach Gerald Alden?" Pete asked.

"No, I had to leave a message, and he hasn't called."

"How about Tim's mother?"

"She called and said they'd hoped to take the boys to Belgrade yesterday, but she couldn't get away from work. They're going this evening."

One hand began wearing a path, moving back and forth through Pete's hair. Doc's description hadn't eased his concerns over Gerald Alden and his friend, Bruce Kinney.

"How are you doing with the other photos—the ones of the friends?" Pete asked.

"I have some, but not all of them. But I don't have someone in Chicago doing the grunt work for me." Martin smiled.

"Look who's talking. You're already delegating to Edgar. By the way, did Edgar find out where Linton is?"

"He said the word is that Linton's too sick to take any calls. As far as his location goes, it seems that everyone assumes he's home, but he's still working on it."

"Once we've accomplished a few other things, I'm going to pay him a visit," Pete said. "I hope to be more successful with Doc tonight. He was acting strange this noon. I wonder if it had anything to do with me. Assuming it didn't, and with a few breaks, we could have the ACS photos, Doc's BCA sketch, photos of Winthrup's friends and one of Dan Felton. Instead of asking the boys to look at photos several more times, I think we'll be more successful if we gather everything first."

"Do you think Doc will cooperate?" Martin asked.

"I don't know," Pete shrugged. "But I hope we'll be ready to meet with the boys sometime tomorrow." Sounding more optimistic he added, "Would you call the BCA and see if Len can work with Doc tonight? We'd best give him a heads-up."

"I'll try to have an answer before you leave. Assuming Doc works with Len, do you think we should have a few other sketches, not just the one of the man that Doc saw?" Martin asked. "That way, the kids won't think there's something special about that person—that they're supposed to select him?"

"Good point, Martin."

Both investigators spent the next several hours on the phone. Pete started by calling Billy's cell, once he got comfortable by tilting back in his chair and resting his feet on his desk. "How's the jewelry situation?" he asked, when Billy answered.

"Everything's cool," Billy laughed, "thanks to you." He said Tim's mom was taking them to Belgrade after work.

Although anxious to get the work or cell phone number for Tim's mother, he listened while Billy told him about their plans and their schedule.

Billy said they'd leave around 5:30. At first he wasn't happy about spending time on a farm, but their parents were letting them take their bikes, and Tim's mom said there were lots of places to explore up there.

At the first break in Billy's running commentary, Pete asked for a number where Tim's mom could be reached this afternoon.

Billy picked up his home phone and called Tim. In a minute, he returned with the number.

Pete wrote it on a piece of paper and handed it to Martin.

"Why do you want her number? Is there a problem?" Billy asked.

"We have a couple of questions." Pete debated over saying more and decided to give Billy a heads up. "We may want to delay your trip for a day. I think we'll soon have some more photos for you and Tim to look at. We'll work it out with Tim's mom. If necessary, we'll drive up to see you."

"Awesome!"

Pete hoped he'd feel that way when all was said and done.

THIRTY-FOUR

Martin called Tim's mother. After hanging up, he told Pete, "She said she'll drop everything and contact her sister."

While waiting to hear from her, Martin followed Pete's recommendation and called Tim, giving him a rundown of what Pete already told Billy.

Pete believed Billy would tell Tim about his call, and he didn't want Tim feeling like the odd man out.

When Tim's mother called, Martin included Pete in a conference call. She said that neither her sister nor brother-in-law knew Bruce Kinney—Gerald Alden's friend who farmed near Watkins. But Tim's mom had a few concerns. One was that he might see the boys while driving past the farm or in town. Her sister thought it unlikely that Kinney spent any time in Belgrade, and that reduced her nervousness.

Even so, Tim's mom said her sister worried that having the boys at their farm might endanger her family. She wanted to know if the police had any recommendations for protecting themselves.

Pete weighed the options. Tim's mom mentioned family in Rochester yesterday, but told Martin they were no longer a possibility. There was no demonstrated reason to be apprehensive about Gerald Alden's friend, Bruce Kinney. But at this time, they were taking every precaution. Also, the killer had no reason to look for the boys in Belgrade.

Pete and Martin said they should be notified immediately if anything raised her suspicions or concerns. Pete also said he and Martin had already advised the boys to do that.

"Belgrade is a viable spot as long as the boys take some added precautions," Pete told her. "They should stay away from any major roads between Belgrade and Watkins, especially Minnesota Highway 55, at least until we have more information about Kinney and his Twin Cities' connection. We'll let you know if and when Kinney is cleared."

Tim's mother decided to stick with Belgrade, and the next question was whether they'd leave today or delay the relocation until Friday. She said she couldn't take them on Thursday.

Waiting two days suited Pete and Martin's schedule. By then, they hoped to have the additional pictures and the artist's compilation to show the boys. But that wasn't a good enough reason to change the family's plans or keep the boys in town.

As Pete prepared for Reaching Out, Martin asked if he should call Bruce Kinney about Alden taking target practice at his farm.

Pete suggested they wait. "The return trip from Belgrade provides an opportunity to meet with him, and that might be more worthwhile."

Martin changed the subject. "On Monday, after you ran into her in the skyway, it sounded like you were seriously considering calling Katie Benton. Have you gotten off dead center?"

"Not yet. I haven't had time."

If you want kids, don't forget that her biological clock is ticking."

"How do you know about biological clocks?" Pete asked.

"You're kidding, right? Michelle and I have one child. Every so often, she reminds me that we have to hurry if we're going to have another, because her 'biological clock is ticking.' I'd like to remove its batteries."

"Where did you and Michelle go on your first date, Martin?"

"To the State Fair. I bought her a corn dog and stole her heart."

"You devil, you. It's too early for the fair. Do you think I should postpone until then?"

"If you do, not even the promise of a corn dog and walleye on a stick will get you a date with her."

THIRTY-FIVE

A FEW PEOPLE WERE OUTSIDE the building when Pete arrived at Reaching Out for the second time today. Apparently most had either an alternative option or better sense.

He enjoyed walking in a slow soaking rain like this one. Standing in it for a prolonged period, however, was much less inviting.

After entering the yard, he found a place where he could lean against the building and catch a few less raindrops. Several people nodded at him. He responded in kind, but didn't join them.

Where were they? Would the rain keep them away? He didn't want to believe it. He had a lot riding on Doc and was anxious to keep things moving.

Scrutinizing each new arrival, while looking indifferent, wasn't getting easier, but he wouldn't be deterred. Once again, ears had top billing—or was it side billing? Across the street, the ears of a man, standing under a tree in the yard of a church, grabbed his attention. But when the man turned, Pete saw that his ears weren't particularly large. Like Alden's, the way they stood out accentuated them.

The closer it got to five o'clock, the tenser Pete became. Would Doc and Stew forego supper here tonight? The last two days, they were here by this time. Did they come this noon because they heard the forecast? Did they prefer sleeping in dry clothes to a meal? It made sense. If they didn't show, should he leave without eating? Would the others think anything of it? Would they even notice?

The door opened, and those gathered outside hurried in, even though most of them were already beyond wet. Pete continued leaning against the wall, hoping.

Twenty minutes later, with his spirits sinking faster than the unseen sun, he made a final review of his options. Then he looked down at his shoes. One by one, he forced some of the water out of them, using compression. In the middle of this process, he heard an ear-piercing whistle.

Looking up, he saw a man a block down West Seventh Street waving at him. The man bore a remarkable resemblance to Doc.

Pete smiled and waved back. Then he resumed the resuscitation of his shoes. He didn't want to look too eager.

"Didn't your mother teach you to get in out of the rain?" the much drier Doc asked as he parked next to Pete.

"That and lots of other things. I was beginning to think you weren't coming, Doc. I haven't been around long enough to learn your schedule, but it didn't look good."

"Do you anticipate you will be?"

"I beg your pardon?" Pete asked.

"Are you planning to come here long enough to learn the ins and outs of my schedule?"

The way Pete read that remark, it wasn't a question. It seemed Doc was calling him out on the carpet. He decided to find out. "I don't know. What do you think?"

"It's hard saying."

He's clever, Pete decided and said, "I'm really happy to see you, Doc."

"Same here. I don't like eating alone—not that it's possible here. Why don't we go inside? The rain isn't letting up."

"I have some questions, and I don't want anyone to overhear us." Pete said. "Speaking of which, where are the other guys?"

"Stew's coming. We're supposed to save a place for him. Benny will probably be along shortly, but there are no guarantees with him. I'm not sure about the others. Sometimes they prefer to patronize other establishments—for comparison purposes." Doc laughed.

"I've been thinking about our conversation, Doc. The one about Brad. Do you mind if I ask a few more questions?"

"That depends."

"We're good friends, and I'm worried about him," Pete said.

"Understandable."

If Doc knew it was a lie, his expression didn't reveal it.

"I wonder about the man who gave you the note for Brad. Showing up a few days before Brad disappeared seems too coincidental. Would you describe him again?"

Doc listed the same traits, ending with, "But he didn't appear a few days before Flash disappeared. He gave me that note, and I passed it on the same day. That was the last time I saw your friend."

Pete skipped over Doc's correction, not wanting to bring attention to the reason for his error. "I keep thinking there's a link between that man and Brad," he said. "I might be crazy, but I have this feeling."

"And you're going to be a detective in your next life?" Doc asked.

"Do you think I have what it takes?"

Doc locked his eyes on Pete's and said, "Yes. I think you're better at that than at being down on your luck."

"None of us are good at that, Doc. We just have to survive it."

"Pretty much."

"Are you trying to tell me something, Doc?"

"I heard about Brad. I know he was murdered. I can't prove it, but I think that, rather than being down on your luck, you're a very dedicated detective, trying to solve the murder. It's commendable. How many police officers would come here this many times, trying to get information?"

"When did you figure it out?"

"Today. Had I known it before, I may not have told you about the note."

"Are you angry with me for deceiving you?"

"Originally, I was put off. After mulling it over, I realized why you're doing what you're doing, and I want you to find whoever killed Brad. By the time I'd gone over all of that, I understood. But why did you return? You got what you needed, didn't you?"

"Yes and no. The information you gave me may be sufficient, but it may not. A few other things would be helpful."

"Such as?"

"You hadn't seen the man who gave you the note before that night, and you haven't seen him since, correct? I mean anyplace, not just here."

"No. I don't believe I'd seen him before, and I definitely haven't seen him since. I'd remember."

Reaching into his hip pocket, Pete pulled out his new, old wallet and extracted the ACS picture of Brad. Protecting it as best he could from the elements, he held it out to Doc in a cupped hand.

"You said he showed you a photo of Brad. Is this it?"

"I believe so. If not, it was very similar. He wore a light-blue shirt and a tie, as in that picture."

"How was the man who gave you the note dressed?"

"He wore dirty blue jeans, dirtier than what we usually see around here, and a T-shirt."

"Do you remember the color of his T-shirt?"

"No, sorry. I tried to remember, but I can't."

"How about his voice? Do you remember how it sounded?"

"There wasn't anything special about it. It wasn't abnormally high or baritone. He didn't have an accent, and he didn't stutter. I can't think of anything that makes it stand out, other than the absence of those things."

"Do you remember his ears?" Pete asked.

"They stuck out more than most people's. Is that what you mean?"

"Yes. Did Brad have any enemies around here, Doc?"

"I don't know that he had enemies, but I'd heard a few of the men talk about his ring. It made me nervous. I suggested he ask a friend or a family member to hold onto it for him—for safety sake."

"And what did he say?"

"He said it wasn't leaving his finger, no matter what. He said it was symbolic of the healing that took place between him and his dad."

"Might someone around here have killed him for it?" Pete asked.

"The people who come here are no different from the people who don't. Most of us are good and honest. Some are not. But even good, honest people get desperate and do things they otherwise wouldn't. Most of us have a breaking point."

"Can you identify the men you heard talking about Brad's ring?"

"Yes, but I haven't seen them all week."

"Do you know their names?"

"Sorry, no."

Both men were getting wetter, and Doc was beginning to fidget, but Pete was determined to maintain their privacy. "Did Brad ever mention enemies or being afraid of anyone?" he asked.

"No, but he was a very private person."

"This helps, Doc. I have one more question. Actually, it's more of a request than a question. Will you work with a forensics artist to create a likeness of the man who gave you the note for Brad?"

"I'll have to think about that."

"Can you tell me why?"

"I'd rather not."

"I'm worried about two eleven-year-old boys, Doc. They saw the murderer, and that concerns me. Doing this could be critical to solving the case, and solving it could be the only way to protect them."

"How often have you used that line?" Doc asked.

"First time, I swear. But if it works, I'll tuck it away for future reference."

With that incentive, Doc agreed to do as Pete asked, provided it didn't require going to headquarters or one of the precincts.

Pete asked for a suggested location, and Doc said, "Let's eat first and I'll think about it."

"Otherwise, Doc, I'd be happy to buy dinner for you."

"Thanks for the offer, but here comes Stew. I'll tell him we waited out here for him. I've done crazier things than standing in the rain waiting for someone."

The three men ate together and discussed many things. Bradford Winthrup wasn't one of them.

Doc finished first and, for the second time today, broke with protocol when he got up and announced, "Sorry to desert you, but I have to catch a bus over on Robert Street. I promised to meet a friend in Maplewood."

"Don't worry 'bout it. I'm almost finished. See ya tamorrow?" Stew asked.

"That's my plan," Doc said.

Pete wondered what Doc was doing. Pete lived in Maplewood. Did Doc know that? How could he? Was there a message in his selection of that location or was it coincidental? His heart and his feet wanted to run after Doc. To take his mind off it, he asked Stew how he stayed dry on nights like this.

"Usually don't."

Eventually, Stew finished eating, wrapped his leftovers and they bussed their trays. Few people remained.

Thanks to the continuing rain, Stew said goodbye before they walked outside. He went west and Pete went north, then east. If Doc was truly going to Robert Street, he would head east or southeast.

After passing St. Joseph's Hospital, Pete picked up the pace. When he reached Tenth and Robert, he looked left, turned right and slowed to a brisk walk. His mind raced. There's a major bus shelter at Sixth and Robert. Would Doc be there? Was he already on a bus? What did he expect Pete to do?

Approaching Sixth Street, Pete saw Doc. He stood outside the bus shelter, protected by the overhang of a building, talking with another man.

Passing Doc, Pete stepped inside the shelter and checked the schedules for the two buses that stopped there this time of day—the 68 and the 71. The schedule for the 71 said it went to Little Canada, and the next bus came in five minutes. The 68 went to Maplewood. Bingo. And the next bus arrived in six minutes.

Stepping out of the shelter, towards Doc and the other man, Pete asked, "Do you know if there's a pay phone nearby?"

"The closest one," the other man said, "is in the Transit Station on Minnesota and Sixth. Right over there," he said, pointing.

"Can you keep an eye out for me?" Pete called back to the two men. "I should be back in time. If you see me coming and the bus is going to take off, can you ask the driver to wait?"

"Sure," the unknown man called after him, "but what bus are you trying to catch?"

"Maplewood," he called over his shoulder, sprinting for the Transit Station.

When he reached Minnesota and Sixth, he glanced around and saw the Transit Station. He charged through the doors and looked for the phone. Bus schedules stood in a rack along the wall. After grabbing one for the 68, he reached into his pocket, pulled out several coins, plugged the phone and dialed.

Standing there, he knew he looked as antsy as Martin did last Sunday. He had to complete this call and catch the bus, and the second hand spun around the clock face with little consideration for his needs. Thankfully, Martin answered on the first ring. "Were you able to reach Len at the BCA?"

"Yeah, he's waiting for me to set a time."

"Terrific! Go to his office and wait until you hear from me." Pete spoke so fast that he had to repeat it for Martin.

Frantically searching the bus schedule, he continued, "Doc and I are catching the 68 bus, going north from downtown. We'll be to the end of the line by, one second, umm, 6:35, but don't leave unless you don't hear from me by 6:45. We might get off before the end of the line. I don't know yet. Gotta go. I can't miss that bus. And Martin, bring the photo line-up of the ACS employees, the friends, and Alden, Felton, and Kinney."

"But, Pete," Martin said. He spoke to a dead connection.

Out the door and running back to Robert Street and Doc, Pete saw a bus go through the intersection. It headed north on Robert. He had a half block to go, so he turned up the pace and ran across Robert, against the light, slowing only to look for oncoming vehicles.

Thankfully, downtown St. Paul was near dead by six o'clock most evenings—unless the Minnesota Wild was playing hockey or there was a performance at the Orpheum Theatre, or some other special event.

Doc wasn't at the bus stop, so Pete sprinted after the bus he just missed. A sign in the upper right corner of the bus's back panel read "68."

He should have gambled on a pay phone at the end of the line, but he had no idea where the intersection of Carmen and Camelot was, other than in Maplewood.

More a distance runner than a sprinter, Pete didn't know how long he could maintain the current pace. Why were lights always green when you needed them to be red, and vice versa?

Thirty-Six

Buses, at least most buses, stopped for red lights. Pedestrians, especially sprinting ones, were often not so inclined. After all, it wasn't as easy for them to shift gears and get back up to speed, especially when the sky was leaking.

Pete got a break when the light on Robert at Eleventh Street changed, and the 68, which he hoped held Doc, shuddered and stopped.

Reaching the bus's front door, he skidded to a stop.

Nothing happened. The bus stop was thirty feet behind him. Did the driver ignore him, because he wasn't at the official location?

Pete knocked on the door and flashed his most plaintive look.

Following a sound that reminded him of one of his mother's most dramatic sighs, the door sprang open.

"Thanks," he inhaled the word with a breath of air, working to catch his breath.

With a flash of relief he saw that the fare box accepted dollar bills. When did riding a bus get so expensive? Before inserting his money, Pete looked for Doc and saw him sitting near the front. He fed the fare box, accepted a transfer and sat in the seat behind his reason for being there.

They passed Regions Hospital and, in one short block, a hotel where the goings on are a bane to the existence of far too many St. Paul cops. By then, they were two blocks from the State Capitol building, and not much further from Casey Winthrup's office.

The bus wound through a brief residential area, passed the Minnesota Transportation Museum, which had the relics of some ancient city buses in the yard, and moved along past Oakland Cemetery.

By the time they arrived at Maryland and Jackson, Pete knew they were behind schedule. He figured Martin was getting nervous. What he wouldn't give to have his cell phone right now.

M EANWHILE, MARTIN AND LEN sat in Len's car, behind the Taco Bell at the end of the bus route. Len had been on his way to dinner when Martin lassoed him, explaining they had to leave immediately to meet with Pete and the other man.

Based on the time Pete said the bus would reach the end of the line, Martin figured that he and Len had barely enough time to get there before the bus. If Pete and this guy, dubbed Doc, got off the bus before the end of the route, he and Len wouldn't be far away.

A roar and diesel fumes announced the impending arrival of the 68. The bus pulled over, and two men exited. They walked towards the apartment complex to the east. A woman carrying a baby and a collapsed stroller followed. Next came Doc, and Pete was right behind him.

"What now?" Len asked after Pete and Doc got in his car.

The four men conferred and decided the best place for them, from the standpoint of comfort, privacy, and convenience, was Pete's house.

Len drove, and Pete asked Doc to look at the lineup for a photo of the man who gave him the message for Brad.

Pete owned a rambler, circa 1960s, at the end of a cul-de-sac. He and Andrea had bought the house two years after they married when they began planning additions to their family. It was a wonderful house in a terrific neighborhood for raising kids. They'd planned to have their kids walk to the parochial grade school less than a half-mile away.

By the time they reached Pete's house, Doc was finished looking at all but two pages of photos.

The four men sat at Pete's kitchen table while Doc completed the process that might preclude the need for Len. It didn't.

Pete moved Doc and Len to the den and filled their drink orders. He and Martin stayed in the kitchen, and he got a can of pop for each of them. After Martin pointed out the photo of Gerald Alden's friend, Bruce Kinney, Pete breathed a sigh of relief. His ears were anything but prominent.

Pete silently noted Doc's failure to recognize the photos of Alden and Felton. That might be good news, but the murderer wasn't necessarily working alone.

Before long, Pete realized the futility of holding Martin captive to this time-consuming process. "If you like, you can head back to headquarters."

Martin glanced at his watch, even though he knew the time, and accepted the offer.

Pete checked on his remaining guests. They didn't need him, so he left them to their work.

Taking advantage of the down time, he went through the non-time-sensitive mail that had accumulated on his kitchen counter. With that task completed and no word from the den, he washed the dishes that seemed to multiply like rabbits in his kitchen sink. As he dried the last few, he reviewed his options.

He could call Katie Benton. Martin was pushing for that. The number of hours he spent on this case gave him an excuse for procrastinating, but it was a flimsy one. Even after all this time, the idea of dating felt disloyal to Pete. He knew it was crazy. Andrea would be the first to tell him to stop hanging on to the past. Easier said than done.

He still dreamt about her. She'd always had a fresh, clean fragrance that reminded him of spring. He'd wake up talking to her and reaching for her. Finding nothing but emptiness on the other side of the bed always left a gaping hole in his heart.

He'd recently learned the meaning of "Communion of Saints" as defined by the Catholic Church: people who'd died could communicate with those they left behind. Pete wondered if that was why he sometimes caught a whiff of Andrea's scent. Was she trying to tell him something or simply trying to comfort him?

How he missed her. He couldn't walk into their bedroom without thinking of her. Did that mean he wasn't ready to move on? He wondered if he was attracted to Katie because she reminded him of Andrea. He also wondered if he was more interested in kids than a wife. If either proved to be true, it guaranteed misery for everyone concerned.

As if that wasn't enough, what about his job? Andrea didn't mind his irregular hours and cancelled plans, but she was unique. His eyes grew moist and he wiped them with the heel of his hand.

If Andrea was alive, he wouldn't be trying so hard to find ways to entertain himself while Doc and Len did their work. Had all gone according to plan, he and Andrea would have had a child by now. How different things would be if he had a son or daughter.

This was craziness. As a diversion, he went to the bedroom and got a book. Back in the living room, he lost himself in someone else's story.

"We're finished," Len said, startling him.

"It isn't perfect, but I think it's a pretty good likeness," Doc said. "If you showed it to me and I knew the man, I think I'd recognize him. I don't think I can do any better, because I can't get the nose quite right. There are so many choices and, try as I might, none of them seems right."

Len handed the sketch to Pete. The man wasn't anyone he'd seen at Reaching Out—or anywhere else. His ears fit Billy's description. Pete hoped Billy would recognize the man. Then the challenge would be determining who and where he was.

"Doc, I'd like to get you and Len some food. You didn't eat much tonight, and he said he stopped you on your way to dinner, Len. Then we can drop you off wherever you like, Doc. What do you say?"

"If Len doesn't mind, I think that would be nice."

"Do you have a hankering for anything in particular, Doc?" Pete asked.

"If you don't mind, I love the French toast at Perkins."

"Good selection," Pete said.

Len agreed.

They headed to the restaurant. While they ate and talked, Doc contemplated the best place to catch a return bus. He decided at the Kmart, located along the route.

Pete still had the schedule in his pocket, so he checked the times.

"The next bus is in about forty-five minutes," he said. "I'll drop you at the Kmart."

Arriving with time to spare before Doc's bus, Pete offered, "If there is anything you need to pick up here, I'd like to buy it for you— as a token of my appreciation for what you've done."

"Thanks, but that's not necessary."

"No, but I'd like to do it. Besides, it'll be an economic stimulus and give you something to do before the bus comes."

Both men smiled at the reference to the economy.

Doc picked out a few toiletries, and Pete paid for them and added some snacks.

At the bus stop, Pete said, "I know your transfer expired. Here's bus fare and a twenty to tuck away for an emergency, or a celebration, or whatever."

"I don't need your money."

"But I needed your help."

Doc smiled and slid the money into his pocket. "I'll miss you, Pete."

"Probably not as much as you think." Pete smiled.

Doc responded with a questioning look.

The old man was bleary-eyed when they shook hands and he boarded the bus. He selected a seat on the side where Pete stood and maintained eye contact as the bus pulled away.

Watching the bus depart for downtown, Pete thought about Doc. He was obviously educated—over and above his stint in the school of hard knocks.

THIRTY-SEVEN

THURSDAY MORNING, PETE CALLED EDGAR, who answered, "Ah, Culnane. This is Edgar. It's getting so I talk to you more than I talk to my wife."

Pete skipped a smart retort and told Edgar about his plans to fly to Chicago. He requested Edgar's assistance in questioning the company VP, Walter Linton, and the brother of the victim's girlfriend, Dan Felton. "If I'm able to wrap up a few things around here and fly in tomorrow morning, can you fit it in your schedule?"

"If you're flying in for the pleasure of my company, the least I can do is see you."

"You're unbelievably accommodating." Pete said.

"We like to call it 'Chicago nice.' Ever hear of it?"

"No, but it's good to know. It makes me less nervous about asking for another favor."

"And what would that be?" Edgar asked.

"Would you mind trying to get some information out of Linton's friends at ACS and their HR department? I have his home address, but I'm not at all confident we'll find him there. The captain doesn't mind my taking a short vacation, but he'll get a little testy if I stay more than a day or two."

"That's hard to understand. It's not like you St. Paul cops have that much to do. Last time I talked to someone out that way, he said he protected the citizenry by reporting icy patches on the sidewalks."

"This is summer. But you have no idea how many of us it takes to keep an eye out for uneven sidewalks. 'Minnesota nice' dictates we do everything in our power to insure a smooth walking surface."

Next Pete called Billy to make sure the boys would be at the farm when they arrived around ten.

The investigators took interstates northwest towards St. Cloud. Heading that direction spared them from having to stare into the sun on another cloudless day. En route, the ever-growing metropolitan sprawl continued for several miles after the north and south bypasses of I-94 merged. It was replaced by rolling farmland, interrupted only by the outskirts of a few towns.

Along the way, Pete saw the current version of hay bales. Intermittently, these white plastic-covered cylinders, like PVC pipes that appeared to be about six feet tall and at least fifty feet long, stood in parallel rows near barns. Some of the corn was tasselling, and the soybeans were thriving.

Once they reached St. Cloud, they resorted to Minnesota highways and sixty-five and fifty-five miles per hour speed limits. The posted speeds had little decipherable effect on the pace of travel, and Martin maintained an average speed of seventy. They drove west for the next forty-five miles. The terrain remained rolling until they reached Paynesville.

On the way, Martin brought up something he'd been contemplating. "Do you think the guy who shot Winthrup saw him taking target practice?"

"Good question. Say you're supposed to meet Bradford at the Upper Landing, and you arrive a little early. Lo and behold, when you look down at your meeting place, the guy's taking target practice. Would that make you a little nervous, put you on edge?"

"Hell, yes!"

"Yeah, me, too."

"But I wouldn't have shot him in the back."

"Under any circumstances?"

Pete and Martin arrived in the tiny town of Belgrade shortly after ten o'clock. The first thing they noticed as they approached the farm of Tim's aunt and uncle was a large, L-shaped building. It sat on the edge of a field, a good five hundred feet from a two-story, white farmhouse, and its sides appeared to be canvass. Beyond a smattering of out buildings, in the distance, a few cattle grazed in a pasture where shade trees provided a bit of protection from the summer sun.

Three mixed-breed dogs came charging from behind the house, barking as Martin and Pete pulled into the farmyard. Getting out of the car, Pete held out a hand, allowing the dogs to sniff.

Pete went to the side door of the farmhouse, while Martin checked behind it.

When his knock went unanswered, Pete called Billy's cell, thinking the kids must be helping with chores. Pete bit his lip when the call transferred to voicemail after the first ring.

"That might be the dairy barn," he said, pointing at the L-shaped building. "I wouldn't think this is milking time, but what do I know? Let's see if they're there."

They walked to the building Pete correctly pegged as the dairy barn and found a man setting out feed. When they introduced themselves, he said only that he was Bob.

Pete wondered if their suits had something to do with Bob's reserved manner. Pete asked about the boys, and Bob said he hadn't seen them in hours and wouldn't hazard a guess where they might be. The next milking was hours away, and that seemed to dictate the boundaries of Bob's interests.

Pete asked, "Should someone escort us on our search? I figured we shouldn't be walking through the buildings here without talking to someone first."

"You talked to me," Bob said turning back to his chores.

THIRTY-EIGHT

As HE AND MARTIN APPROACHED a sizable, metal pole barn that stood with several other buildings near the dairy barn, Pete heard muffled voices. Moving a few steps closer, he put a finger to his lips, signaling Martin.

The whispers grew to a crescendo, followed by silence.

"Billy? Tim?" Pete called softly, uncertain what he was interrupting.

A voice whispered, "Be right there." It might have been Billy, but Pete wouldn't put any money on it.

Seconds later, Billy came running around the shed, eyes dancing and a broad smile across his face.

Tim followed, but with a little less energy. He wore more of a smirk than a smile. Pete wondered if Tim might view their arrival as an imposition. Or perhaps he didn't like being chased, then coerced, and finally visited by police—twice—all in four days. The kids would have some great stories to tell, and embellish, once school resumed, assuming a paper on "How I Spent My Summer Vacation" was still an annual requirement.

"My cousin wanted to come, too. I said he should stay with his mom. Am I right?" Tim asked.

"Good thinking," Pete said. "If you like, you can introduce us later."

In response to Pete's inquiry about how they were doing and how things were going, Tim ran through an exhaustive list of the pluses and minuses of spending time on a farm.

After Tim finished, Pete explained that Billy should come with him, and Tim should go with Martin, so they didn't influence each other's recollections of the man who threatened them on Sunday. "Where would you like to go with Martin?" he asked Tim.

"Can we have the house? It's cooler in there."

"You've earned some points with me by selecting a cool place," Martin said.

Tim shrugged and a smile cracked his frown.

"How about you, Billy?" Pete asked.

"I think it's cool enough in the shade. Is that okay with you?"

When Pete nodded, Billy asked, "How about if we sit on the grass in the backyard? There aren't any lawn chairs, and the picnic table's in the sun."

"The grass is good, but I'm going to put my jacket in the car."

The men and boys walked back towards the house, Billy and Tim out front.

When they reached the car, Pete held a stack of pages out to Tim and said, "Take these. We'll keep the others for now." He handed the rest of the photo lineup and the sketches to Billy. "If we finish first, we'll come in the house, and if you finish first, come out here. Then we'll trade pages. But this isn't a contest. Take your time and look at them carefully."

Billy took his pages to the selected place, shuffling through them as he went. Reaching the shade of a large elm, he plopped down and propped his back against it.

Taking his lead from Pete, Martin left his suit coat in the car. He hated to miss out on any opportunity to get more comfortable. He followed Tim into the kitchen.

The house seemed empty. When Martin asked about it, Tim said his aunt and cousin were in the machine storage building, because Buffy was having kittens. "It took some convincing," he explained, "but my aunt got Billy to stop watching for you guys and come see. Everyone else is doing chores."

They sat at the kitchen table, in air-conditioned comfort.

Switching gears, Tim asked, "Are you close to catching him?"

"Closer."

"Do you know how much longer it'll take?"

Sensing the boy's fear, Martin said, "It shouldn't be much longer. Do you feel safe here?"

"Sorta, but I'd rather be home."

"I understand, and we're doing everything we can."

The warm smile Tim delivered in return for the reassurances surprised Martin.

After placing the stack of pages on the table, Tim carefully worked them into a neat pile, then repeated the ritual he used on Monday when examining the photos of Gerald Alden and Casey Winthrup.

Martin slumped in a chair, observing the process and watching the boy's face, looking for any hint of recognition. At the current pace, he figured he'd be lucky to get home before dark.

"They use computers for everything here," Tim said, perhaps uncomfortable with the lack of conversation. "Do you know that my uncle's milk cows don't even get to go outside? How crummy is that? The only thing is that they never get too hot or too cold. It only takes about fifteen minutes to milk a cow. I haven't tasted unpasteurized milk. I asked to, but they won't let me. Did you ever drink it? My mom said she used to."

The only time Tim looked away from the photos or ceased the monologue was when he glanced at Martin, hoping for some assurance that he wasn't taking too long.

Outside, Pete selected a spot where he could track Billy's eyes as he examined the pictures and sketches.

Billy made his way through the photos, occasionally covering the hair to get a better idea of how the person looked with a do-rag. His eyes jumped back several times to one of the photos. Finishing with that page, he kept it apart from the others.

Pete watched him go through the same careful process with the last page of photos. He didn't ask about it. Instead, he handed Billy the sketches and asked if anyone there looked familiar.

Billy flipped through them quickly, then took more time. The second time through, he removed the sketch Doc helped create. He placed it on top of the two pages of photos he'd separated from the others.

"See these three guys?" Billy asked. "See how they have the same ears?" He pointed to the photos of Walter Linton and Gerald Alden and a sketch. "Mostly, I think he looked like him," Billy said about the composite Doc helped create, "just not quite, and the sunglasses weren't like these."

"Any idea what makes him different from the guy at the Landing?"

Billy looked at the composite for a long time. When he looked back at Pete, he shook his head and said, "I just don't know."

"That's okay, Billy. It's hard work."

Pete collected and shuffled the photo lineup and the composites, and they went in the house.

Tim still poured over the pages he'd been given, but was nearing the end. When he saw what lay ahead, he groaned.

"Bear with us, Tim," Pete said. "You're halfway there."

"Did Billy find anything?" Tim asked.

"I'll tell you when you finish," Pete said. "I don't want you thinking there's a correct answer. All we want to know is what you remember. Different people see things differently. Are you finished with these?" Pete pointed at the pile to Tim's right.

"Uh-huh," Tim sighed, "and if you hang on a second, I'm almost done with this one."

Pete picked up the completed pile, placed the remaining pages for Tim to look at on the table and waited.

Reaching back over his shoulder, Tim handed Pete the other page.

"We'll be outside," Pete said. "Join us when you're finished."

Tim sighed like it was his last breath and went back to work.

It took less time for Billy to go through the new stack. He seemed to have a more distinct idea of the image he sought. When he finished, he looked up and said, "Nothing. The other three I showed you were for sure the closest, especially the sketch that I said had the wrong glasses. Do you know where to find him?"

"Not yet, but we found someone else who may have seen him. That's how we got that composite." Pete explained about forensic artists. "Creating that composite took much longer than it took to look at all these pages," he added. "We wanted you and Tim to look at the photos and the composites to find out if you saw the same man."

Watching and waiting for Tim and Martin, Billy shared a secret with Pete. "I was going to run away if my parents decided to send me to Rochester or Brainerd. My cousins in Brainerd spend the whole summer in the lake, and I can't swim that well. They think that's hilarious. My aunt and uncle in Rochester don't have any kids. Can you imagine me hanging around the house all day by myself, while they're at work? I wanted to stay with my grandparents, but Mom said it would be too hard on them. She didn't care how hard it was going to be on me.

"Tim said if I ran away, he would, too. I was glad. I knew it would be easier if there were two of us. When your partner wouldn't tell us where Tim's parents were sending him, we started planning what to take, and when and how we'd get away. Then Tim's mom mentioned this place, and that both of us could come and bring our bikes. It isn't as good as staying with my grandparents, but it's a lot better than being alone in Rochester or in Brainerd with the fish."

Pete would have laughed at that last remark, but Billy didn't smile when he said it. "If you took off, where would you have gone?" Pete hoped he wouldn't have to use the information later.

"I can't tell you," Billy said, diverting his gaze from Pete. "Tim would kill me if he knew I told you any of this."

"Promise you'll call me if you start thinking about taking off again, Billy. At least give me a chance to try to help you find another solution. Will you do that?"

Billy considered it for several seconds, brows furrowed deeper than Pete thought possible for a kid his age. "I'll try, but I can't promise."

"Let's shake on that." Pete held his hand out, hoping that the handshake would force the boy to think longer and harder before failing to call.

Billy smiled and shook hands with a firm and prolonged grasp.

It made Pete wonder if Billy was happy to get all of that off his chest. Less satisfying, he also wondered if he was getting a heads up.

Motivated by the latter possibility, Pete tried to drive home a few points. "I'm glad you didn't run away, Billy. Your help is critical to solving this case. No one else can help in the ways you and Tim have. My partner and I appreciate it. Also, I think you should know that I'd be worried sick if I didn't know where you were."

"Your kids are pretty lucky." Billy smiled sheepishly.

"Yeah."

The tone of Pete's voice confused Billy, but before the boy could ask about it, Tim and Martin came around the corner of the house.

"Any luck?" Pete asked.

"I think he looks most like this guy," Tim said. "But like I told you before, I'm not really sure. I didn't really look at him. I think I'd recognize his shoes though."

Tim was pointing at the photo of the victim's brother-in-law, Gerald Alden.

Thirty-Nine

PETE THANKED THE BOYS, held up both hands to give them each a high five, and asked if they still had his and Martin's business cards.

Billy produced his from the back pocket of his shorts. Tim said his were in the bedroom.

As Martin drove towards the Twin Cities, via Kinney's farm in Watkins, Pete told him about Billy's selections from the photo lineup and the one composite.

"Billy picked the photo of Alden the last time, too," Martin said. "Linton looks at least ten or fifteen years older than Alden or the man in the sketch. What do you make of that?"

"It's possible that between the do-rag and the sunglasses, the ears made the overriding impression. Also, we don't know when the photo of Walter Linton was taken."

"So you're not going to Chicago?"

"Yes."

Martin rolled his eyes. "Yes, you're going or, yes, you aren't?"

"Yes, I'm still going. You know something, Martin? I really like those kids."

"Yeah, I know. They know it, too. I can tell."

As they worked their way southeasterly on Highway 55, Pete called the Meeker County Sheriff's office. He advised them of the planned visit to Bruce Kinney's farm and gave them an opportunity to participate.

After hearing the county didn't feel compelled to be represented, he called Kinney's home number. It was almost noon, and he hoped Kinney would be inside for lunch.

Kinney said he was just leaving; it wasn't a good time to meet.

And Pete said they'd see him shortly.

When they arrived, Kinney stood in front of the house, arms crossed, feet spread, looking belligerent.

Pete and Martin took turns asking questions. They learned that Gerald Alden arrived around noon last Saturday and left late that afternoon. Kinney said no one could back him up on that because he lived alone and none of his hired help was around at the time.

Pete asked if that was unusual, and Kinney said it wasn't.

Kinney couldn't remember, but thought Alden called Thursday or Friday to plan the trip. He showed Pete and Martin where they took target practice and correctly identified the type of gun Alden said he bought.

Kinney said he hadn't been in or through the Twin Cities for more than a month and hadn't met any of Megan's brothers. He claimed that the only handgun he owned was a .45 caliber Smith and Wesson, and he'd advised Alden to purchase the same.

When Pete asked if it was a good gun for a woman, he seemed surprised and asked what that had to do with anything.

FORTY

E N ROUTE TO REACHING OUT, Pete contemplated his initial appre-
hensions about going there. Acceptance no longer concerned him.

When he arrived, Stew and some of the others held their usual
spot.

He joined them. Watching for Doc, he examined the ears around
him. It qualified as an obsession.

Seeing no sign of Doc, Pete asked Stew.

"Don't know," Stew said, accentuating it with a shrug.

Overhearing them, Benny spoke up. "He's in the hospital."

"What happened?" Pete asked, masking the depth of his concern.

Based on the way other members of their group moved in to better hear what Benny said, Pete assumed many of them hadn't heard
about it.

"Doc was attacked this afternoon just after he left here. Last I
heard, the guy who did it got away. Someone saw it happen and ran
back here. Ray, from the office, called 911."

"Any word on how he's doing?" Pete asked.

"No, that's all I know," Benny said.

"When they open the doors, I'd like to find Ray and see if there's
anything we can do for Doc," Pete said. "What do you think?"

He directed the question at the group, looking for an endorsement to take the lead.

"That would be good," Benny said, and the others nodded. They
seemed happy to give him their proxy.

"Where can I find Ray?" Pete asked.

"His office is to the left when you get inside," Benny said, pointing with a curved index finger.

When the line began forming, worried more about Doc than about food, the group pushed Pete to the head of the line. He was one of the first in the door.

Following Benny's directions, he found an office. The lights were on, but it was empty. Pete walked back into the hall and looked around.

Finally, a middle-aged, balding man in khakis and a polo shirt entered the hall along the same path Pete followed earlier. As he approached, he smiled and asked, "Are you looking for me?"

"Are you Ray?"

"I am."

"My name's Pete Culnane," he said softly. "I spoke with you last Monday. Can we go in your office? I have a few questions about Doc. I understand he was attacked today."

"Yes, I remember you. Please come in and have a seat."

The office was even more meager than Pete might have anticipated for someone in Ray's line of work.

"Where did you get your information?" Ray asked.

"One of the guys who usually eats with Doc told us, while we were waiting to get in. Can you tell me what happened?"

Ray said that another man who eats at Reaching Out saw Doc lying on the sidewalk, about five blocks from there. He also saw a man running away. After checking on Doc, he ran back for help.

"He came in my office and said to get an ambulance right away. I called 911 and went with the man to try to help Doc, until the ambulance arrived, but they were there by the time I was. He had a pulse, but his eyes were closed and he didn't respond to the paramedics' questions. They took him to Regions."

"Do you know the name of the man who found him?" Pete asked.

"The police questioned him. They have his name and a description of the man who ran away. I understand he only saw him from the back, so the description's pretty sketchy. According to the police, it's possible the man who ran away didn't hurt Doc—that he discovered him, got scared and ran."

"Have you heard any more about Doc?" Pete asked.

"No, but it's only been a few hours. I also doubt they'll tell me anything if I call the hospital. I wonder if it'll be on the news."

Pete used Ray's phone to call Martin. He told him about Doc, and asked him to grab another phone, call Regions, and get a report. Waiting for answers, Pete strummed his fingers impatiently on Ray's desk.

Martin's report caused the furrows in his brow to relax, slightly. After looking at his watch, Pete said, "I'll meet you there at 5:40."

He shared the news with Ray before joining his friends.

By the time he got his food and reached the usual table, everyone else was finishing their meals. They hung around waiting to hear the news about Doc.

He told them Doc was alive when the ambulance arrived, and he was still in the hospital.

"I won't be here tomorrow," Pete said, "but I'll let you know when I hear anything."

Pete wasn't in the mood for eating. He worried about Doc and wondered if he'd played a role in the man's beating. Did someone other than Doc know he was a cop? Did anyone see them get on the same bus?

Wrapping his uneaten cookies in a napkin for Martin, Pete stood and reached for his tray and the others followed his lead. They walked out together, and the men dispersed in as many directions as there were men.

As usual, Pete walked the first few blocks and broke into a run. Waiting for the traffic at Jackson and Fourteenth Street, he saw Martin standing restlessly near the hospital's revolving door.

"What did you find out?" he asked as he approached.

"He's conscious, and we can see him."

When they reached his room, they found Doc lying flat on his back, eyes closed. He had a bandage wrapped around his head. His face displayed a variety of bruises and his eyes were blackened. Alongside his bed, a monitor beeped at a monotonous pace.

Pete stood next to the bed. Martin hung back.

Bending over, Pete whispered, "Doc?" After a few seconds, he repeated, "Doc?"

A thin smile slowly made a dent in the beckoned man's face, and his eyes opened slightly. "Pete, I'm glad to see you. You were the first person I thought of when I was hit from behind and went flying. I was wishing you were there. I think you'd stand a better chance in a street brawl than I."

"Did you see who did this to you, Doc?"

"Yes, I got a pretty good look at his face. I wonder if it has something to do with that message for Flash, but it wasn't the same man. Please, don't tell me you want me to sit down with another forensics artist."

"Oh, don't worry. Len's our man," Pete said, trying to make light of Doc's comment. "He'll be glad to help out again."

Doc's laugh was a harrumph.

"Did the man who did this say anything to you, Doc?" Pete asked.

"Only that this was but a sample of what would happen if I didn't keep my mouth shut."

"Did he say what you're supposed to keep your mouth shut about?" Pete asked.

"No, but Flash's murder isn't the only possible explanation."

"Will you tell me about the other possibilities?"

"No, Pete. A non-lethal beating is sufficient motivation to remain silent. Can you help me get a drink of water?"

Pete picked up the Styrofoam cup and moved the straw close to Doc's mouth.

After straining to lift his head, Doc took a small sip, said, "Thanks," and eased his head back on the pillow.

"How are you doing with finding Flash's murderer?" Doc's voice sounded a bit clearer.

"I'm going to Chicago and will use the composite you helped with, Doc. Even before this happened, I was concerned someone could link it to you. Now I'm doubly concerned. I want to find a way to protect you, and I need your help. Is there someplace you can go for several days or maybe even a few weeks?"

"The Twin Cities is my home."

"I know, but it may not be safe. You wouldn't have to go for very long. Do you have friends or family you could visit for a while?"

"I exhausted my welcome at the homes of family before I ended up on the streets, and you've met most of my friends."

"I can make arrangements for you to stay in a hotel in, say, Milwaukee. I don't think you want a cop following you around until we get this resolved. How long will you be in the hospital?"

"I'm supposed to be released tomorrow. And no, I don't want to go to Wisconsin or anywhere else. I'm staying right here."

"But, Doc," Pete said, "what if someone comes after you again? I think they'll be less delicate the next time. I'm not saying that to scare you. I want you to know what you can realistically expect. Also think about this. What if he hurts some of the other guys in the process?"

"I'm an old man, Pete. I don't adapt as well as I once did. When you're my age, you'll understand. I need the security of a familiar place and familiar faces. My chances of survival are better here than in strange surroundings. I hope my friends aren't in danger. I don't think they are. When someone came after Flash, no one else was hurt. I have to trust the same will hold true now. Besides, as I said, this may not have anything to do with Flash . . . or you."

"Is there anything I can say to change your mind? Is there anywhere you've always wanted to go?"

"There are plenty of places I've dreamed of visiting, but not any more. There's nothing you can say and nowhere that I want to go. But thanks for your concern."

"Doc, I know you don't want to hear this," Pete said, "but I want you to work with Len again."

Reaching up and massaging the bridge of his nose, Doc said, "Since you're the one who's asking, the answer is yes. But can we wait until tomorrow? I have a headache that's demanding silence and darkness."

"Tomorrow's fine, but I want it to be tomorrow morning. I want this handled before you're discharged. That way we'll avoid having to do it on the sly. Okay?"

"That's fine. The hospital may protest, but I'm awake by six every morning. The closer to that time the better, as far as I'm concerned."

"Thanks, Doc. I know this hasn't been any picnic."

"Definitely not like the ones my mother prepared. I liked Brad. I don't know why he was murdered, but I want you to catch the creep who did it. Brad was a good person. Life isn't always fair."

"You're a wise man, Doc. Have you ever thought about writing a book?"

"I did write a book, but that was in a different lifetime."

Pete waited, hoping Doc would continue.

He didn't.

FORTY-ONE

ON HIS WAY HOME, Pete thought about calling Katie Benton and wondered if the day's events motivated him.

Due to his insecurities, the outcome of that contact was uncertain. They'd never gone out, yet the relationship was complicating his life. He had a bad case of Katie-on-the-brain. Was there a lesson in that? He'd thought about calling her since running into her in the skyway on Monday, but the demands of the Winthrup case and the uncertainties of his schedule precluded setting up a date. Unpredictable schedules were just one of the complications of dating a cop. Pete had seen how often that sort of thing deep-sixed promising relationships. Should he wait until things calmed down at work?

He grabbed the cordless phone, settled in the recliner and put his legs up. After thinking for several minutes about what he'd say, he dialed the number. When he heard her voice, he pushed the lever forward, lowering his legs. "Katie, I hope it's not too late. I would've called earlier, but I've been tied up. This is Pete."

"Pete, hi. I recognized your voice. It's nice hearing from you."

Buying time, trying to decide whether to wait indefinitely or set up a first date, with the understanding he might have to postpone, he took a stroll down small-talk lane. They talked about the headlines and the weather, what each was reading and the books on their to-read lists, the State Fair and the headliners at the Grandstand shows, the new film at the Omni Theater and the latest movie releases. He didn't know her well enough to talk politics.

He asked about her week, and when she asked he told her about his. He told her about Chicago and, finally, broached the subject of a first date—or whatever you call it when you're their age.

"I've wanted to call you ever since I ran into you on Monday, and kept hoping my schedule would get more predictable so I could. I realize this is short notice, and it's possible that something will force me to cancel, but I'm wondering if you'd like to get together Saturday evening."

"I think you just set the record for the most qualifications tacked onto a single question." Katie laughed. "As far as your question goes, the answer is yes, as long as I don't get run over by a truck, stomped by bulls or struck by lightening before then."

"Touché! I hope to finalize tomorrow, but it could be as late as Saturday afternoon. I hope you'll bear with me. I'm not always in control of my schedule. If Saturday falls apart, how about Sunday, or another day next week? Assuming all goes well in Chicago, my schedule should be easing up."

"I understand, Pete. Don't worry about it. If Saturday doesn't work, sometime next week would be nice."

Pete hung up and smiled. It went even better than he'd hoped. Would she be this nice the next time he was so vague? Assuming, of course, that things went well enough for there to be a next time.

FORTY-TWO

"WHAT ARE YOU DOING HERE?" Martin asked when Pete walked into headquarters at 6:45 Friday morning.

"It's nice to see you, too."

"I thought you were on your way to Chicago."

"First, I'm checking up on you. I want to make sure you aren't screwing off when I'm out of sight."

"Thanks a lot!"

"Martin, I'm kidding. You're here mighty early. Were you able to arrange things with Len?"

"We're going over to Regions in a couple of minutes. Doc wanted us there early and, like you mentioned last night, we want to be finished before the hospital releases him. I know they won't be delighted when we walk in this early but, hey, what the hell."

"Do you mind if I tag along?"

"It's fine with me, but we can handle it," Martin said defensively.

"I'm sure you can, but I want to take a copy of the composite with me."

Although the three men arrived at Regions at 7:05 a.m., they went straight to Doc's room. Passing the nurse's station, they raised a few eyebrows and earned at least one frown, but paid no attention.

Len, however, winked at a nurse who smiled at him.

The second bed in Doc's room was, thankfully, unoccupied.

So was Doc's. He sat next to it, in a chair. His eyes looked a little brighter, but his face looked worse. His posture was encouraging, as was the absence of the heart monitor.

Doc smiled when Pete knocked on the open door.

"How are the head and the headache this morning?" Pete asked.

"The headache's better, the head's a little worse. Have you heard you can only feel pain in one part of your body at a time? I think this qualifies as a demonstration of that theory."

"Are you up to a repeat performance with Len?" Martin asked.

"I am, and the sooner we start, the sooner we'll finish."

"Terrific," Martin said. "But first, look at these photos one more time, just in case we have a picture of him."

Doc went through the pages, then looked at Pete and shook his head.

"We'll wait in the hallway," Martin told Doc and Len. "Let us know if you need anything and take as much time as necessary."

Pete went to the nurses' station and checked on Doc's schedule. He found out breakfast would be delivered at 8:30, followed by a bath or shower.

"If necessary, could you please delay his bath until we're finished? I realize you have a full schedule, but I'm on my way out of town, and it would sure help if he's able to finish before I have to leave."

He supplemented his hard luck story with a smile. One or both did the trick.

Pete's flight was scheduled to depart at ten-thirty. In addition to his carry-on bag, he'd have two locking cases—one for his Glock and the other for the ammo. He figured he had to be at the airport by nine to allow time to declare and check the two locked boxes.

While Martin leaned against the wall outside Doc's room, occasionally standing, then falling back against the wall, Pete paced the halls. He extended the distance traveled, when Martin's tension-relieving tactics began irritating him.

Doc and Len were interrupted only once, when Doc's breakfast arrived. It neither stopped nor slowed their efforts.

Smelling Doc's coffee, Martin decided he needed some. After getting directions to the cafeteria, he caught an elevator.

Both Pete and Len were happy when he returned and handed each a large coffee.

Len took his and told Martin they were wrapping it up.

Pete and Martin looked at the completed work, then at Doc.

"What do you say, Doc?" Pete asked. "Are you happy with it?"

"I am. I especially like the mouth and chin. After he hit me in the back of the head and knocked me down, I knew I had to memorize his face. When he came around in front of me and hit me a few more times, I studied his features. It's possible that the way I looked at him irritated him and resulted in a few additional blows."

Doc's smile amazed Pete. More accurately, Doc amazed Pete.

Pete and Martin looked at the likeness. The ears weren't large and the face didn't ring any bells.

"Doc, I hate to keep harping on this," Pete said, "but I'd sure like to do something to protect you. It . . ."

"Stop right there. I appreciate your concern, but everything I said yesterday still holds."

"But . . ."

"Thanks, but no."

Much as he hated to, Pete gave up. "I'll check on you when I get back from Chicago," he said. "In the meantime, please, Doc, be careful, and call Martin if anything happens we should know about."

Onboard his flight and seated seconds before they closed the cabin door, Pete called Edgar. Feeling under the scrutiny of a cabin attendant reminded him of his first conversation with Megan Alden when she tried to talk before her flight departed.

Edgar answered, and Pete confirmed his scheduled arrival time and plans to rent a car. He asked where they should meet. Edgar said as long as they were on his turf, Pete didn't need to rent a car.

"My captain will be sending you a thank you note and putting you on his Christmas card list," Pete quipped. "I'll see you in about ninety minutes."

He spent the flight studying each photo and comparing it, feature by feature, to the new composite. It was a laborious process, and he was happy the man beside him didn't strike up a conversation.

He passed on a beverage, and it reminded him how, according to his dad, there was full meal service between Minneapolis and Chicago "in the good old days." Now you had to pay for a quarter-ounce bag of peanuts.

Pete was sliding the composites and photo lineup into his leather portfolio just as his row began to deplane. Perfect timing.

FORTY-THREE

EXITING MIDWAY AIRPORT VIA the door designated by Edgar, Pete spotted a guy who looked big enough to play defense in the NFL, with a few pounds to boot. He was propped against the front end of a Crown Victoria.

Pete walked over and asked, "Edgar?"

"That's right. Culnane, I assume. I thought they grew them bigger in Minnesota."

Pete stood a good inch taller than Edgar. But he was grossly underweight if the other man's build set the standard.

"The women back home love bodies like mine. They like someone they can wrap their arms around."

"How many times?"

"Only once, but while we're holding a couple of pizzas, piled on a case of beer."

"If that's all you brought with you," Edgar said, nodding at Pete's carry-on, "after a week or two, I'm going to have to start cramming Vicks up my nose."

"If I'm here a week or two, the way I smell will be the least of my problems. The captain gets really testy if I'm gone that long. He can't live without me."

"I did some checking," Edgar said. "Walter Linton's in Allied Hospital. It's downtown. Should we get something to eat first?"

"How about eating after we talk to Linton?"

Edgar gave Pete a "you've got to be kidding" look, and muttered, "No wonder you look like you starve yourself."

Since Edgar knew the room number and the layout of the hospital, they went directly to Linton's room.

His wife was with him when they arrived. Her chair hugged his bed, and she looked worried. Linton looked flushed and his breathing was labored. The IV plugged into his arm delivered a clear liquid at a good clip.

Learning they were police officers, Linton told his wife, "Why don't you get something to eat? This has to do with work, and it won't be of any interest to you. I'll be fine." His tone left no room for discussion.

It appeared she was accustomed to following his orders. She got up and, without saying a word, bent over the bed and kissed him.

"Don't hurry. You have your book," Linton said. "Relax a while and read."

"Not while you're in this condition I won't." Strain marked her features.

It seemed the man's tongue stuck to the inside of his mouth as he spoke. Pete thought he might know the reason. He became more convinced, when he and Edgar pulled up alongside the bed. Linton's breath was sickeningly sweet.

Pete began the questioning. "You fired Brad Winthrup, Mr. Linton. Why?"

"I'm confident you already know."

"I want your version, Mr. Linton," Pete said.

"He threatened me."

"What did he threaten?" Pete asked.

"To destroy me." Linton reached for his glass of water and took a long drink, holding the last mouthful for a moment. Then it looked like he was running his tongue around the inside of his mouth.

"Explain what you mean by that, Mr. Linton," Pete said.

"It's inexplicable. I was good to him. I had him by the hand and was moving him up in the company."

"How was he going to destroy you, Mr. Linton?" Pete asked.

"You'll have to talk to his attorney about that."

"When did you decide that firing Winthrup didn't solve your problems?" Pete asked.

"I don't know what you mean." Linton's expression reflected surprise, ineffectually.

"You know exactly what I mean, Mr. Linton. Who did it for you?"

"I don't have any idea what you're talking about," Linton's hand shook as he reached for his water glass and took another prolonged drink, concentrating on the glass and avoiding eye contact with Pete or Edgar.

"How did you know where to find Winthrup, Mr. Linton?" Pete asked.

"I don't know where he is."

"Since he's out of the loop, let's go in the hall and wait for his wife," Pete said. "I'm sure she's better informed, probably unbeknownst to her. I'm confident we'll get everything we need from her, and she won't know what she's telling us—until it's too late."

"No! Wait!" Linton coughed. He shakily poured more water—as much on the tray as in his glass, and took another slug.

"I did it, okay. I murdered Winthrup. Leave my wife out of it. She doesn't know."

"Stop right there!" Edgar said, a little too loudly. "I have to read you your rights before you say another word."

He pulled a card with the Miranda warning out of his billfold and read it to Linton. When he finished, including getting Linton's agreement that he understood, he said, "Okay, go ahead, Culnane."

Linton continued before Pete could ask another question. "I was saying that everything would've been fine if Brad had just walked away and left me alone. Instead, he forced my hand. I had no choice. I'm sorry it happened. I had no idea it would lead to this. It wasn't worth his life, and it isn't worth mine, but what's done is done. It's over. I can't change that." Again Linton filled his water glass. He drank like a marathon runner on a ninety-degree day.

"You said it wasn't worth Brad's life. What does that mean?" Pete asked.

"Like I told you, I murdered him."

"Where did you murder him?"

"Right where you found his body."

"And that was?"

"In Minnesota."

"Where in Minnesota?" Pete asked.

"At a place called, ummm, the Upper Landing."

"How did you get to Minnesota?"

After another drink, Linton said, "I drove. I'd have flown, but couldn't with a gun."

"When did you drive there?"

"Friday, so I'd have plenty of time to set things up."

"And when did you come back to Chicago?" Pete asked.

"Sunday, right after I shot him."

"How did you know Winthrup was in Minnesota?"

"Because his attorney's there, and I called his mother for the specifics."

"You said you went to Minnesota on Friday to set things up. What did you do to set it up?" Pete pressed.

"I left a message for Brad at a homeless shelter."

"What homeless shelter?"

"The one his mother told me he was often at. I don't remember the name."

"So you met Brad there and gave him a message?"

"No, I gave a note to someone and asked him to give it to Brad."

"Describe the woman you gave the note to," Pete said.

"I gave it to a man, not a woman."

"Okay, describe the man,"

"He looked homeless. He was ragged, and needed a shower."

"Describe his build,"

"He was average. That's all I remember. I was in a hurry. I didn't want to be seen by Brad. I wanted to talk to him when no one else was around. I didn't pay much attention to how the man looked. Once he took the note and said he'd give it to Brad, I no longer needed him. Why would I remember him?"

"If he was homeless, he must've been pretty much a loser," Pete said. "For example, he probably wasn't very articulate."

"True. I remember that part."

"Why would he be willing to give Brad the note for you? He didn't know you from Adam,"

"I made it worth his while."

"By?"

"I paid him to do it."

"How much?" Pete asked.

"I just grabbed a bill out of my wallet. I think it might have been a ten. I was too busy watching the man to pay much attention. I was worried he'd grab my wallet."

"What did the note say?"

"It said to meet me at the Upper Landing on Sunday morning."

"What time?" Pete asked.

"Nine-thirty on Sunday morning."

"Let's go back to Winthrup's threat," Pete said. "What did he say that you decided you had to fire him?"

"He found out about my personal use of the printers at work and wouldn't let it go. He said he was going over my head. Of course I couldn't let that happen."

"He knew you were the guilty one?" Pete asked.

"At first I didn't think so, but when he kept bugging me about it, I knew I had to stop him before he figured it out. I thought I'd gotten rid of him and saved my neck, until I received interrogatories from an attorney in St. Paul. I couldn't let him succeed. My life's tied up in that company. If he exposed me, I'd lose everything—my job, my retirement. Literally everything!"

Pete remembered the letter Brad sent Megan. It said he couldn't identify the guilty person or persons.

Linton refilled his glass and repeated the process with the water. His mouth seemed to crave moisture.

"Why would you risk a vice-presidency for the little you could make doing this?" Pete asked.

"First, the job no longer pays that well. My pay has taken a dive, compared to the other VPs. Then I was screwed over when they gave out the bonuses last year. They didn't give me the money they should have, so I found another way. All I had to invest was a little time. It was almost one-hundred-percent profit—income tax-free profit. ACS supplied the hardware, the software, the paper, the toner, and the electricity. The expenses to the shell company I set up to handle this were nothing, compared with what I made. About all I had to do was get the orders and send them to the printers. Do you have any idea what you pay a commercial printer to print a page with color? Five thousand pages here, ten thousand there—it's a nice chunk of change. It didn't fully compensate for the way I was treated, but it sure helped.

"Tell me you wouldn't do it," Linton continued. "I don't deserve to be treated the way they're treating me. I helped make the company what it is today, and my reward is that they're putting me on the shelf. Do you have any idea how that feels?"

"I still don't believe you'd gamble losing your job over that kind of chump change," Pete said.

"Do the math. The price I charged per page varied, but I was significantly undercutting local competitors. Working with some nice round figures to make the calculations easier, say on an average week I made twenty cents per page on six thousand pages. That's twelve hundred dollars. If that's 'chump change' to you, how the hell much do cops make these days? I risked it because I never thought I'd get caught. Really, what were the chances? They were infinitesimal. Brad stumbled upon what I was doing. I was going to quit right then, but he didn't know who was doing it, and I just wanted to make a few thousand more. Get while the getting was good."

"Who else from ACS was involved?" Pete asked.

"No one. I didn't trust anyone enough to risk it."

"Who did your customers think was doing the printing, and how did you get the orders?"

"As I said before, I set up a shell company and, with a little help, set up a website. If you undercut the local printing companies and advertise on the Internet, you'd be amazed how much business you can generate."

"Who set up your website?" Pete asked.

"It doesn't matter. I'm the one who murdered Brad."

"What did you use for a weapon?" Pete asked.

"For the website?"

"To shoot Winthrup, Mr. Linton."

"A handgun."

"Describe it," Pete instructed.

Winthrup picked up his glass and took a long drink, causing Pete to wonder if he was buying time. After setting it down, he said, "A Glock."

Pete asked what he used for ammo, and Linton said he bought it on the street, loaded. That was one of the specifications when he bought it, and he was only going after one man, then tossing it. When Pete pressed, he insisted he didn't know any more about the ammo.

Pete got up to leave and Linton asked, "What's going to happen now?"

"We'll place an officer outside your door," Edgar said. "How long are you going to be in the hospital?"

"I don't know. They can't get my blood pressure or my blood sugar under control. Maybe, now that I've confessed, things will be different. I can stop waiting for the other shoe to drop. The die is cast." He sucked thirstily on the straw. As they left his room, he pressed the button to call a nurse.

When he and Pete were back in the hallway, Edgar said, "It's really hard to believe that someone in his position would be so stupid and throw it all away."

"I've seen even dumber antics. For example, the guy making more than one hundred thousand dollars a year who lost his job for stealing money out of the coffee fund at work. In comparison, think how little that netted. Oh, the frailty of the human condition. We sometimes do such stupid things. But Edgar, Linton didn't murder Winthrup."

"Say what?"

FORTY-FOUR

WALTER LINTON DIDN'T MURDER Brad Winthrup," Pete told Edgar.

"And you know who did?"

"Not yet, but I hope to in the next several hours."

"Does Linton know?" Edgar asked.

"Would you confess if you didn't know whom you were protecting?"

"No, but if you don't know and he does, why didn't you try harder to get him to tell you?"

"At least for now, I think it works in our favor to have him think we believe him. I want to talk to his wife. We could both go to the cafeteria and risk having her return to his room while we're gone, but I want to talk to her before he does. Would you like to see if you can find her in the cafeteria, while I wait here?"

Thinking he might find something to tide him over while looking for Ms. Linton, Edgar headed for the elevators.

Meanwhile, Pete positioned himself halfway between the elevators and Linton's room, confident this was the best place to intercept Linton's wife, should Edgar not find her. He waited impatiently, and finally saw Edgar exiting the elevator, alone.

"She'll be here in a minute," Edgar said. "I told her we have a few questions."

"Are you sure she'll show—that she won't take off?" If he was Edgar, he'd have walked back with her, rather than risking her slipping away. If she blew them off, it would throw a wrench into his plan—a big fat monkey wrench.

"You know how curiosity killed the cat? Well," Edgar said, "she's more curious about what's going on than worried about us. She'll be here."

"Is there a lounge nearby?" Pete asked.

Edgar didn't know, but went in search of one or a nurse to ask.

When Pete saw him again, Ms. Linton was at his side. She looked panicky.

Pete walked down the hall to meet them, and she greeted him with an emotional outburst. "Before we talk, I have to check on Walter. A nurse said he has everyone looking for me. Something must've happened."

"I doubt it's a medical emergency," Pete said. "If it was, I'm sure they'd have told you that, not that he's looking for you. If it makes you feel better, we'll ask a nurse to check on him and let you know. We don't need much time. We're in a hurry and running late."

Ms. Linton walked back to the nurse's station with Edgar and Pete.

At Pete's request, a nurse agreed to check on Linton, making it appear routine. If Linton asked, she'd say his wife was on her way back from the cafeteria.

Edgar led the way to a small lounge. On the way, she said to Pete, "I'm sorry. I don't know your name."

Pete gave her his name and displayed his badge and ID.

The lounge, probably once a smoking area, had a couch and several matching chairs. Pete was glad it was vacant.

He and Edgar sat in two of the chairs, and Ginny sat across from them, on the couch. Pete wondered, based on her age and figure, if she was a trophy wife.

Ginny had some questions of her own, and before Pete got a word out, she asked, "Is there a problem at Walt's office? Is that why you're here?"

"Your husband was mistaken about the reason for our visit, but after speaking with us, he understands," Pete said.

"That's good."

"I'm sorry your husband is having so much trouble with his diabetes," Pete said. "I know how difficult it can be to control your blood sugars. My aunt has diabetes, and I know it's a constant struggle for her. Did this episode come on suddenly?"

"He's had problems off and on, but at least he was able to manage, until Sunday afternoon. One moment he was fine, and the next he was drinking water like there was no tomorrow."

"I know stress plays havoc with my aunt's blood sugars. Did something happen on Sunday that was particularly stressful for your husband?"

"No, not that I know of."

"How did you spend the day?" Pete asked.

"I've tried and tried to determine what might've set him off. It was just a regular Sunday, nothing special. We got up and had breakfast. No sweet rolls, no donuts, no muffins. Nothing that should've caused it. Then we read the newspaper. We had lunch, and after lunch we went for a walk. While Walt watched golf on TV, I paid some bills. Walt's son, Theo, called and we both spoke with him. I don't think it was more than an hour before Walter became ill. I asked him if he had any idea why it happened. He said he didn't."

She bent forward on the couch, as though seeking solace in her proximity to the two men, and wrung her hands. "Walt's doctor is stumped, too. He's also very concerned, because all of a sudden Walt's blood pressure is off the charts. That presents a hazard to his kidneys. His creatinine levels, a measure of kidney function, have been elevated for the past few years, and elevated blood pressure can damage the kidneys even further. The doctor also has to be careful about how much insulin he gives Walt. It seems like every time they bring his blood sugar down near normal, several hours later it takes off again. I'm scared for him."

"Does he have a brother or someone to confide in?" Pete asked.

"Yes, he and his brother Scott are very close. Walt's been helping him out. Scott's going through some rough times."

"Where does Scott live?" Pete asked.

"Right now, he's staying with us."

"Did your husband speak with anyone other than Theo and you on Sunday?" Pete asked.

"I'm sure he spoke with Scott, but I don't know of anyone else."

"Was Scott around all day Sunday?" Pete asked.

"No, he was gone most of the day."

"Do you know what time he returned?" Pete asked.

"I think it was late afternoon."

"Was it before or after your husband became ill?" Pete asked.

"I'm not sure, but I think before."

The nurse who checked on Linton stuck her head in the door and said, "Your husband's fine, Ginny, but he's rather perturbed about wanting to see you ASAP."

The way Ginny got to her feet looked like she'd been bounced up and off the couch. "I'd better go!" she said breathlessly.

Pete stood even quicker. It seemed he'd anticipated her actions. "Please, Ginny, just thirty more seconds. When was your husband hospitalized?"

"On Wednesday. He finally got things under control on Sunday, had a few setbacks on Monday, then he seemed to do okay until Wednesday morning. That morning, things got so out of control that he was hospitalized."

"Can you think of anything that happened Tuesday night or Wednesday morning?" Pete asked. He thought he knew. Assuming he was right, Edgar should also know. Edgar's visit to ACS on Wednesday was probably the cause.

"No, he was home all week. He may have spoken with someone at the office. I don't know. I honestly don't know. I have to go now."

"If you answer a few more questions, I'll only keep you another minute. Do you and Walt have any children?"

"Walt has two sons and a daughter."

"Where do they live and work?" Pete asked.

Ginny raced through the answer. "The youngest son, Theodore, lives in Chicago and has his own business—a small publishing company called Linton Press. The other son, Gary, is a veterinarian in Mankato, Minnesota. Walt's daughter, Diane Porter, is an emergency room physician at Danvers Hospital in Chicago. Can I go now?"

Pete thanked her for taking the time to speak with them, and told her that he hoped Walt turned the corner and felt better soon. Eyes floating, she left them and returned to Walt's room.

Pete felt bad for her. Her husband wasn't the murderer, but his level of involvement remained to be seen.

FORTY-FIVE

"NOW WHAT?" EDGAR ASKED PETE on their way to the parking ramp. "How about if I call my partner and update him, while you drive to Theodore Linton's office?"

"Whatever you say. You're calling the shots."

When he reached Martin, Pete told him about Linton's health and his confession, as well as the Minnesota connection—his son, Gary. He asked Martin to drop everything and pay Gary a visit and make sure he took the sketches.

Contrary to Edgar's comment, Pete wasn't calling all the shots. At Edgar's insistence, they stopped for lunch on their way to Theodore's office. Pete wasn't happy about the delay, but they made short work of the meal and arrived at their next stop just before three o'clock.

Edgar did the honors, displaying his badge and asking the receptionist to see Linton.

Looking surprised, she said, "He's in a meeting. His briefcase is here, so I'm sure he'll be back. I just don't know when."

Pete and Edgar settled on a couple of deceptively comfortable-looking chairs, immediately inside the door of the sparsely furnished but tastefully decorated office. They saw rush-hour traffic out a picture window, and the congestion served as a source of amusement, at least for Pete, reminding him why he had no desire to live in Chicago.

It was nearly 3:30 when Pete heard footsteps and saw the receptionist signal someone in the hallway. She looked from the doorway to Edgar and Pete, then back out the door.

Pete excelled at nonverbal communications, and he understood hers. She conveyed something on the order of, *there's someone waiting here that you probably don't want to see.*

In a nanosecond, Pete was out of the chair and in the doorway. The only person in sight, a man, was hurrying down the hall, away from Linton Press.

Pete caught up with him in a few strides, grabbed him by the shoulder and spun him around. "Theodore Linton, right? It's nice meeting you, as well. I'm Peter Culnane. I came a long way to see you."

"I don't know what you're talking about. I forgot something upstairs, and I'm on my way to get it."

"Great. We'll come with you."

Edgar stood in the doorway, arms crossed, watching the proceedings and looking amused.

"That's okay. I'll get it later." Theodore Linton looked resigned. He also looked like his father. Most notable were the protruding ears that father shared with son. His hair was dark brown, thick and propped behind his ears. It hung in a mass of waves down to his shoulders. Billy and Tim would've remembered hair like Theodore's—had it not been for the do-rag. Wouldn't Doc have said something about it? Had Theodore concealed it under the baseball cap?

"There's no sense in wasting your time," Theodore said. "I'm sure you're a busy man. Let's go to my office."

He led Pete and Edgar to a compact office with a view of the Sears Tower.

"You're too gracious," Pete said, while he and Edgar showed Linton their badges and IDs.

"Where were you last Sunday, from eight a.m. until eight p.m.?" Pete asked.

"Why do you want to know?"

"I'll get to that later, Mr. Linton. Just answer the question."

"I was home with my family."

"Can you prove that, Mr. Linton?" Pete asked.

"If you're willing to accept the word of my wife and children, yes."

"I understand you spoke with your father that afternoon," Pete said.

"Yes, so?"

"I also understand that conversation upset him, Mr. Linton," Pete said.

"That's not possible. We talked about my kids and our vacation. I can't think of anything else, other than maybe the Cubs."

"Take a few minutes and think harder," Pete instructed.

Theodore sat behind his desk, looking both impatient and nervous. He rearranged the papers on the surface. He closed his eyes and rubbed his neck. "Do you mind if I go get something to drink?" he asked.

"Yes, I do, Mr. Linton," Pete said. "You'll have plenty of time for that after you answer my questions.

"Is it okay if I ask Barb, my assistant, to bring me something?"

"No, it's not," Pete said.

That elicited a smile from Edgar.

Theodore tilted back in his chair, put his hands behind his head and stared at the ceiling. After a minute, he said, "I don't know what you're looking for."

"Only the facts, Mr. Linton," Pete said.

Theodore said he'd already told them all he remembered about that conversation, and Pete asked if he and his father were close.

"I'd say, very."

"And you know about his current condition?" Pete asked.

"Of course. Dad wouldn't try to keep that from us."

"Do you have any idea what sent your father into this tailspin?" Pete asked.

"He and Ginny can't figure it out. How could I possibly know?"

"I can't answer that, Mr. Linton, but figuring it out might save his life," Pete said.

Theodore was obviously concerned about his father. It was just as apparent that this line of questioning wasn't getting Pete anywhere. It seemed that Walter kept much of his family in the dark.

"What kind of business is Linton Press?" Pete asked.

"We assist authors seeking to be published."

"Are you a vanity press?" Pete asked.

Theodore Linton looked repulsed. "No way! We're involved in what's commonly referred to as 'self-publishing.'"

"Do you do color printing, Mr. Linton?" Pete asked.

"Generally, only the covers."

"So you actually print and bind the books?" Pete asked.

"Correct."

"That's all, for now," Pete said. "Would you give him one of your cards?" he asked Edgar.

Turning back to Linton, he said, "Don't leave the city without first calling Edgar. Understand, Mr. Linton?"

"No, I don't understand. Are you accusing me of something?"

"Not yet."

FORTY-SIX

WHILE PETE AND EDGAR WORKED their way through the Chicago Lintons, Martin drove to Mankato, on a mission to question Theodore's brother, Gary.

Martin estimated that Mankato was eighty-five miles southwest of St. Paul, give or take a few kilometers, so he'd arrive by mid- to late afternoon. Before leaving the office, he went online to find directions to Gary Linton's office and home. He also called the Mankato Police Department. Out of courtesy, he informed the officer to whom he spoke that he planned to question Gary Linton about a St. Paul murder.

His contact opted out on participating, but he asked to be notified of the outcome. The man informed him that Gary Linton was a respected and valued member of the community.

Gary Linton must provide free vet services to law enforcement, Martin decided.

Because he was in for the duration, even if it meant waiting in his car in front of Linton's home or office for hours, Martin laid in a few provisions before setting out. In addition to a couple of bottles of Coke and a bag of chips, he bought a bag of peanuts and two candy bars.

This time, he also brought his matrix. Given the opportunity, while waiting around, he'd review and update it. Keeping it current was becoming a full-time job. Things were happening so fast.

On the way to Mankato, he gleefully contemplated the feather in his cap that he'd earn by arresting the murderer without Pete's help. He assumed it fair to define it that way. After all, Pete was in Chicago, gathering information, while he was here, alone, on the front line. That drew a broad grin and a chuckle.

Gary Linton's animal hospital stood on the southern edge of Mankato, and several times Martin had to refer to the directions he'd printed. The building, a compact brick structure, was freestanding. Several cars occupied the parking lot, so he anticipated not only Linton's presence, but also that clients might complicate the situation.

Seeking protection from the heat of the sun, he found a spot in one of the few shaded parking spaces and began contemplating all of the possible ways this might play out. Once he stepped out of the car, he wanted to be prepared for every eventuality.

What were the chances that Linton had a gun in there? He reached inside his suit coat and touched his own gun.

Was Linton crazy enough to try to escape by taking a hostage? Maybe he should have insisted on backup from the Mankato P.D. Now in place, he didn't want to regroup. If all went smoothly, doing anything other than staying the course might make him look foolish. What were the chances that a respected member of the community, and a veterinarian, would emerge with guns blazing anyway?

As he prepared to leave the car, a woman exited the building and started walking towards the lot. She looked at him, turned and went back into the building.

He couldn't help it. He wondered if that was relevant. Was she sent to check him out? These days, any idiot could recognize an unmarked car. What would she report? How would she describe him?

Martin peeled back the wrapper of a candy bar. He needed to take on some sustenance before he faced Gary Linton and, possibly, his defenders.

After pulling the last bite from the wrapper with his teeth, he crumpled the wrapper, stashed it in the plastic bag that hung from a knob on the dashboard and brushed the back of his hand across his mouth.

Taking a deep breath, he reached for the door handle. "T minus one minute and counting," he whispered.

FORTY-SEVEN

DOC STOOD IN FRONT OF REACHING OUT, a little worse for the wear. A gauze bandage encircled his head, and his face looked like he'd done a face-plant off a loading dock. Staring at the ground, he waited for his friends and thought about Harry, better known as Pete in some circles. He missed the cop. Harry had been a terrific diversion.

Those thoughts reminded Doc of Harry's question. Were there places he dreamed of visiting? Of course there were, beginning with Ireland and Italy—the birthplaces of his mother and father. It didn't matter how old or how rich you were, did it? Weren't there always places you wanted to see? There had to be for as long as a person drew breath. When that stopped happening, life must sink to some level of hopelessness. Even though he'd never again leave the Twin Cities, he still dreamt.

"Just the man I'm looking for," an unfamiliar voice said, startling him.

Doc had never seen the man before, and the first thing to cross his mind was Harry's concern for his safety.

"Sorry, my friend. I think you have the wrong man. I don't know you."

"That's right, but I know you. I had an excellent description. It couldn't have been more accurate."

Doc back-pedaled slowly away from the stranger, hoping to surreptitiously stretch the distance between them. He'd been this scared before, but never more so, and he'd lived through some frightening moments in six-plus decades.

"I didn't see you this noon. Were you here this noon?" asked the man.

"No, I wasn't here." In a half-hearted attempt to delay the inevitable, Doc said, "My friends will be here any second. Would you like to join us for dinner?"

"You seem nervous, Doc. I didn't mean to scare you."

Worse yet, the stranger knew his name. *What does that mean? The guy with the note knew Brad's name. Am I about to buy the farm?* "No," Doc said. "Why would I be scared? But you didn't answer my question. Would you like to join us?"

Before the man responded, Doc regretted asking. What might happen to his friends if the offer was accepted?

"Yes, I'd like that," the man answered.

The gauze bandage around Doc's head did an inadequate job as a sweatband, but it was one of the drier places on his person. He fidgeted, stepped from one foot to the other, clenched and unclenched his fists in his pockets and continued looking, desperately, for anyone who might be able to stand up to this stranger. Harry was the first person who came to mind. He could handle this guy. Doc was sure of it. This man looked to be about the same age as Harry. He was a bit shorter and a few pounds heavier, but then who wasn't?

But Harry was gone, so he needed either one young and vital person or a gang of friends. At the moment, Doc's altruism was slinking into the backseat, succumbing to fear. It was still too early for his friends—or too late, depending on your perspective.

He realized that he should have given a little more consideration to Harry's offer. When his wife walked out on him and his career tanked, he didn't think he cared if he lived or died. Had he miscalculated? Why did death seem so much less ominous when it wasn't staring you in the face?

"Relax, Doc. I'm here for a friend."

Like I didn't know. And you're here to finish the job, right? Was this friend the one who killed Brad—or the one who beat me up yesterday?

"He asked me to check on you," the stranger continued. "He's worried about you."

Worried about me? Or worried about the problems I'm creating for him? Doc wondered, but asked, "Does this friend of yours have a name?"

"Most people do, don't they? His is Pete. Pete Culnane."

Letting out a deep breath, Doc said, "Tell Pete Culnane that his efforts to protect me almost resulted in my demise. Between raising my suspicions about strangers and sending a stranger to check on me, he almost gave me a coronary."

"Sorry, Doc. Guess I didn't go about it very well. Based on what Pete said, it didn't occur to me that you'd be jumpy. It only makes sense though, when I look back on what he said. If I'd given you a heart attack, he probably would've killed me."

"Are you sure he wouldn't have settled for turning you over to the judicial system?"

"Not in this case. He'd have wanted to handle it himself, all by himself. You don't know the side of him I know. He can be a real hardass."

"No kidding? I haven't had a glimpse at that."

"I'm surprised you didn't see it when you wouldn't let him protect you. I ran right smack into it when he decided I was trying to kill myself."

"What do you mean?"

"There was a time when I wouldn't have told anyone about that. Pete and I were partners, until I drank my way out of a job. Then things really went sour."

He winked before continuing.

"Pete grabbed me by the throat and shook me back to reality. He stood by me when the rest of my "good buddies" abandoned me. He's helped me through some tough times. I love him like a brother . . . better than a brother."

"Do you mind if I ask your name? I want to thank Pete and compliment him on his taste in friends."

"I don't mind a bit. I'm Chris, Chris Gannon."

Chris stayed for dinner, and Doc took care of him. So did Stew.

When they finished, before driving home, Chris watched Doc from a distance until he reached his final destination for the night. He understood why Pete was fond of the man.

Forty-Eight

"W E SEEM TO BE RUNNING OUT of people faster than we're getting useful information," Edgar said as they got back into his car. "Does that worry you, Culnane?"

"Not yet. Ask me in a few days."

"Where do we go from here?" Edgar asked.

"How about if I update my partner and see what's happening with Gary Linton while you drive us to visit with Scott Linton?"

"To protect and serve, that's my mission. You say drive, and I say where and how fast. Just one thing, though. We could have saved a lot of time if we'd gone to Linton's home first. Driving into downtown at this time of day is a good thing to avoid."

Pete snapped his fingers and shook his head. "I think all of the radio signals in the Chicago area are interfering with my telepathic waves. But don't worry, I'll keep working on it."

Walter and Ginny Linton and hence Walter's brother, Scott Linton, lived in a condominium in the middle of downtown Chicago, and Pete was no more pleased than Edgar with the traffic. But Edgar was more successful in reaching Linton's home than Pete was in reaching Martin.

When they finally arrived, they walked into the entrance and viewed the elaborate lobby. A baby grand piano sat in one corner. Sofas and high-backed chairs provided seating for several small groups. Beautifully arranged flowers adorned the end tables. Bookcases held leather-bound editions and perfectly symmetrical, potted trees were grouped in balanced patterns.

"Sooner or later we have to strike oil so, in hopes it's here, let's discuss strategy," Pete said.

When Pete felt they were as prepared as they reasonably could be, Edgar stepped up to the security desk. He exchanged a few words with the woman stationed there, and his badge bought access to the elevators. Before long they were on their way to the thirty-second floor.

"Does she think he's here?" Pete asked.

"Said she doesn't know. She hasn't seen him today."

It felt a little over zealous under the circumstances, but more than one dead cop would still be around if he or she had been more cautious. For that reason, the two men stood on either side of Linton's door, and Edgar knocked. There was no response. He knocked a second time, and this time he put more of his weight behind it.

"Is that you, Ginny?" a man's voice called out.

"No," Edgar said.

The man who answered the door was about the height and build described by Billy, and looked a year or two younger than Walter Linton. His ears were large, his hair was black and sparse, and his eyes drooped. He was tying his tie when he opened the door.

"Police!" Edgar barked, backing the man, none too gently, into the living room.

An elegant Persian rug decorated the hardwood floors. It matched the burgundies and golds on the four chintz-covered Louis XV armchairs and sofa. Occasional tables held Waterford crystal lamps. The arrangement of the furniture took advantage of the view of Lake Michigan, visible through the sliding-glass doors.

Edgar's eyebrows went up as he observed the furnishings. "There's nothing to get excited about. My friend here has a few questions for you. You're Scott Linton, aren't you?"

"How did you get in here? This building has a security system. No one is supposed to get in if I don't buzz them in. I'm calling the desk. You sons of bitches can't barge in here. I have rights!"

"File charges later," snapped Edgar. "In the meantime, are you Scott Linton?"

"Who wants to know?"

Pete and Edgar displayed their badges and IDs.

"One last time," Edgar snorted. "Are you Scott Linton?"

"Yes, so?"

"You're going to answer our questions," Edgar said. "You can do it here or at the precinct. Take your pick."

Scott Linton deflated. His shoulders slumped and appeared to absorb half of his neck and several inches of his height. He aged ten years in five seconds.

"Sit down," Edgar instructed, pushing him towards a chair that looked rarely, if ever, used.

After Linton did as instructed, Pete sat facing him, and Edgar stood behind Linton's chair.

"If you cooperate, Linton, this will be more pleasant," Edgar advised. Turning to Pete, he said, "Go ahead, Culnane."

Pete was confident that in any other situation, Edgar would make it nearly impossible not to play the good cop. Today, he seemed destined to be part of a bad cop/bad cop team. Under different circumstances, he might have felt sorry for Scott Linton.

Before Pete uttered a word, Linton shouted, "I don't know why you're here! I didn't do anything. I don't even have an unpaid parking ticket!"

"How long have you been staying with your brother and sister-in-law?" Pete asked.

"What does that have to do with anything?"

"Just answer the question," Pete said.

"Or else we'll cuff you and haul you in," Edgar chimed in.

"About a month."

"It was good of your brother to take you in when you needed a leg up." Pete said.

"It was."

"You must feel fortunate. Not everyone would open their home to their brother. Don't you agree?" Pete asked.

"Yes."

"Do you have other siblings?" Pete asked.

"Yes, two other brothers."

"But you're closest to Walt?" Pete asked.

"Yes."

"Does that go both ways?" Pete asked.

Edgar shot Pete an inquisitive look.

"Definitely." Linton appeared to be settling in and relaxing a bit.

"So you felt compelled to help him, didn't you?" Pete asked.

"I don't know what you're talking about," Linton said, tensing.

"Sure you do. Think about it."

Moving his hateful stare from Pete to the floor, Linton sat there. He didn't speak and he didn't move.

Confident he could wait the man out and hoping Edgar wouldn't ruin it, Pete remained silent.

Edgar looked quizzically at Pete.

In response, Pete shook his head. As far as he was concerned, the longer this took the better.

Edgar shrugged and returned his attention to Linton.

Linton resurrected the bluster and snarled, "If you expect me to know what you're talking about, you're crazy."

"Let me help you out," Pete said. "Bradford Winthrup."

"What about him?" Scott asked.

"What about him and your brother?" Pete asked.

"You'll have to ask my brother."

"I did," Pete said. "It's making him sick. It's probably killing him. This much stress isn't good for anyone, especially someone with diabetes. This is your chance to repay him. You can save his life."

That little speech seemed to affect Linton. His head and shoulders slumped, and he went back to staring at the floor.

"You tried to help your brother," Pete said. "Generally, that's a noble thing. In this case it wasn't."

"I don't know what you mean." Scott looked frantic . . . and trapped.

"I know you do," Pete said. "You're not getting out of here until you tell us."

Or after Culnane tells us, Edgar thought. He sure wouldn't be handling it this way.

"He was trying to destroy my brother," Linton said. His face was painted with hate.

"How so?" Pete asked.

"I thought you said you knew all about it?"

"I do. I just want your version. I got your brother's when he confessed to Winthrup's murder."

Linton was up and out of the chair, yelling, "He didn't do it!"

"Yes, Scott, he did," Pete said, "and he confessed a couple of hours ago."

Linton shook his head forlornly.

Pete gave him time to contemplate it.

The opportunity was interrupted when someone knocked on the door.

FORTY-NINE

GARY LINTON'S VETERINARY CLINIC was neat and modest, painted in shades of blue and green. As Martin waited for the woman behind the counter to notice him, he wondered if the color scheme sought to calm the animals by resembling grass and sky. He scanned the room looking for the woman who started out the door and returned. He didn't see her. *Curious . . . very curious.*

The half-dozen patrons accompanied their menagerie, and most of these animals looked reasonably tame. In one corner, Martin saw a lady holding an elderly miniature poodle with one leg in a cast. A pair of cocker spaniel puppies tugged on the ends of a rope toy while a woman clutched both of their leashes close to her chest. A kid held a lizard that must have been two feet long. The reptile gave Martin the evil eye. A huge golden retriever looked big enough to carry his son, Marty, on its back. A tiger-striped cat sat on an old woman's lap and a couple of small animal carriers on the floor at her feet appeared to hold another cat or two. The lizard was still staring at Martin.

"Are you here to pick up your pet?" asked the woman behind the counter.

After saying no, that he only needed a few moments to speak privately with the vet, the woman suggested he take a seat to wait for a break between appointments.

Martin selected a seat that maximized the distance between himself and the others. It didn't help. He felt a sneeze coming on and his allergies acting up. Only he didn't have allergies.

For more than thirty minutes, he sat in the waiting area—an appropriate moniker, for wait he did as his discomfort grew. The lizard was still waiting, too, and the creature continued to stare at Martin and snap his tail in slow motion.

Martin felt restless. *Could Linton have left through a back door?* He decided to give it a little time. He didn't want to overreact. If all else failed, he had Linton's home address.

Martin hadn't flashed his badge because he wanted to avoid causing a stir or hurting someone. Too many innocent people were already in danger, and Pete would have handled it this way.

Maybe the woman at the desk assumed he represented a drug company. No, that couldn't be. Those people received more friendly greetings. They brought enticements. He should have done that. He could have handed the woman a bag of cookies.

Back on his feet, intent on asking how much longer he had to wait, he finally heard his name. Following a vet tech down the hall, he felt his cell phone vibrate. *Great! It never failed. It has to be Pete.* But Martin couldn't stop and look. He had to be fully aware of his surroundings and the layout. His life might depend on it.

His escort's uniform looked like surgical scrubs and matched the waiting room colors. She ushered him into Gary Linton's office and instructed him to have a seat.

He watched her turn and walk back down the hall.

Now alone, rather than sit with his back to the door, Martin stood with his back to the desk and faced the door for several minutes. Suddenly considering that being asked to wait there might be a ruse to provide Linton with an escape route, Martin decided to return to the reception area.

As he rushed out of the office, he nearly trampled Linton, as the other man came around a corner.

"Sorry to keep you waiting," Dr Linton said as he bumped into Martin—or vice versa. "Come in. Have a seat. What can I do for you?"

The veterinarian looked to be in his mid-thirties. Check. He was about Martin's height and had an average build. Check.

Martin stared at him. Gary Linton didn't have large ears like the sketch of the murderer, and he bore no resemblance to the composite of the man who attacked Doc. His nose was too small and his face was too long and narrow.

"I believe you know one or both of these men." He handed the material to Linton. When Gary looked back at him, Martin continued. "Take your time. This is very important."

"Important because?" Gary returned his attention to the sketches.

"One of those men murdered a man, the other beat up his friend."

"Why would you think I know them?"

"I'm asking the questions here," Martin said and crossed his arms.

The vet shrugged and resumed looking at the composites. When he looked up he said, "I'm sorry, but I don't know either of them."

"Let me make this clear. Telling me the truth is in your best interest. I don't think you want to be hauled in on charges of obstruction of justice or as a co-conspirator. That's what you're up against."

"I understand what you're saying, but that doesn't change anything. Unless these likenesses bear a poor resemblance to the men they're meant to portray, I don't know either of them."

Martin was exasperated. "Look at the features one at a time. These likenesses are rarely perfect. Do any of the features resemble anyone you know?"

"First, the only thing that's distinct about this guy," Linton said, holding up the composite of the murderer, "is his ears. But at least five percent of the population must have ears like that."

"Fine. List all of the people you know with ears like that."

"The sunglasses don't help, you know. If I could see his eyes . . ."

"Tell me everyone you know who has ears like that," Martin said, growing restless.

"Well, my dad, one of my uncles and my brother. I know some of my cousins have ears like that. We refer to it as the haves and have-nots in the Linton family. Just so you know, other than the ears there's no resemblance to the people I mentioned. If you want to leave it here, or if you let me make a copy, maybe someone will come to mind later."

"This one," Linton continued, holding up the other composite. "I don't see anything distinctive about him. He looks like John Q. Public. He looks like a hundred guys walking down the street on any given day. I don't know what else to tell you, except, again, if I keep a copy, maybe someone will come to mind."

FIFTY

"IF YOU'LL TAKE HIM INTO A BEDROOM and keep him from making a sound," Pete told Edgar, tossing his head in Scott Linton's
direction, "I'll get the door."

After looking at Pete like he'd asked him to throw Linton off the
balcony, Edgar placed his hand on Linton's shoulder and applied
pressure.

Scott's eyes went wild, and he called out, "Joey . . ."

Just those two syllables escaped, before Edgar covered his mouth
with a meaty hand. Holding it there proved challenging, as Scott
struggled feverishly, to free himself.

Edgar half-helped and half-lifted Scott out of the chair, knocking
it over with a bang. Then he strong-armed him down a hallway to
the last bedroom.

Being no match for Edgar's size and strength didn't deter Scott.
He flailed desperately, kicking wildly and trying to grab hold of each
door frame as they passed, occasionally succeeding in getting enough
of a grip to slow their progress.

A nervous voice called, "Dad, are you okay?" from the hallway
outside the apartment.

After walking to the door and waiting for Edgar to get in position, Pete placed his right hand on the butt of his Glock and braced
for an onslaught from the man on the other side. Grabbing the handle with his left hand, he flung the door open.

The man standing there looked to be in his late twenties—Brad's
age, of average height and a muscular build, with dark curly hair and
Walter and Scott Linton's ears. He looked shocked. Without a word,
he spun and ran.

Certain that words wouldn't stop the man who had to be Scott Linton's son, Pete ran after him. He paused long enough to yell over his shoulder that Edgar should call for reinforcements.

Pete and Edgar had scouted the building before barging in on Scott, so Pete knew there was a bank of four elevators and two stairwells.

Joey Linton passed the elevators and raced to the stairway. A logical move for someone bent on escaping. He grabbed the doorknob, turned it and yanked. He had so much adrenaline behind the pull that his hand flew off the knob. Frantically, he grasped it again, this time opening the door.

Pete dove at it, hoping to slam it closed before Joey got through. He succeeded, halfway. The door slammed, with Joey on the other side. Pete seized the knob and jerked the door open.

Joey was fast. By the time Pete was inside the carpeted stairwell, Joey was rounding the corner onto the landing for the thirty-third floor.

"Stop! Police!" Pete yelled.

The words had no visible effect on the other man's actions.

As he ran up the stairs, Pete tried to anticipate Joey Linton's plan. At the same time, he wished Joey had run down, rather than up the stairs. At some point, it might have given him a vertical advantage.

He wondered if the reason Joey went up was because he believed he was in far better physical condition than his pursuer. If Pete was right about Joey's age, relatively speaking, Linton had roughly a ten-year advantage. Pete was in good shape, but the additional years threw the overall advantage to Joey.

There was a laundry room and a trash room on the thirty-second floor, Walter Linton's floor. *Was there one on every floor?* Pete wondered. *Was there a pool? How about an exercise room? What else?* Undoubtedly, Joey knew more about the building than he, and that was significant. Pete wished he'd more thoroughly investigated the layout. Forewarned is forearmed, but thinking of that now contributed nothing to the effort.

Could Edgar get reinforcements here in time to make a difference? Would the few seconds delay caused by calling for Edgar's help insure Joey's escape? Probably.

"Stop! Police!" Pete shouted again when he reached the landing for the thirty-third floor.

Joey rounded the corner and began his ascent to the thirty-fifth floor.

Pete decided to shed his suit coat. In the process, he hoped to cool down a few degrees and improve his flexibility—just in case. That also meant it wouldn't be an impediment, if he had to draw his Glock.

He told himself that the two additional steps Linton gained on him were attributable to that action. It was more encouraging than the alternate explanation—that it reflected the superiority of pursued over pursuer.

Would he be doing better if he'd trained for Grandma's Marathon this year? He decided to stop wasting time on unproductive thoughts. Either Linton believed he could put enough distance between them in ten stories or he had another plan. Pete, too, had to devise a plan.

Putting aside the current lack of justification, and looking at it only from a technical standpoint, drawing the Glock was ill-advised. Linton was so far ahead of him, he didn't have an unobstructed shot. And what if someone stepped into the stairwell at the most inopportune moment? He didn't want to have to live with what that might mean.

Pete did his best to take each turn as tightly as possible, grabbing the railing with his inside, left hand and using centrifugal force to accelerate in the turn. He was panting, but not gasping. He didn't hear Joey's breathing, so he couldn't judge the other man's level of exhaustion. He wouldn't let that discourage him.

Initially, Pete yelled, "Stop! Police!" at least once each rung. By the thirty-seventh story, he cut that by half. He didn't want to waste the breath, since the command wasn't stopping or even slowing his adversary.

Pete didn't pour everything he had into this chase. Not knowing Joey's plan, assuming he had one, Pete had to conserve energy and strength. If he reached the final floor on the other man's heels and was too spent to prevail, the outcome might not be pretty. He knew he could run up ten stories. He didn't know how much energy he could muster afterwards, let alone how much he'd need to overcome Joey. He couldn't be totally reliant on his gun and wished he knew how tired Joey was now, and would be by the time they were face to face. That would be soon, Pete hoped.

He wondered if Joey knew Pete had a gun and decided he must, unless he thought Pete was lying about being a cop. But then, why was Joey running?

Trailing by nearly a story and a half, judging from the sound of the other man's footfalls, Pete resolved to stay the course and watch for any cute moves by the other man. The only sound he heard, assuring him that Joey remained in the stairwell, was the pounding of feet that were not in synch with his.

Almost to the landing for the thirty-eighth floor, Pete saw the door begin opening. "Close that door! Police!" he yelled.

The door began closing, slowly, and Pete sped up the process, taking the turn wide and giving it a good shove. "And keep it closed!" he added, thinking how right he'd been about being extra cautious with his gun. He also felt lucky that the door began opening well after, rather than before, Joey passed. It would have been too easy to grab the person on the other side of the door and turn this into a hostage situation. *Was Joey crazy enough to pull a stunt like that?* Pete wished he knew.

As he neared the thirty-ninth floor, the sound of Joey's footsteps ceased. What the hell? Did he stop? He couldn't possibly be to the forty-second and final story, could he? No way. Pete knew Joey was very close to a story and a half ahead of him. He had to be between landings. Maybe he collapsed? Pete gained a few seconds of encouragement from that possibility before discarding it. Were it true, he should have heard something.

Maintaining the same, sure pace, Pete continued his pursuit. That was his best bet.

He wondered who benefited more from the adrenaline rush, the pursuer or the pursued. Believing it was the latter was preferable from the standpoint of his ego. But that didn't bring him an inch, much less one flight, closer to Walter Linton's nephew.

Undaunted, aside from placing his right hand on the butt of his Glock, Pete continued, at the same time doing his best to muffle the sound of his footsteps and labored breathing.

Considering Linton's possible escape from the stairwell, Pete tried to remember if the door on the thirty-second floor made a sound as it closed behind him. A hydraulic device insured it didn't remain open, but how tight was the tension on it? He'd been in other stairwells, on other chases, when the sound was loud enough that it had to be obnoxious for the residents. He didn't remember that being the case here. Would he remember? Or was he so involved in the chase that he was oblivious to everything else?

What about Joey? He wasn't crazy, or arrogant enough to burn time easing it closed, was he?

As Pete reached the landing for the fortieth floor, he heard swift footfalls. It sounded like they were approaching. There was no time to act or react. All he saw was a flash of color—Joey's tie—as he flew at and landed on top of Pete with enough momentum to knock him to the floor.

Both men were sprawled on the fortieth floor landing, and Joey had the advantage. Not only was he on top, he also had Pete's left arm pinned under his right knee.

Punches flew, as both men fought to gain the upper hand.

Joey delivered two quick right jabs to Pete's face, and Pete felt the bursts of pain.

With his left arm pinned, Pete grabbed Joey's necktie with his right hand and pulled as hard as he could to the right. Simultaneously, he tried to buck Joey off his chest and arm.

That infuriated Joey, who connected twice with Pete's jaw.

Pete still held onto the tie and, after the failed attempt to use it for leverage, gave it a swift yank and let go.

Trying to resist the pull, Joey was thrown off balance when Pete released his tie.

Pete made use of that, connecting with Joey's jaw. It was as close as he could come to a roundhouse from this position.

Joey's head snapped back.

Pete's upper-body strength contributed to the effort as he utilized the marginal shifting of the other man's weight. By rolling himself and Joey to come out on top, Pete regained the benefit of two hands and arms. He instantly punched Joey's face, twice, with his right fist. He threw two quick jabs to Joey's jaw with his left, while pulling his Glock from the shoulder holster with the right. He believed Joey was sufficiently dazed for him to succeed.

He was wrong.

The Glock had barely cleared his holster when Joey knocked it away.

Furious, Pete delivered an uppercut that sent Joey's chin towards the ceiling. Not taking any chances this time, Pete hit him once more in the face, then put everything he had left into three punches to Joey's belly.

When Linton gasped for air and began coughing, Pete hurtled down the stairs to retrieve his Glock. Gun in hand, he worked his way back up the steps at a measured pace, taking deep breaths.

Joey was on hands and knees, watching him and coughing.

Several steps away, still beyond Joey's reach, Pete thundered, "Stay on your hands and knees. Back up—slowly—until you reach the wall. When you get there, sit down and put your hands in the air. If you resist again, I'll blow your damned head off!"

Whether exhaustion or belief in the spoken word was the deciding factor, Pete didn't know. Either way, Joey Linton followed the instructions to the letter, without taking his eyes off the Glock.

Interpreting that stare, Pete growled, "If you're thinking about going airborne again, my face will be the last thing you see this side of hell."

FIFTY-ONE

WHILE THE MIND GAME PLAYED OUT, Pete pulled his cell phone from his pocket. Glock and eyes on Joey, he maintained a cautious distance plus a buffer.

Flipping the phone open, thankful for the redial feature, he found the only recent call with a 312 area code. After highlighting the Chicago number, he hit the talk button. All of that took substantially longer than normal, because he had to keep transferring his attention from Joey to the phone and back.

Edgar answered, saying, "He get away?"

"Too close for comfort." Pete explained where he was and added, "Can you secure his father and help me? If not, can you send someone? Minimally, I need cuffs and a tape recorder."

They waited so long for Edgar or backup from the Chicago P.D., that Joey began complaining that he couldn't hold his hands up any longer.

With a measure of pity, Pete instructed him to rest them on his head.

The words were barely out when Edgar entered the stairwell.

Pete glanced over his shoulder, insuring the new arrival was Edgar.

"Judging from your face, I'd have guessed he came out on top," Edgar said. "I better get you through security when you fly home. I don't think they'll be able to match that face to your ID."

While Edgar climbed the few stairs to reach his side, Pete told Joey to stand slowly, staying close to the wall, turn, face the wall and put his hands behind his back.

When he'd done so, Edgar and Pete walked to the fortieth floor landing. Pete pressed the barrel of the Glock into Joey's back and whispered, "Don't even think about moving. I'm feeling jumpy."

Edgar whispered, "Miranda?" and Pete nodded.

"Don't say a word until I read you your rights," Edgar barked. Before Joey could blurt out a confession and turn all of this into a wasted effort, Edgar took care of the Miranda warning.

Pete asked, "Where do you want to take him, back to Walter Linton's, to the precinct or . . . ?"

"Since we don't know when Ms. Linton will return, let's go to the precinct."

Edgar used his cell to arrange transportation for Scott. He told whomever that he and Pete would take Joey with them.

When they arrived at the precinct, with the legal formalities already out of the way, Pete got started. "Where were you last Sunday, between 6:00 a.m. and 6:00 p.m.?"

"Home with my wife, except when we went out to lunch and picked up some groceries."

"She'll vouch for you?" Pete asked.

"Of course."

"Give me a number where I can reach her," Pete said.

"She's at work for another four hours. Her number's in the contact list on my cell."

"Four hours is a long time," Pete said. "We'll do that later. We may as well continue. Listen, Joey. Joey Linton, right?"

No reply.

"Anyway, Joey, I know all about your uncle and his problem, and I know how you tried to fix it for him. Who'd have thought that a couple of simple cops like Edgar and me would figure it out, huh?"

"My uncle's in the hospital. How could I fix that? I'm not a doctor."

"That's not the problem I'm talking about. Walter confessed. He now has a couple of cops outside his hospital room. Do you feel guilty? You caused his current health problems. Your aunt's scared, with good reason. What do you think the chances are that he'll survive until the trial? If he does, I can pretty well guarantee he won't survive the sentence, even with time off for good behavior. Since you put him in this predicament, don't you think you should 'fess up and give him a break?"

The fifth Linton he and Edgar had questioned today appeared to be thinking.

"How did you find out that Winthrup was in Minnesota?" Pete continued.

"I don't know who you're talking about. I don't know anyone by that name."

"That's strange. I met someone who swears they saw you running from a location by the Mississippi. The part that's in Minnesota."

Joey shook his head.

Pete looked at Edgar and said, "I wonder how they're doing with his dad. If he confesses, we can let this guy go. My main mission is to get a conviction. I have a track record to maintain, and I'm working on a promotion. The way prices are going up, I need it just to stay even."

"I'll check," Edgar said. Leaving Pete and Joey, he got a cup of coffee and drank it at a leisurely pace. He wanted Joey to have plenty of time to think, and worry, about his dad and his uncle.

Pete sat at the table, facing Joey, with an ankle braced across the other knee and his fingers laced behind his head. He didn't take his eyes off Joey, but his gaze was a lazy, nonchalant one. And he didn't say a word.

Edgar interrupted the standoff when he returned, wearing a satisfied grin. "Joey can go," he announced. "His old man confessed. It's being typed up, and he'll sign it. He has all the details, down to a gnat's ass, so he's our man. Sorry, you got messed up needlessly, Joey. It wouldn't have happened if you hadn't run. Keep that in mind the next time you decide to run from the police. Follow me. I'll get you out of here."

Joey did as Edgar instructed. But halfway through the door, he gave Edgar a shove and yelled, "My dad didn't do it, you stupid son of a bitch!"

"Like I told you," Edgar said, "we have our man."

"I know this is a game. You can't do this!" Joey sputtered.

"Let's go. You need to find a way home, and don't touch me again," Edgar warned, walking away from him.

Joey turned to Pete and said, "Is he crazy?"

"Follow him," Pete said. "We need to get rid of you, so he can take me to the airport. I don't want to miss my flight."

Joey's face grew red with anger and frustration. "Find someone who will listen, would you?" he shouted. "My dad didn't do it. He doesn't have all the facts. I do."

Pete only shrugged.

Edgar was out of sight.

"Ask Dad where he got the gun. Did he tell them what kind of gun he used?"

"I don't know," Pete said. "Even if I did, I couldn't tell you."

"Look, neither my dad nor my uncle did it. They're trying to protect me."

Edgar returned in time to hear that and said, "You're no prize. Why would anyone confess to a crime he didn't commit to save your sorry ass?"

Joey's head dropped. Edgar must have hit a nerve.

"You've got five minutes to convince me you did it," Pete said. "Otherwise, Edgar's going to get his way. I have to catch the 9:00 flight home, and you know how the lines are at airport security. Start with what you did, when and how."

Joey told them, in detail, how he went to St. Paul a week ago and gave a man at Reaching Out a note for Brad Winthrup. The note said to be at the Upper Landing at ten o'clock on Sunday morning.

"How did you know Winthrup was in Minnesota?" Pete asked.

"From some of the guys at the company where my uncle works."

"And how did you find out that he was living on the streets?" Pete asked.

"His friends at ACS knew his parents' names. I got the phone number, called and asked for him. His mother said he wasn't there anymore. I told her Brad and I were buddies, and I was going to help him. I said I'd be in St. Paul and asked where I could find him. She told me he often went to a place called Reaching Out, and she looked up the address for me."

"What happened at the Landing?" Pete asked.

"I got there early, and two punk kids were hanging around. I scared the hell out of them, and they took off. Winthrup was already there with another man, and he had a gun. That screwed up everything."

"And?" Pete asked.

"I waited for the other man to leave. I didn't want to hurt him, and I didn't want to hurt the kids. I didn't even want to hurt Winthrup. All I wanted to do was scare him into dropping the lawsuit against my uncle. Walt's been good to Dad and me. He put me through college, and he's helped Dad several times. My dad hasn't been as lucky as Walt—at least as lucky as Walt was until this guy decided to destroy him. I wanted to repay my uncle. He didn't deserve what this wise guy was doing."

"By the time Winthrup finished, Uncle Walt and Aunt Ginny would've been out in the street. Winthrup didn't understand anything, and he didn't care. He didn't have the years my uncle has with the company. My uncle helped build ACS Marketing, but none of that mattered to Winthrup. The self-righteous bastard wanted to take him down. I just wanted to scare him enough to keep that from happening. When I saw the gun, I freaked. I shot him. I didn't intend to kill him."

Joey looked remorseful, but Pete couldn't tell if it was an act.

"How many times did you shoot him?" Pete asked.

"I only fired once."

"Where did you hit him?" Pete asked.

"In the back."

Edgar flashed Joey a look of utter disgust.

"Then what did you do?" Pete asked.

255

"I ran to him. I couldn't believe he was dead. I didn't even know how many shots it would take for me to graze him. All I wanted to do was wound him and tell him to drop the lawsuit or else. When I realized he was dead, I grabbed his gun and took off. I ran all the way to my car, got in and drove away. I drove straight home, stopping only once, for gas."

"You went to the Upper Landing with no intention of hurting Winthrup?" Pete asked.

"Right. I already told you that."

"But you took a gun. Why?" Pete asked.

"Insurance. Don't you have insurance on your home and your car? I took an insurance policy along. I wanted to scare him. I thought the gun would prove I was serious about the threat."

"How did you know he was dead?" Pete asked.

"From the way he crumpled and fell forward. But I felt his neck for a pulse, just in case."

"Just in case what?" Pete asked.

"In case he wasn't dead."

"What would you have done if he wasn't?" Pete asked.

"I'd have whispered 'Drop your lawsuit!' and taken off. Then, first pay phone I saw, I'd have dialed 911."

"What kind of gun did you use?" Pete asked.

"A .45 caliber Smith and Wesson."

"Where are your gun and Winthrup's gun now?" Pete asked.

"Sunday night, I threw mine into Lake Michigan. The other's at my place."

"Where were you standing, when you tossed yours?" Pete asked.

"At the Forty-Ninth Street Bridge."

"What part did your father play in all of this?" Pete asked.

"He told me about Uncle Walt's problem with Winthrup. That's all. He didn't do anything, and the only thing Uncle Walt did was complain to Dad about Winthrup. Walt had just heard from Winthrup's attorney, and he was a basket case. I swear! I wanted to be a good nephew. Like I told you before, I only wanted to scare the guy. I was blinded by the sight of that gun—of Winthrup standing there with a gun. Why would he bring a gun? I panicked. I lost sight of my reason for being there. Suddenly, it was a matter of kill or be killed. Tell me you've never been in a situation where you just reacted—where you didn't think beyond that moment!" Joey hissed.

If he did, Pete knew he'd be a bold-faced liar. He hadn't killed anyone with a knee-jerk reaction, but he remembered the time he was grocery shopping with his grandmother. She was counting out the exact change—but not fast enough for the guy behind them. That guy was so put out by the ten-second delay that he was hemming and hawing, sighing and rolling his eyes. Even at seventeen, Pete was large enough to block his grandmother's view of the creep, and her hearing was compromised enough to protect her from all of this.

As the man started to voice his complaint more loudly, Pete felt his hands tighten into fists. He took a step forward and was about to deliver a strategically placed punch to the guy's mouth when Pete realized he'd only make things worse. But that didn't stop him. It only changed the delivery of his message. He'd lifted the guy up with a stranglehold on his shirt, backed him further away from Grandma, and whispered, "If you shape up, maybe you'll be her age someday. If you make it, I hope someone treats you this badly, you sorry son of a bitch. Now, if you do anything to hurt her feelings, I'm going to knock you on your ass!"

All Pete said to Joey was, "You could have walked away."

"No way! I had to help Uncle Walt. When I saw Winthrop taking target practice, I knew Uncle Walt was in danger."

"So you shot him in the back?" Pete asked.

"I knew he was so much better than me with a gun. He was an excellent marksman. I figured I had to shoot first—just to injure him. It surprised the hell out of me that he went down the way he did."

"When did your uncle find out?" Pete asked.

"I called Dad when I stopped for gas on the way home. I had to talk to someone. I was pretty shaken up. Like I said, I never planned to kill him. I don't know when Dad told Walt."

"One last thing, at least for now," Pete said. "What were you wearing when you went to the Upper Landing?"

"Jeans, a black T-shirt, hiking boots, a do-rag and sunglasses."

Pete motioned Edgar to follow and they exited the room, leaving Joey behind.

"How did you know it was him?" Edgar marveled.

Pete pulled the sketch of the man who gave the note to Doc out of his leather portfolio and handed it to Edgar.

Edgar studied the composite, then looked at Pete and said, "I thought you had a special knack, but it was only a sketch. His age and the ears are a tip-off. Still, based on what you said, you only saw him for a second, before he took off. How did you know it was him?"

Pete shrugged and said, "I was running out of suspects. Had to pin it on someone."

FIFTY-TWO

WHILE JOEY LINTON WAS BEING booked, Pete made a reservation to return to Minneapolis that night. He felt lucky to get a seat on a 10:30 flight out of O'Hare. Once home, he'd begin the extradition process.

He and Edgar had dinner in downtown Chicago at one of Pete's favorite German restaurants, the Berghoff, before Edgar took him to the airport.

"You're not half bad for a Minnesota boy," Edgar told Pete as he got out of the car. "The next time you need to tap into my vast expertise, give me a call."

"I will, if I can stand the intimidation," Pete said, sealing it with a smile. "Seriously, thanks for all your help. It wouldn't have happened without you, Edgar. By the way, I've spent most of the day with you and I don't know your first name."

"That's easy. It's Edgar."

Pete shook his head and closed the car door.

Once he'd explained his way through security and was at his gate, he called Martin.

Martin answered, "Why didn't you tell me that Gary Linton didn't do it?"

"Because I didn't know that until about four o'clock. When I called, I got your voicemail."

"What do you mean you didn't know before then?"

"If you don't interrupt, I should be able to tell you most or all of it before I have to hang up. I'm flying in tonight."

"What time will you arrive? Need a ride?"

"No thanks. I won't be there until about midnight. Now let me tell you about it."

Pete leaned back in a chair and relaxed. He spent the time before boarding, telling Martin about his day.

"Oh, Martin, do you have Billy and Tim's parents' home phone numbers handy?"

"Yes, why?"

"Great. I have Billy's cell phone number, and I'll call him next. It's late, but will you let their parents know we arrested the man they saw? I'm sure they'll want to know, despite the time. Also tell them he doesn't know they worked with us. Gotta go. I'll call you tomorrow."

One down, two to go. Pete looked up the number and dialed Billy's cell.

When Billy answered, he told him about arresting the man from the Landing. He ended with, "Tell Tim we're sure we have the right guy. He confessed. I'm afraid we're going to forego the lineup."

"Oh, okay. Thanks for everything."

While boarding the plane, he had time for one more quick call. It wasn't too late now, but it would be when his flight landed. He highlighted the name in his cell directory and pressed TALK.

FIFTY-THREE

DOC'S FACE LIT UP AND A SMILE emerged when he saw Pete approaching. It was just past eleven on Saturday morning.

Pete walked up and patted him on the back.

"I owe you big time, Doc. You solved the case for us."

"I'm glad I helped you find Flash's murderer, but what happened to your face?"

"I wanted to better understand how you felt when you became a punching bag."

"I think you went overboard."

"How did you like Chris?"

"Aside from that initial scare, I like him. He took good care of me. I know it was your doing, but it was all for naught. Obviously my beating wasn't related to Flash's murder. So my private bodyguard was superfluous."

"Not a chance," Pete said. "When I arranged it, I had a valid concern. I'm glad my fears weren't realized."

"I've survived out here for more than three years, and you don't think I'm capable of taking care of myself?"

"Not against a man set on revenge. But let's drop that for now. I have something else I want to talk about."

"Oh?" The word was laced with curiosity.

"Yes. I'm planning a victory celebration with you and Chris, and another friend of mine. If he can make it, Martin will also be there. Will you join us?"

"I like celebrations," Doc said, nodding.

"I want you to pick the location. We can have it at my place, or we can go to a park for a picnic, or we can go to a restaurant of your choice. Which do you prefer?"

"They all sound good. How about if we have it at your house? Do you know how to cook?"

"Steaks on the grill with a salad is my specialty. How does that sound?"

"Like a real treat."

"I know it's short notice, but can you do it this afternoon? If not, we can do it tomorrow or any day next week? At least for now, they all work for me. What's best for you?"

Doc looked delighted. "Today's good, but so are tomorrow and all of next week. My appointment book is wide open."

"Great! Hang on while I check with Chris."

He dialed the number on his cell, wanting to arrange everything while still with Doc. Time was at a premium. He'd asked Katie about it last night, and she bought in on this strange twist to their first date, pending his ability to hook up with Doc. He sealed it saying, "I know it's unusual, but I owe both of them and this will take me off the hook."

She sounded fine with it, but he didn't know if she really felt that way.

Chris was available, so Pete told him to be at his house anytime between 3:30 and 4:30. "If I'm not there when you arrive, make yourself at home and I'll be there shortly."

Pete dialed Metro Transit, got the bus information for Doc, and they set a meeting place and time.

"Here's a bus card and a phone card," he told Doc, handing both to him. "Brad told his sister that they come in handy."

Walking back to his car, Pete dialed Katie's number. When she answered, he told her, "We decided I'll throw some steaks on the grill at my place. Do you mind?"

"That sounds like fun, Pete. What's the dress code?"

"Knowing my friends, casual to ultra-casual."

"Can I bring something?"

He told her he was serving steak and salad, and left it up to her. She gave her okay for his 2:30 arrival at her house. That gave them time to drop off whatever she brought and get to the bus stop in time to pick up Doc.

Pete didn't know how Katie might react to Doc, but he was pretty sure he'd pegged her correctly.

Next, he checked in with Martin. "I've been thinking about your matrix," he said. "Sorry the Linton's weren't in Minnesota. If they were, you could have applied it right up to the end. I'd like to have seen that happen. How about if we sit down Monday morning, and I go through everything that happened in Chicago with you?"

"So you think it has possibilities? I'd like that, Pete."

"Yeah, and I don't think you should give up on it before you've fully tested it. I know it's the eleventh hour, but are you doing anything this evening?"

"Marty has a game at six. I think he's making progress."

"That's great, Martin. Say 'Hi' to him for me, and I'll see you on Monday."

KATIE WAS READY WHEN PETE ARRIVED. She kept him waiting only long enough to get the twice-baked potatoes, minus the final step, from her refrigerator. She wore shorts and a tank top, and he thought the potatoes looked almost as good as she did.

They drove to his house, and he gave her a quick walk through.

"I love it," she said. "It doesn't look much like a bachelor pad. Are you sure you live here?"

"Just a second."

He walked into the living room, opened the front door, stepped out and looked at the house number. Coming back in, he closed the door and said, "Yup, it's mine all right."

Katie laughed, and he liked the sound of it.

"We better go," he said. "We have to pick up the guest of honor."

On their way, Katie broached the subject of the bruises on Pete's face.

"I got them on a trip to Chicago. I think they add character. Don't you?"

He appreciated it when she let it go at that.

Arriving at the bus stop, they got out of the car and waited on the bench.

"Why didn't you pick the guest of honor up at his or her home?"

"Security there is tight. They wouldn't let me through with this face."

She was still trying to decipher that when the bus arrived.

Pete stood, and she followed his lead.

It took a minute for Doc to emerge, and Katie kept watching.

"Doc, I'm glad you made it. I'd like you to meet a friend of mine, Katie Benton. Katie, this is Doc."

Katie smiled, held out a hand and said, "Glad to meet you."

"I know you," Doc said. "You've worked at Reaching Out, haven't you?"

A delighted grin covered Pete's face as Katie said, "Yes. I'm sorry, Doc. I didn't recognize you."

Doc was smiling, too. "No problem. I have a way of blending into a crowd. That's the way I like it."

Chris arrived right after they returned to Pete's, and everyone adjourned to the living room. Doc did much of the talking, telling first how he met Pete, then how Chris almost killed him. There were plenty of anecdotes and even more laughs.

When it was time to put on the steaks, Chris huddled over the grill with Pete while Katie kept Doc company.

Pete waited for Chris's assessment of Katie, but Chris talked about everything but her. That meant either Chris didn't like her or he was yanking Pete's chain.

As he transferred the steaks from the grill to a platter, Pete said, "Okay, Chris, tell me."

Chris grinned. He loved making Pete sweat, and he had so few opportunities. "I think she suits you—the poor thing."

"Now that's a rousing endorsement."

"The decision isn't mine to make. How long do you think she'll put up with you?"

"I'd say through dessert, if she's smart."

The group had a pleasant and prolonged dinner, and Chris left when Pete and Katie took Doc to catch the bus.

After Doc boarded the bus, Katie said, "I'm impressed, Pete."

"Oh, why?"

"That you went out of your way to be so kind to Doc. It's a nice touch."

"If you think that's a nice touch . . ." He brushed a few strands of hair off her forehead, took her face gently in his hands, bent down and kissed her.

ACKNOWLEDGMENTS

My thanks to Tom Motherway for sharing his experience and expertise in law enforcement; thanks to Felicia Donovan, a fellow member of Sisters in Crime, who likewise contributed law enforcement advice; and thanks to Don Gorrie, chief investigator for the Ramsey County Medical Examiner, who patiently and graciously answered a bushel basket full of questions. Thanks to Dayna Kennedy, who answered my questions about Saint Paul schools (regarding the two boys in this story); and thanks to Brian McCord, who coached me about eleven-year-old boys. Thanks also to Marly Cornell, Debbie Harper, Pam McCord, and Ann Williams. I accept full responsibility for any errors in the application of information from these professionals.